Praise

"From the very first few pages of the nocturnal stirrings of a raccoon until the final climax, Gowers has woven an intriguing first novel of the struggle for life or death of his protagonist, Francis. From one foreshadowing to the next, the reader's anticipation and increasing foreboding is never relaxed.

Instead, Gary subtly heightens it as he moves Francis from one resolution to the next while his shadow of depression continues to dog him as Francis struggles to escape the ravages of his guilt and shame. It is as if some deep and cosmic retribution is part of Francis' karma; unshakeable no matter all the allies he gathers around him hoping to save him.

Unfortunately and very sadly, what Francis carries unforgiven inside of himself has to find its mate from outside to balance his yin and yang."

-Dr. Paul J. Kachoris, M.D.

"Gowers provides us with something that we desperately need in our busy, self-centered lives; a warning and a reminder. The warning that life is fragile; in an instant tragedy can strike, altering our lives or the lives of our loved ones.

He helps us to see that we shouldn't take even the smallest parts of it for granted. And he reminds us that, in most cases, we have no idea what a person has been through in their life. They may have had personal tragedy that has caused them to be unsociable or considered a weirdo, even mean or disrespectful.

He weaves a story that causes us to realize that we personally have the ability to do good or bad. Help or harm. Give hope, or take it away. This book was one of internal reflection for me, and hopefully it will do the same for you."

-Brandon Shaw, Co-Host of *Brothers on Whatever* CBS Sports Radio

5th Floor Francis

Gary R. Gowers

Happy Duck Publishing
PO Box 607
Belle, MO 65013

Genre: Fiction, General
ISBN: 978-0-9861182-1-0
First Edition.
Printed in the United States of America.

This book is dedicated to
Cho Kyung-sook
The love of my life and the most beautiful, wonderful
woman on my planet.

And to
The love that got away:
MCG

ACKNOWLEDGMENTS

I would like to thank my brother, Billy, for his encouragement, moral support and for not giving up on me when my life took a turn for the worst. His patience during my many rants and his concern for his big brother were invaluable during a terrible time.

My sister-in-law, Cally, was also supportive to the max and went beyond the call of duty to lend support to a mere brother-in-law. She is truly a sister, and the "in-law" can be dropped altogether.

My grandmother, Ruby, turned me into a heavy reader at an early age and for that she deserves much credit in fostering my love of books. Every kid should have a person with whom they can sit quietly with and read.

My mother, Debbie, went head-to-head with my father every time the book order form came around at school. The tab got paid in coins sometimes, but she always made sure I had plenty of books to read. She also did her best to keep things quiet around the house as I sat at my desk working this novel out.

My brothers from different mothers, Jean-Xavier and Peter. They have their own struggles with the demon depression. Their conversations with me went a long way in helping me figure out what was going on in my own head. Additional thanks to Peter for nagging me to write more.

Thank you to Dr. Park So-yeon and Dr. Cho Ky-young for listening to me babble about my depression and my novel when we should have been studying English!

And thank you to all the family and friends in the USA, South Korea, New Zealand, and France who looked forward to and supported the publication of this book. I hope you enjoy reading it as much as I enjoyed writing it. I'll go ahead and apologize in advance to Norma, Aunt Ruth, Aunt Marie, Moira, and Grandma for all the curse words; not everyone is as classy as you ladies!

Finally, I'd like to thank my friend and editor, Ed, and his charming wife, Eva. Without the interest you expressed in *5th Floor Francis* it never would have been realized. For that I am ultimately grateful.

In addition to those who helped, and continue to help, me with my problems with mental illness and through the development of this novel, I'd like to acknowledge the millions of people around the world who are suffering from the various forms of illnesses called all-too-plainly depression.

Depression sucks the life out of you. It causes you to suck the life out of those around you. It causes you to do things you could never imagine yourself doing. It causes you to seek relief in narcotics or alcohol or your own death. It is truly an illness, as real as cancer or diabetes or any of the physical diseases that claim countless lives every day.

If you know someone with depression, don't discount them. Don't shun them or play the "they'll get over it" game. It's not the flu. You don't just get over it. It is inside them, eating them alive, and only assistance from those outside their head can help them. They might surrender to help immediately or they might fight it tooth and nail, but help them even if it draws their ire.

I'd like to also acknowledge and dedicate this novel to two people from the public spotlight.

Robin Williams: One of the greatest entertainers of our time. He lost his life-long battle, but he kept up the fight for so long even when most of the public didn't even realize he was in a fight for his life.

Nicholas Brendon: An actor/writer of my own generation. He has recognized his problems and taken the steps to heal. In addition, he is putting his name to good use by promoting and drawing attention to mental health issues. Who knows how many people have been helped, or will be helped, due to his efforts?

Prologue

The raccoon awoke in the pitch black of the attic and immediately came alert to the sounds and smells around him. The mice nesting in the insulation were stirring, the mother probably nursing her litter before she left the safety of the attic in search of crumbs and morsels left behind by the large animals living below.

The raccoon had attempted to find and eat the litter after they were first born, but he received a nasty surprise when the insulation got in his eyes and up his nose. It was too bad, because there was nothing much better than a meal of soft, fresh pinkies.

In addition to the mice, a small colony of sparrows was perched just out of his reach twittering softly to each other as they groomed and realigned their feathers. The sparrows knew he slept there during the day and were always on the lookout for him. One of them always stayed awake until he had left in the evening to do his overnight foraging.

He could smell squirrel droppings, but no squirrels were in the attic. They would come in during the day, discover the sleeping raccoon and then exit back out into the sunlight in search of a safer nesting spot. While the raccoon would not try to eat one of the full-grown squirrels, he would definitely eat their young if a litter were produced. In the attic the raccoon was the top of the food chain.

He waddled over to the attic vent and squeezed through the space left by a missing slat, emerging onto the shingled roof overhanging the backyard deck of the two-story home. Once he was out in the open night air he yawned, tongue lolling out while he stretched his limbs and arched his back; loosening up for the night's search for a meal, or meals, which he preferred.

He made his way over to where the gutter met the drain pipe, his downward route to ground level. After a short and sweet shimmy down the metal he hit the ground at a gallop and made for the tree line. It was still too early to raid the garbage cans at the actual home where he nested. They were always his last stop in the wee hours of the morning before he went back to the attic to sleep the day away. At that time of the morning he could count on the large animals living inside to be sleeping. He had made the mistake of making a ruckus with the garbage cans early in the night when he had first nested there. He had knocked over one of the cans and this resulted in a large male storming out of the structure in his direction howling at the top of its lungs. But as long as he waited until just before dawn the large animals would not disturb him.

He tended to avoid garbage cans in general during the first few hours of his search for food, unless the can had no lid and he caught the smell of something choice wafting on the breeze. No, during the first few hours he would comb the wooded areas around his nesting spot searching for ripening fruit, rodents, snakes, and frogs in the underbrush or litter left by other large animals like the ones living in the lower stories of his nest.

He was picking up a scent now of such litter. He followed the smell, which was easy. Unlike the prey in the brush and the fruit, the litter left by the large animals had underlying smells he could not recognize. But whatever these smells were; he was fairly sure they were responsible for keeping the food edible, even after it had been laying out in the sun all day, unless another scavenger got to it first.

The scent took him to the side of a road only a couple of blocks away from his attic. He found the paper bag in the grass next to the road and started to rip into it with his dexterous claws. He found the food which had drawn his attention and as he started to chew bright lights fell upon him, prompting him to quickly make for the trees. No sooner had he escaped the lights he heard the roar of the machine to which the lights belonged moving down the road at great speed. The machine flew past where the raccoon hid, hunkered down behind the trunk of a small tree, and the machine seemed confused. It was moving from one side of the road to the other, a high squealing sound coming from the frightening hulk before it left the road completely, flew over a ditch, and went nose first into a stand of larger trees. The noise of the impact caused the raccoon to stand up on his hind legs, head cocked, ears perked, and masked; twinkling eyes wide in the direction of the commotion.

All went silent. After a short wait the raccoon chanced a scurrying over to the litter again. He grasped the paper bag in his jaws and dragged it back into the relative safety of the tree line to finish his meal. As he chewed he could hear the howling of one of the large male animals coming from the direction of where the machine stopped and smelled smoke moving with the early night breeze. And just under the scent of smoke he detected the sweet odor of blood.

I

"*Exactly what are you trying to say? Are you saying he's better?*"

"*Better is a relative term, Mister Tower. However, I can say with confidence, a cautious confidence, that he has made a significant breakthrough. I've conferred at length with others on staff who are familiar with your brother's history and his resulting condition and we are in unanimous agreement that my plan bears significant merit.*"

"*But a steak knife under his mattress? How can you call that a breakthrough or a sign of progress? Isn't he still a danger to himself?*"

"*Yes, certainly, but the fact that he didn't use the knife! Therein lays the breakthrough.*"

"*Okay. But, honestly, that seems a little weak.*"

"*For a healthy mind, yes, it's a little weak. But for your brother it would be like me asking you not to think of a pink elephant if I say 'pink elephant'. You can't help but involuntarily picture a pink elephant in your mind. What your brother did was very deliberately place a pink elephant under his pillow and then not think about it. You see?*"

"*Believe it or not, I actually got that.*"

"*Now, I just need you to trust me and follow my lead. Did you bring what I asked?*"

"*Yes, I left it at the nurses' station like you told me to.*"

"*Excellent, I am going to go on in now and talk to him. I want you to bring it back here to the observation room and wait for me to call you in. A wave from me to you through the mirror will be your signal.*"

"*Okay, Doctor. But do you actually think something this simple, something like this, could actually make him better after all this time?*

Relatively speaking?"

"Mister Tower, after all this time, the therapy, and the medications we know nothing for sure. But this is certainly worth a go. This has been the one and only course of treatment that has shown any real possibility of working at any level. The different combinations of medications, the antidepressants, sertraline, trazodone, venlafaxine... all the others; the different dosages and combinations, even when we get him to take them as prescribed, the best results weren't good enough to allow him to live on his own as a normal, functional member of society. His problem goes far beyond a simple brain chemistry imbalance or deficiency. I know you don't want your brother to spend the rest of his life confined here and medicated to the gills, am I right?"

"Of course, of course, that's right. I just worry about him, that's all. What if it doesn't work as you, sorry, as WE hope? What if the first thing he does on the outside is head for the nearest bridge or slash his wrists with a chunk of glass or something?"

"Again, Mister Tower, I'll admit there are no guarantees here. But if he wants to kill himself, even here under our constant surveillance and care, eventually he will find the means. I'm going forward on a huge hunch here, but based on recent events I think it's worth a try. I know you've already signed the waiver as legal guardian, but if you are having second thoughts it is most assuredly your call. We can call it all off and continue the current course of treatment."

"Second thoughts? Try third and fourth. But, if you really think... okay, Doctor. I'll trust your judgment, but I can't help having my doubts."

"I completely understand, but smile when you bring it in. Your brother needs all the positivity we can muster. For his sake we cannot afford to display any doubts. Understand?"

"Certainly, Doctor. I'll be all smiles and rainbows on your signal."

Francis Tower sat in Interview Room B on the third floor of the Harper Institute attempting to find something new to look at.

He had been slouching there in one of the two white plastic chairs and resting his elbows on the matching table for nearly twenty minutes. He had been in this room, and others exactly like it, countless times over the past five years or so and they hadn't changed a whole hell of a lot.

It never ceased to amaze him that these rooms were always graffiti-free. Not a scuff on the floor or a scratch on the table. Never a "Joanie loves Chachi" or a "call Tiffany for a Good Time" or the big nose of Kilroy to be seen. The same squeaky-clean white plastic furniture, the same white-painted concrete walls, the same white-faced clock with black numbers and hands hanging on the wall enclosed in a clear plastic cage, the same spotless mirror taking up an entire wall of the room.

He was aware, of course, that the mirror was there so that people could look him over, but he no longer thought or cared about that. Someone was always watching him. He couldn't remember the last time he'd eaten a meal, brushed his teeth, took a shit, or even slept, without an audience. He had grown so used to the stoic presence of the white-clad orderlies that he no longer bothered to tell them apart. They were just as assembly-line-standardized as these interview rooms.

Francis thought he could hear people talking on the other side of the mirror, but that could have just as easily have been residual effects from the cocktail of meds he had habitually swallowed that morning. Actually, it was more the habit of the nursing staff to give him the pills and watch him like a hawk until he swallowed them than it was his own habit of taking them. He'd just as soon not take them at all. Or, if he had his choice, he would have taken them all and licked the dust out of the bottles for good measure. Either or. Pills or no pills, he often heard murmuring that he couldn't account for.

Old Martin told him once, in all whackadoo seriousness, that the murmurings were Francis' personal demons plotting and conniving with each other, and that it was best not to try to hear what they were saying for they surely didn't have their host's best interests in mind. Francis could imagine that being the case. So if not the meds, maybe it was his demons. Or maybe both; maybe the meds made it possible for him to hear the demons. He knew, though, that the murmurs were merely the muted conversations of real people conversing behind the mirror.

He didn't give Old Martin's paranoid talk of demons any real consideration. Furthermore, why is it that people always have demon voices in their heads anyway? *Why is it you never hear about people hearing the voices of lemurs or fire hydrants or cans of spray cheese?* He'd have to ask Doctor Singh about that. Francis was the first to admit that he had problems to deal with, but he knew he wasn't crazy; not like Old Martin, a guy who was scared of the voices in his own head and a man who had made the mistake of listening to the voices and acting out violently to placate them, thus earning himself a padded room at The Harper Institute.

Francis wasn't privy to all the details of Old Martin's history, but he was fairly certain it involved Old Martin's wife, two neighbors, an EMT, may they all rest in peace, and a nail gun. But Francis knew the voices in his head and they didn't scare him, they were merely the product of his own subconscious reminding him of things he'd rather not remember. Simple as that.

He turned from his thoughts to resume his cursory examination of the blank surroundings of Interview Room B. His eyes had just settled on the brass doorknob and started to muse that the doorknob was the only non-white object in the room when it turned with a quick twist and Doctor Singh came sweeping through the door in his white coat and flashing his patented smile. He could imagine him as Fred Astaire in the part of a singing, tap-dancing medical professional.

Francis liked Doctor Singh for the most part, considering their medical relationship. He didn't wield the same sterile, clinical persona as most of the other medical staff members at the institute. He was always smiling and never came across as condescending when he talked to the people under his care, so unlike many of the medicos Francis had met over the past several years.

Some of Francis' more undesirable fellow inmates, like Old Martin, called Doctor Singh "The Stinkin' Injun." It is true that Doctor Singh often smelled of spices, such as cloves, saffron, cardamom, and others that Francis could not identify, but it was a pleasant, subdued aroma that Francis rather enjoyed and not a stink at all. Besides, Francis had never asked, but he had always been under the impression that Doctor Singh might be Pakistani, not Indian.

"Good afternoon, Francis. Sorry for the wait, I was conferring with a colleague."

"About me, or some other loon?"

"Yes, as a matter of fact, about you. And you know I don't appreciate that term."

"Sorry, Doctor Singh. Behind the mirror?"

"The mirror? What about the mirror?"

"Never mind, it's nothing." *Ha! Not demons after all, crazy Old Martin.*

"Francis? Would you happen to know why I wanted to talk to you today?"

"I think I have a pretty good idea. I'd have to say it's about the steak knife the orderly found in my room, right?" Francis knew as soon as he was escorted to Interview Room B after lunch that the doctor wanted to talk to him about the knife.

There had been a surprise room inspection of Ward C that morning and Francis hadn't had the time, nor the inclination, to stash the knife in a better hiding place. He knew when he was asked to leave the room for the duration of the inspection that the knife would be found by the ever-thorough orderlies and that a trip to an interview room would follow close behind the discovery. Frankly, he was surprised he was able to even sneak the knife out of the cafeteria in the first place. The eagle-eyed orderlies usually watched the silverware like the couch potatoes in the common room watched reality television, intently and without blinking.

"Yes, that's right, the steak knife."

"No harm, no foul."

"Well, that is sort of what I wanted to talk to you about, Francis. No harm, that is. You had the knife in your room for three days. Did you not?"

"How can you be sure it was only three days?"

"Tuesday was—"

"—steak night. The orderly found the knife this morning. I get it. Yeah, I had it for three days. Sorry, Doctor Singh. I should know better than to try to play games with you. You don't deserve that."

"You don't have to be sorry. But I want you to understand how important this is. Don't you see how significant this is in terms of recovery, Francis? Can you see how this can be viewed as a sign of great progress?"

"Significant progress? How so?"

"Over the three years that you have been with us, you have attempted suicide on at least eleven separate occasions."

"Well, most of those were during the first year or so. Do you see the reduction in attempts as a sign of this recovery?"

"No. The reduction in attempts is because you have been on twenty-four hour suicide watch for most of your stay and the staff, as I'm sure you have noticed, is very good at picking up on possible incidents before they are actually carried out. The frequency of your attempts diminished as we gained an understanding of your habits and learned to recognize the warning signs concerning your behavior. Even those with erratic behavior have patterns. Nobody is completely unpredictable. You have been fortunate. As you are well aware from your time with us, we don't always catch on in time, you know."

Francis thought about the bodies he had seen leaving Ward C, not on their own feet but stretched out on gurneys with crisp, white sheets hiding the fatal damage they'd done to themselves.

"Yes, your staff does seem to know what I'm going to do before I know I'm going to do it sometimes. So, what's the point? I've stopped being a challenge or something? Do I need to spice it up some? Make your job more interesting?"

The memories of the crispy, sheet-covered dead making his words come out harsher than he intended. He instantly regretted speaking to Doctor Singh in such a way. He knew the doctor took the demise of patients personally and to heart. He had even witnessed the man staunching tears as he bent over the bodies declaring the suicides deceased.

"Francis, don't be that way. You are better than that. What I'm trying to get at is that you had the knife in your possession for three days and made no attempts to end your life. It's been a long time since you had such an opportunity, and you didn't take it. And I think you can understand why I view this as significant." Doctor Singh locked eyes with Francis as if willing him to understand the point he was he was trying to express.

"Wrong, Doctor. I thought about it. I thought about it a lot. And I had the knife out several times intending to do it."

"There is nothing dangerous in thinking about it or even preparing to do it. People who have experienced far less trauma than you can have suicidal thoughts and even act out the first preparatory acts of suicide; the planning, acquiring the essential *equipment*, and so on. You didn't so much as scratch yourself with the knife. I believe there is more to it and I think I know why you didn't use it on yourself."

Doctor Singh leaned back in his white chair and looked at Francis, letting out a deep breath through his smile. "Francis. What activity do we have you scheduled for later today?"

"It's pet therapy day, at two o'clock. You know that. You scheduled me for it yourself."

"Yes, I know; just thinking out loud. I looked over the attendance for pet therapy day, and I noticed that you have not only attended every session I and others have scheduled for you, but you have also requested to be present for additional sessions on several occasions. I even learned you bribed other patients with desserts and packs of cigarettes in exchange for the extra time slots they had acquired. According to Martin, you gave up a week of desserts in exchange for two of his hours."

Damn that Old Martin and his motor mouth!

Truth be told, Francis always looked forward to the days the pets came to visit the residents. The Patients 'N Pets Program began about seven months ago and he found the time he spent with the dogs, cats, rabbits, and other animals very pleasurable; much more so than weaving baskets and playing bingo with the other patients. Francis even grew to enjoy the touch and companionship of some of the more exotic and less desirable creatures, like the iguana and the tarantula. He even saved the tarantula's hairy little hide on one occasion when Cicely Nelson tried to stomp it. Cicely was limited to dogs and cats after that incident. And, as a reward for his service to the arachnid, Francis was always given first crack at the multi-legged animal during therapy sessions.

The whites of Doctor Singh's eyes grew larger as he raised his dark black eyebrows. "It is my professional opinion, Francis, that the reason you stashed the knife under your mattress instead of making a suicide attempt at the first possible opportunity is that you look forward to the time you spend with the animals. What do you think of that?"

Francis did know that he looked forward to the animal therapy, but could it really have thwarted his urges to do himself in? The urges which had grown to define him? Those squirming, vile feelings that had become the focal point of his dismal, pointless life. The urges that had put him in this hospital in the first place.

Come to think of it, when he took the knife from the cafeteria he did it more out of an impulse based on years of looking for an avenue out of this life rather than through conscious planning. After all the therapy and medications designed to put an end to his all-consuming want for a final end, could the animals be what he needed? It seemed too easy.

"Uh... I don't know, Doctor Singh. I do look forward to seeing the animals, but—"

"And that," Doctor Singh waved one hand towards the mirror, "is why I have decided to discharge you under your brother's supervision at the end of the week. Congratulations, Francis."

Francis could hardly believe what he was hearing. They had to be out of their minds. After all this time they were going to let him out just because he liked petting bunnies, holding tarantulas, and playing fetch with terriers! Just like that? The fear of what he would do to himself once he was out on his own rose up in his chest.

"Now hold on. Wait just a minute, doctor! I'm not ready to leave. I can't be alone! I... what if I... when I'm alone—"

"Francis, I didn't say you would leave here alone. And, I have to add I'm doubly encouraged by your reluctance to leave and for the fear you are showing for your own life. When was the last time you feared for your life, Francis?"

As that thought did frantic laps in Francis' head a sound came from the white door. Doctor Singh and Francis turned their heads to watch it open. Francis squinted curiously at the sight of his brother standing there smiling and holding a small wire cage.

Inside the cage was a wheel spinning and squeaking with frantic rodent exertion. On the wheel a little brown hamster was running as if its life depended on it, like it was being pursued by demons of its own.

II

"Hey, buddy. Do you have any spare change that I can borrow? Maybe a buck or two? I'd like to get me and my dog here something to eat."

"No. I don't have any money to give you, but I have a cheeseburger in my bag that the dog is welcome to. Here you go, boy. Good boy, you like that? When was the last time you ate? Huh? Poor little guy."

"Hey, man? What the hell? What about me?"

"What about you?"

"If you can't give me any money, then do you have another cheeseburger I can have? The mutt isn't the only one that hasn't eaten in a while."

"No, just enough for the dog."

"What kind of fuckin' asshole are you? You'll give the mutt something, but not me?"

"What kind of asshole am I? If you didn't have the dog tied down with that leash he could surely find his own food somewhere on his own. You are holding him back and forcing him to go hungry. What's your excuse for going hungry? I can see the neck of your leash sticking up out of that paper bag in your pocket. You're the asshole from where I'm standing."

"You son of a bitch! You think you're better than me or something? You got no right to talk to me that way!"

"Oh, is that right? So you're saying that you have the right to let your dog suffer and starve because you're a lazy boozehound? Additionally, is it your right to harass strangers who are walking down the street and minding their own business? But I don't have the right

to tell the truth as I see it? I don't have the right to call a worthless scumbag a scumbag? How about this, why don't you just untie the dog, then you can crawl under a refrigerator box and die somewhere. Do yourself, the dog, and everyone in this city that favor."

"You rat bastard son of a bitch, I'm gonna' stomp the shit outta' your motherfucking ass!"

"Hey! Get your hands off me! What are you doing? NO!"

Officer Chavez stood against the white wall across from the waiting room vending machines doing his best to keep his considerable bulk out of the way of the teeming hospital staff and milling patients. His head pivoted on his thick neck towards the air-sucking sound of the automatic doors of the hospital emergency room for what seemed like the millionth time since he finished the interviews: first with the homeless transient suffering from severe dog bites and manic temperament, then the quiet, uncooperative pedestrian who was hit by the taxi, and finally the flustered cabbie who had been driving the taxi.

The transient, one Lawrence McPhee, would remain in the hospital for a couple of more days while the doctors observed his wounds for infection, checked his blood for rabies, and did a psych eval for good measure.

The banged-up pedestrian, one Francis Tower, would be released once his ride arrived. The cabbie, a legal immigrant named Ngbodi Houndou was interviewed and cleared of any wrongdoing at the scene of the incident. The whereabouts of the dog were currently unknown and no efforts were being made to track it down.

Officially, Officer Chavez was finished with his shift at the time he accepted the dispatcher's call to respond to an incident a block from the big pet supply place on Sycamore. The transient had been ranting and uncooperative, the pedestrian had been tight-lipped and the cabbie was just plain confused and scared, probably afraid that Immigration and Naturalization would get involved. But, with the completion of the interviews finally accomplished, Chavez had finally finished his shift. The incident allowed him to log two and half hours of overtime, so he wasn't really complaining, though he was now ready to sit back in his recliner and call it a day. Maybe stop by the gym first on his way home. However, the tight-lipped Francis Tower's emergency contact Terrance Tower, the pedestrian's younger brother, wanted to speak further with Chavez about the incident that had landed his brother in the emergency room. It was the imminent arrival of the brother that kept Officer Chavez's head swiveling towards the swish of the automatic doors. He had already clocked out via radio, so this was now officially a favor. *Above and beyond the call of duty*, he turned again at the sound of swishing doors.

Terrance whipped his two-year-old BMW into the hospital's emergency room parking lot and lucked out in finding an empty space right across the ambulance lane from the large double doors of the ER entrance. He had been in the middle of the weekly meeting with his sales staff when his receptionist buzzed through the call from an Officer Chavez, who told him simply that his brother had been injured in some sort of altercation while walking down Sycamore; only a block from Francis' apartment. Chavez had attempted to give further details, but in his distress Terrance had failed to hear the first few sentences spoken by the policeman. Officer Chavez seemed to take Terrance's panic under consideration and was kind enough to agree to stick around until he could get to the ER for a more detailed explanation of the events that had landed his brother in the hospital.

This wasn't Francis' first visit to the hospital since leaving Doctor Singh's care, but it was the first time he had been admitted to the emergency room. Terrance had been so busy lately with the day-to-day operations of Tower Properties that his weekly visits to check up on Francis had lapsed into once-a-month visits and brief, weekly phone calls. Francis was easy to overlook because he never used the phone himself. Terry already felt guilty about not seeing his brother as often as he thought he should, though Francis had said on more than one occasion that the visits were unnecessary, and even kind of bothersome, so the call from Officer Chavez served to heighten his feelings of negligence to a level of panicked worry.

Terrance had no trouble spotting Officer Chavez as he entered the emergency room; six-foot-plus-change Hispanic policemen are not an everyday sight, even in a hospital ER. Besides, the hulking policeman's eyes had immediately zeroed in on Terrance as he came through the doors which meant Chavez had been on the lookout for a frantic man in a business suit. The two men faced each other in front of the nurses' station.

"Mister Tower?"

"Yes, that's me." Terrance extended his hand. "Can you tell me where my brother is?"

"First, Mister Tower," Chavez shared the handshake, "your brother is fine."

"Yes, I understood that much when you called, but what happened?"

"Well, we received two and a half versions of the story," began Officer Chavez while taking a small notebook from his breast pocket and consulting it.

"Two and a half? What do you mean?"

"Yes, sir. Mister McPhee, that would be the homeless man, claimed that your brother tried to steal his dog which resulted in a struggle that caused your brother to go stumbling into the street."

"That's ridiculous!"

"I'm inclined to agree with you, sir, and I've stated so in my report. This was my first encounter with the transient, but McPhee is no stranger to the department. In fact, he has been charged with harassment and public intoxication on several occasions and has served time for assault once before; domestic assault actually. Besides, the man was severely bitten by his own dog, which leads me to believe that he was the aggressor in the situation. That's how it all adds up in my head anyway."

"I assume the half version of what happened came from my brother?" Terrance gave a half-embarrassed roll of the eyes.

"Correct, sir. For a wronged party he certainly offered very little in the way of information. He refused to elaborate on what led to the incident and he has no wish to press charges against Mister McPhee. It was all I could do just to get him to tell me his name and to get in the ambulance. And even with his injuries his only concern was with his shopping bags and his wish to go home."

Terrance shook his head and spoke in a low, irritated voice, "That doesn't surprise me in the least."

"Sir?"

"Ah... nothing, Officer Chavez. I suppose if my brother doesn't want to press charges then we ought to let it go. Once he makes up his mind there is really no use in talking to him."

"If that is how you would like to play it, sir, but I'm willing to testify before a judge concerning McPhee's criminal record and I am certain that the taxi driver would also cooperate. He said he saw McPhee doing the shoving right before your brother went into the street."

Terrance chuckled. "Officer, you'd have to know my brother. You see, he has an... um... a condition. He dislikes interacting with people and never leaves his neighborhood. Legal action would require that he appear in a courtroom, there is no way in hell he would go along with that. It really is best for everyone if we just let it go."

"I see. If you believe he cannot be encouraged to press charges, then I suppose my job here is done. If he changes his mind, be sure to give me a call. This is my contact information."

Terrence took the offered card from Chavez. "Thank you for your time, officer. But I assure you that this is the end of the matter. I, we, appreciate all of your help. Thank you very much for waiting here for me. I'd like to get in and see my brother now."

"I understand, Mister Tower. You can find your brother straight down the hall, third examination room on the left. Have a nice day, and please ask the other Mister Tower to be careful out there. He's not the only one on the streets with a condition."

Terrence entered the third examination room on the left to find his brother sitting upright on the paper-covered examination table with his shirt off. "Like meat on butcher paper," their father used to say. A large, beefy nurse with a pleasant smile and nimble fingers was just finishing up taping Francis' ribs

"Hey, big brother. How are you feeling?"

"Your brother is going to be sore for several weeks," Nurse Beefy chimed, "and he's going to have some trouble getting around. He's not feeling anything right now though; he has some pretty strong painkillers flowing around in there."

Francis sat quietly, with no overt signs of discomfort while the nurse finished up and then left the room with a nod.

"Francis? What the hell happened?"

"Nothing, really. I fed a dog a cheeseburger; the dog's owner got pissed, and pushed me in front of a taxi. Now I have four cracked ribs and my left thigh is bruised to the femur, from the hip to the knee. They said they'd give me a cane. Oh, and six stitches on the back of my head. Not much blood, though."

"Come on, Francis. He didn't push you just for feeding the dog. You must have said something to get him all riled up."

"I just told him the truth; pointed out that he was inferior to his dog."

"Well, that would do it." Terrance sighed. He had noticed before that he tended to sigh a lot when he talked to, or about, Francis. Francis had a way of saying things in a straightforward fashion that was both insulting and perfectly logical at the same time. But that isn't how most people think, in black and white like that. Most people think in shades of gray, come up with excuses for their behavior or try to explain themselves in a way that puts their behavior in a better light. If you asked most people, "Why do you smoke," they would reply, "Oh, it relaxes me" or "I'm trying to cut down." But, Francis, who smoked no less than two packs a day, would answer, "Because I'm addicted to nicotine." His cut-to-the-quick, no bullshit style of communication made Francis hard to talk to sometimes.

"Hey, you ready to get out of here? The doc said you were good to go once the nurse finished up."

"Yeah, I'm ready. I didn't want to come here in the first place, but that large peace officer made me."

"Well, that's his job."

"I know. They put my things in that closet there."

"What things?"

"Some sacks of supplies. I was walking home from the Sycamore Pet Emporium when this happened. A water bottle and some vitamin supplements were smashed under the taxi tires, so we have to make a pit stop at the Emporium on the way to my apartment."

"You're lucky it wasn't your head that got smashed. Don't worry we can stop on the way."

"I'm not worried. Can you go in for me? I'll write down what I need if you'll go in for me. I'm starting to feel a little sore, besides, that teenager is working the counter today. She always asks too many damned questions about things that don't concern her."

"Like what?" Terrance felt another sigh rising up out of his chest.

"Like if I'm having a good day or not."

The sigh didn't make a wasted trip up from his chest. "Sure Francis, I'll go in for you."

"Thank you, Terry. And hurry, please. I have a lot to do."

Terrance Tower had bought the seventy-year-old, five-story, red brick apartment building at 517 Sycamore and managed it through the family business, Tower Properties. The

Gary R. Gowers

business focused primarily on buying, renovating, and selling commercial properties; but Terrance purchased the ten-unit residential building in order to provide Francis with a spacious residence near the well-stocked Sycamore Pet Emporium. The Emporium was open for business seven days a week with extended hours Monday through Saturday, and boasted an in-house veterinarian for limited hours each day.

Francis visited the Emporium nearly every day and the sprawling store was pretty much his only social contact. However, Francis avoided the employees as much as he could and probably knew the store's stock and layout better than the manager. This was intentional, for if he knew what was available and where everything was located he wouldn't have to ask for help.

Francis had the entire fifth floor of 517 Sycamore, as well as the building's roof, for his own use. The two units he had initially occupied had been renovated in order to provide one huge apartment, and most of the walls had been removed in order to open up the space. The high ceilings of the old building gave Francis' apartment the feel of a medium-sized, rectangular cathedral. It even retained some of the original stained glass in the upper panes of the huge, floor-to-ceiling windows. If so inclined, Francis could have put in pews, placed a statue of whichever deity he chose, or created, and formed a cult.

The fourth floor was unoccupied and the two empty units were used as storage by the Tower family. Storage space was not really a concern and no one had been in the units for some time. Francis just didn't want to be bothered by the sounds produced by neighbors, so very little was actually stored in the two apartments. Not that the building was especially loud anyway. Most of the residents were older, if not at the elderly end of the aging spectrum, and there were only two or three child-aged residents living in the building. Though Francis had offered no input as far as the screening process for prospective residents, he made his wishes and wants known to Terrance, who went along for the sake of his brother's comfort.

The building not only provided Francis with a place to live, but also an income. After his stay with Doctor Singh ended four years ago, Francis showed absolutely no willingness to return to the family business, but was still eligible for an income provided by its activities. The rent collected from the occupied units went into Francis' bank account, while all monetary issues were taken care of by the company's accounting department.

Terrance didn't like visiting his brother at 517 Sycamore. In the first place Francis didn't like to be visited; he was always busy with his own home-bound activities and offered very little in the way of brotherly conversation. But, what Terrance truly disliked about the property was that there was no elevator, which meant Francis' insistence on living on the fifth floor called for a breath-stealing hike up the long staircases for anyone who wished to see him. With his cracked ribs and injured leg the five flights of stairs were going to be a problem for Francis.

After parking in the landlord's space in front of 517 Sycamore, Terrance moved around to the passenger's side to open the door for his injured brother. The ride from the hospital to the Sycamore Pet Emporium, to replace the water bottle and vitamin supplements, and then to Francis' building didn't seem to be too uncomfortable for Francis. Only a few potholes spotted too late to avoid had caused him to wince through his teeth. The painkillers were starting to wear off and before long every movement would bring a new surge of pain. It was going to be a long climb up to the fifth floor.

Once Francis was out of the car and deposited on the sidewalk leaning on his cane in front of the building, Terrance moved to the trunk and heaved out the two large, plastic sacks – each bearing Pet Emporium's logo of a smiling non-breed specific canine, though Terrance always figured it was a collie.

Lassie used to smile like that, and Flipper. Never noticed the similarities between collies and dolphins, mused Terrance.

A smaller bag containing the replaced water bottle and vitamin supplements was perched on top of the articles in one of the larger bags. Francis was right about that young cashier. She does ask a lot of questions and talks a lot in general.

"Okay. You ready Francis? This isn't going to be a walk in the park."

"I'm ready."

"Just take it slow and easy. No rush."

"I know. You can carry the bags?"

"I got them. You just worry about hauling your carcass up the steps."

"Are you pissed off about something, Terry?"

"No. No, big brother, I'm not. Sorry. I just don't care for all the stairs."

"I guess I'm used to them."

The two brothers went up the four steps to the front double doors, entered the building and headed for the first flight of stairs. Terrance took a peek at Francis' mailbox as they passed, but it was empty. It was usually empty, and not because Francis checked it regularly. His brother just didn't get much mail.

Terrance remembered coming by the first New Year's Eve Francis was in the building to visit and found Christmas cards from various family members getting dusty in the mailbox. Mail was another thing Francis had no interest in, so all bills for the building were forwarded to the accounting department at Tower Properties. As far as the personal correspondence, such as the Christmas cards, Terrance made sure to let people know their thoughtful envelopes had arrived, but had long ceased bothering to give them to Francis.

"Move."

"What?"

"Not you. Her." Francis was staring at the bottom step of the first flight. Terrance hadn't noticed because of the armfuls of bags and his mailbox peeking, but there was a young Asian girl sitting on the steps. The girl looked to be about eleven or twelve, but she may have been older; maybe a little small for her age.

She wasn't taking up much space on the step, but just enough that Francis would almost have to turn sideways to get past her without making any sort of contact.

"Come off it, Francis. Hi, little lady. Could you move so he can get past? He's not feeling very well."

"Sure." The girl stared up at them meekly.

"Thanks," Terrance turned to his brother, "Francis, you go ahead and get a head start. I'm going to get a better hold on these bags and talk to your neighbor for a minute. Do you have your keys?"

Francis lightly patted his pocket in confirmation. "I have them," and then started slowly up the stairs with a muted grunt.

"Remember, slow and easy. I'll be right behind you."

Terrance and the Asian girl watched Francis' back for several minutes until he got to the top of the first flight and was mostly out of hearing distance. Then Terrance turned to her with a slight smile, "Sorry about that, hon. You must think he's pretty rude, huh?"

"Yeah. But that's the most I've ever heard him talk."

"Oh? He's talked to you before?"

"No. I used to say hi to him when I saw him, but I gave up after a couple of months. He never answers. Everyone in the building thinks he's crazy. He just walks up and down the stairs once a day or so carrying those bags like you're holding, the ones with the smiling dog."

"Nah, he's not crazy. He has just had some problems and he's not very good around people. I've known him my whole life and he doesn't even talk to me all that much. He wasn't always like this though," chuckled Terrance. "So, which apartment do you live in?"

"Right here," She pointed at the door next to the stairs. "101. Me and my mom live here, and her boyfriend sometimes."

"Ah, then you must be Susan Lee's daughter. Right?"

"Yeah, I'm Chava Lee. How did you know that?"

"I'm Terrance... Terry Tower. That guy limping up the steps is my brother, Francis Tower. We own the building. Well,

Gary R. Gowers

he does officially. But I remember looking over your mom's rental application and she came by my office to sign the lease and pick up the keys."

"He's our landlord? But he's never even talked to us."

"Like I said, he's not good with people. What are you doing sitting out here anyway?"

"My mom is sleeping. She works the night shift in the Paramount Hotel laundry. She doesn't like me going outside by myself and I don't like sitting in the apartment being quiet while she sleeps. So I just sit out here and talk to the neighbors when I see them. Everyone is pretty nice. Well, almost everyone." She quipped, gesturing up the stairs out the corners of her eyes, "It's not so boring when school is going on, but with it being summer vacation there is nothing much to do."

"Yeah, you must get pretty bored all by yourself."

"And it's only the first week of vacation," she sighed, rolling her eyes.

Terrance adjusted the bags for a better grip and put his foot on the first of many steps. "Well, hang in there Chava. It's been nice talking to you. I'm sorry again for my brother's rudeness. But keep on saying 'hi' to him. Just 'cause he acts like that doesn't mean we have to, right?"

"Right, Mister Tower." Chava smiled up at him.

"Call me Terry if you want. He must be getting near the top by now, so I'd better get up there. He'll be needing these bags. See you around, Chava. Tell your mom hello for me."

"Okay. See you Mister Tow— Terry."

III

"I'm telling you, I don't need anyone. So just drop it, Terry."

"I'm well aware that that is what you think. But face it, you're hurt; hobbled even. How often do you go to the pet supplies store?"

"Almost every day. You already know that."

"Almost every day. That's a lot of walking up and down those stairs. How are you going to carry bags up those stairs in the shape you're in?"

"I'll manage."

"Oh, yeah? And how are you going to do all your work, huh? The cleaning? The feeding? There is no way you can keep up with it in your condition."

"I'll manage that too."

"No, I don't think you will. You need someone to help you. At least until you are back to your old self. Besides, it will do you some good to have some company up here! Some human company for a change."

"And if I refuse? I'm not a goddamned child you know. I'm a forty-five-year-old man. And contrary to what everyone, including you, thinks, I'm perfectly sane and capable of taking care of myself."

"I don't think you're insane, Francis. But I do know that you're sick. And you know it too. Sick and now temporarily disabled. You're getting a helper. That's all there is to it."

"I don't need no fucking 'helper'. They'd just get in my way. I won't allow you to come in here and mess everything up."

"You won't allow? Hey, do I need to remind you that you were released under my supervision? One phone call and I can have you back in that hospital with Doctor Singh and Old Martin... and the *therapy sessions... and the meds... and the suicide watch. Don't think I won't do it... one call. Now, what's it going to be?"*

"Fine, Terry, fine. You don't have to hold the supervision bullshit over my head. Who—"

"Well, I'll have to call an agency or something, maybe I... wait! I think I have the perfect person in mind. Big brother, you're going to hate this, but I need you to cooperate with me. Listen..."

Terrance left Francis' apartment with the same gnawing feelings of frustration and helplessness that he experienced pretty much each and every time he visited with his brother. There were times when he thought it might actually be better to re-institutionalize Francis. Sure, he wasn't trying to kill himself anymore, but he only traded one sickness for another. Wasn't this seclusion, this total sealing of his shell, just another slow method of suicide?

At least when Francis was plotting to die he showed some amount of zest. A zest for escape, a zest for death sure, but it was something. Doctor Singh had explained to him that the suicide attempts were an effort to escape the pain caused by personal tragedy and now, this closing off from the world, from other people; it was an effort to escape the possibility of additional pain. The hamster, Little Demon as Francis named him, was supposed to be therapy that would lead Francis back to the mental health thoroughfare. But the therapy had expanded on itself, gone beyond its own bounds, and now Francis was stuck on the back roads, and he wasn't looking for directions. In a nutshell, Francis was afraid and unwilling to give a shit; and he had become very good at it.

When Terrance talked to Doctor Singh about what Francis had morphed into the doctor was understanding, but not even the slightest bit perturbed by the outcome of the introduction of Little Demon. He even went so far as to state that Francis may never be normal again, that he would never be the big brother that Terrance had known up until that fateful night so many years ago. Doctor Singh's immediate goal in treating Francis, and Terrance had agreed at the time, was to find a way to stop the suicide attempts. But was this any better, really? His brother lived like a ghost on the fifth floor. The kid, Chava Lee, had even said that everyone in the building thought he was crazy.

This wasn't the first time Terrance had run through this gamut of thoughts. He went through it every time he came to visit; it had become his own obsession: how best to help Francis. This parade of thoughts normally ended with the same question: how can he stop his brother from slipping further and further away into the muck of secluded depression and detachment, out of the reach of normal, without getting his own feet stuck in the sucking mud and joining him there? After all, he had the right to live his life too. He has a wife and kids to think about. What about them? Even though his wife Lorraine never complained about his pre-occupation with Francis, should she and the kids take a backseat to Francis' problems? And, as usual, he had no answers for his own questions.

Right now there was a more immediate problem to address, a problem in the realm of the physical for a change. Contrary to Francis' vehement protestations, it was obvious he would not be able to deal with his daily routine in the shape he was currently in, especially once the non-refillable prescription of painkillers ran out. Hell, with Francis' intense dislike and distrust of medications, he may have already flushed them by now anyway.

By this time tomorrow the five flights of stairs, the walk to the pet supplies store and back, the bags of supplies hanging off his bruised and battered body, and all the movement Francis' activities required would make the tortures of the Spanish Inquisition seem like a tickle fight in comparison. But Francis would endure it rather than ask for assistance. That is why it was up to Terrance to head the bulk of the pain off at the pass. He had an idea, a good one in his estimation. He just had to get everyone to go along with it. Francis was reluctantly on board, though it would have been better if it hadn't been against his will. Terrance hated playing the "released under my supervision" card and threatening to put his brother back in the Harper Institute, but strong-arming was the only thing Francis gave in to.

Strong-arming however, was not going to work on the other two participants in his plan. A call on basic human compassion, and an offer of money, was going to have to do the trick.

Susan Lee answered the door on the third knock; still in her bathrobe and with a towel wrapped around her wet hair. She had to leave for the Paramount Hotel to start her shift in the laundry in about an hour and a half and was still in the middle of getting ready to go, so she didn't look exactly friendly when she swung the door open and found a stranger looking down at her with his right hand in a fist, poised for a fourth knock. She instinctively drew her robe tighter with her left hand and gripped the knob of the door, ready to slam it on the stranger if he turned out to be some kind of weirdo. *He looks harmless, but you never know.*

"Can I help you?"

"Oh, I'm—" the man was obviously embarrassed to have caught her fresh out of the shower, which she took as a sign of normalcy, "I'm sorry. I caught you at a bad time. I was looking for Chava."

Suspicion flooded over her. "She's my daughter."

"Yes, and you are Susan Lee."

"How did you? Oh, wait! I recognize you now. You're our landlord, Mister Tower, right? I remember you from the real estate office. How can I help you?"

"Yeah, that's me, but you can call me Terry. I can come back, I'm really sorry to bother you." He gestured apologetically with both hands and started to back away from her door.

Susan's face softened at Terry's discomfort and she quickly worked to repair the awkwardness caused by her brusque behavior. "No, it's fine, really. I was just getting ready for work and wasn't expecting anyone. Chava is in her room. May I ask why you need to see her? Has she been bothering the other tenants? I've asked her to leave the old folks alone."

"No. No; nothing like that at all. Actually, I'd like to speak to both of you if you could spare a moment or two."

"Uh… sure, have a seat while I put something on and get Chava. But I only have a minute, my shift starts soon."

"Thanks a bunch."

Susan shuffled quickly down the hall in her bare feet towards the apartment's two bedrooms and called for Chava as she shut her own door behind her. Terry took a seat in a brown, overstuffed chair opposite the matching sofa and took a moment to look around. It was obvious the Lee's were not well off, not a lot of unnecessary or luxurious items that people tend to fill their homes with, but they seemed to appreciate cleanliness and basic comfort, and it looked like Susan did what she could with what they had. There were several framed prints on the walls: children playing with kites, a boy riding an ox while playing a flute, farmers in a rice paddy. The writing at the bottom of each print looked Chinese. Was Lee a Chinese name? He thought so, maybe Korean. There was only one photograph hanging in the living room and it was of a man. He was smiling in the photo and looked like a nice, gentle guy… also Chinese or Korean. The picture frame had a black ribbon running diagonally across the photo. Terrance was pretty sure that the ribbon signified that the man was dead. Was that Chava's dad? That would explain the girl's earlier comment about a boyfriend living there with them sometimes.

Terrance's contemplation of the photo ended when he heard Susan and Chava entering the living room from the direction of the bedrooms. He turned to see Susan fully dressed in a white laundry uniform and Chava standing there in her socks with a puzzled expression on her face.

"Terry? Um… you wanted to talk to me, to us, about something?"

"Hi, again. Yeah, I wanted to run something by you and your mother. Please, have a seat. It'll only take a minute."

The Lees sat on the sofa across from Terry as he spoke. "You both know my brother; he lives up on the fifth floor."

Chava nodded. "Yes. I was wondering, what happened to him anyway? Why was he using a cane?"

"He had sort of an accident today. Actually, well, he was hit by a taxi cab. And that's what I wanted to talk to you two about."

Susan's voice held real concern as she spoke. "That's terrible. And I don't mean to sound cold, but what does that have to do with us?" She also sounded like she meant the last part.

A blank look came across Terrance's face. *She's right. What does this have to do with them? Why am I inviting them into any kind of interaction with Francis? He is not the least bit pleasant to be around, even as his brother. How is he going to talk to these two? Will he even talk to them at all? I know that Francis will allow them to help him, but not 'let' them, and he definitely wasn't going to show any signs of appreciation. He's going to do it because he wants to avoid even the most remote of chances of ending back up in the hospital; a basic fear. I suppose offering the Lees cash to help him out is basic, as well... the basic desire for money. And it's not like they couldn't use it. I'm prepared to make them a very sweet deal. And if it gets to be too much, well, they could always quit and he wouldn't blame them or hold it against them.*

"Well, Missus Lee—"

"Please, call me Susan."

"Well, Susan, you're right. You are right; it isn't your problem in the least. What I wanted to talk to you about is a job; jobs actually, for the both of you."

"I have a job already. It doesn't pay much, but still—"

"Chava would actually be doing most of the work. I was just going to ask you if you could do a little cooking and maybe some light housework for Francis. Chava would be doing errands and helping my brother with his hobby."

"Light housework? Doesn't he use the whole fifth floor? That's a huge area."

"True, and the roof, but Francis' actual living area is very small; one room where he sleeps and a kitchen and a bathroom, and he is very tidy. The rest of the space is dedicated to his hobby. That would be Chava's department. I'm prepared to pay you, Susan, two-hundred and fifty dollars a week to cook him at least one hot meal a day and pick up after him in his living space. If he takes to the home cooking and isn't opposed to more meals, I'll up the pay. As for Chava, that is going to be much more work. I just thought that seeing as it is summer vacation and she needs somewhere to be during the day while you sleep after your shifts, she could make some money for your family. I'll start her off at three-hundred a week."

"Three-hundred a week!" Chava's face immediately lit up. Terrance could see the little girl's wheels turning, thinking about what she could get with all that extra money.

"Wait, Chava, wait; what exactly would she have to do up there? I mean, you keep mentioning your brother's hobby. Could you be a lot more specific? That's a lot of money to pay a kid to help with model airplanes or scrapbooking, you know."

Terrance sat quietly for a moment. He didn't like talking about Francis and his activities out loud. It always felt like he was betraying some nasty family secret, it also made his brother sound like he was a loon and that made HIM start to question Francis' sanity too. But the Lees would quickly learn the truth if they worked upstairs anyway, so he may as well come clean about it now.

"Well, first of all, it is not exactly a hobby in the strictest sense. It is actually a form of therapy that has sort of… um… sort of ballooned."

"Therapy?" Susan looking slightly alarmed. "What is wrong with him exactly? You said he wasn't dangerous."

"He's not dangerous, not at all. Not to others. He's a danger to himself. I mean he WAS a danger to himself. He has pets. Taking care of the pets helps him cope with his problems. The welfare of the animals, the feeding, the cleaning, the caring, it gives him a focus, something to care about, something besides the desire to… well, to do himself harm."

"Oh. Wow, I don't know. It's a generous offer, but —"

"Hold on." Chava stared at him with wide eyes. "You want to pay me three-hundred dollars a week to help him take care of some pets. What? Does he have rattlesnakes or black widow spiders or something up there?"

"No! Well, maybe. I'm not sure. It's just that he has A LOT of pets. You've seen him with the bags of pet supplies? He goes to the Sycamore Pet Emporium almost daily. He spends his time taking care of the animals. And with his injuries, he's going to need help. You'll also have to go down to the grocery store for him, but that won't be more than once a week or so. He gets most of his food delivered. If he has any dangerous animals up there, you won't have to get anywhere near them. I guarantee that."

"How many pets exactly?" Chava sounded intrigued.

"I really don't know. He doesn't invite people into that part of the apartment, not that he has anyone to invite, and I haven't been in there for some time now. So, what do you think? Try it out? If it is too much for you we can call it off, no hard feelings. We can even deduct most or all of the money you make from your rent. However you want to do it."

Chava and her mother looked at each other, their eyebrows arching quizzically, before finally turning and smiling at Terrance.

"When do we start?" Chava beamed.

IV

"Well, he has me by the short and curlies—"

"Damn him. I can take care of things myself—"

"A helper is just going to get in my way; have to show them, teach them, look at them, talk to them—"

"And they're going to talk back, going to talk about their day, what they like, what they don't like—"

"Asking questions; and more questions, and MORE QUESTIONS—"

"Questions about me, why this and why that, what I like, what I don't like; QUESTIONS… and looking at me, watching me—"

"Then they'll leave and talk about me; talk about you—"

"Going to have to show them how to change your filters, how to trim your nails, how to scratch your belly without scaring you, how to spread your supplements evenly, how to feed you, how to know when you're hungry, how to apply medications, how to know when you aren't feeling well—"

"They won't get it the first time; I'll have to repeat everything over and over and over again… and AGAIN—"

"They won't know how to hold you, how to pet you, how to make you feel safe, HOW TO TAKE CARE OF YOU—"

"They won't know what to do first, what to save for last; they'll screw everything up—"

"I'll have to explain everything, more than once; have to re-explain every single day; the same questions every single day. EVERY SINGLE DAY—

"I'll be talking all damned day! I'll have to hear them and see them ALL DAMNED DAY—"

"Damn you, Terrance—"

"Why are you doing this to me? Why is he doing this to me, to us? Why can't he just let me be—"

"Maybe he'll put me back in the hospital anyway. No, no he wouldn't do that to me, to us. He's just trying to help me, to help us. It's not his fault, it's my fault. It's ALL my fault—"

"He's always been there for me, for us. He's been a good brother. I've been a ton of bricks on him for years! I've been a burden on him, a fucking thorn in his side! A constant toothache—"

"I'll teach the helper the best I can. I'll teach them; maybe they'll be a fast learner, catch on quick. Maybe they'll understand me, understand us. Please, learn, catch on! Please understand—

"I just hope they don't talk too much; look at me too much, ask me questions. No questions, please—"

"Damn you, Terrance! Thank you, Terrance, you are a good brother. I wish you would leave me alone, leave us alone—"

Francis sat at the small kitchen table centered exactly below the one bare light bulb used to illuminate the space, his aluminum cane leaning against the table on his left. The light fixture was actually capable of holding up to four bulbs, but one was easily enough to see by and he never bothered to change out the bulbs until all four were dead. Then he'd put in a fresh foursome and start again. The first time he had to remove the fixture cover he never bothered to put it back in place. He didn't know what became of the cover, probably went out with the trash, and he never gave the light fixture another thought until the fourth bulb burned out and he could no longer see. He had simplified his life greatly in this way, why bother worrying or thinking about something until it makes itself obvious?

The rest of the kitchen was as bare as the bulb. There was a white enamel double sink, with no dirty dishes in it. His one of everything: plate, coffee cup, fork, and so on, were in their proper places in the white cabinet. A white coffee maker sat on the counter beside the sink, with the pack of filters and a can of coffee sitting beside it. The humming refrigerator, also white, stood in one corner. It held only mustard, cheese slices, milk and frozen ground beef. On top of the fridge was arranged a row of loaves of sliced white bread and a stack of corn flake cereal boxes. A stove sat in another corner, though he never used the oven, just the range for cooking cheeseburgers. This was also white.

The kitchen table and chair were arranged so that he could look out over the rest of the wood-paneled apartment. Off to his right immediately past the kitchen entrance was the bathroom. The rest of the apartment could be seen from the kitchen. But there wasn't much to be seen. A single bed neatly made up with a small end table next to it to hold the telephone. An easy chair placed next to a small shelf of books, all of them about pet care except for a stack of *National Geographic* magazines stacked neatly next to the shelf, and a wooden shelving unit that held all of his clothing, neatly folded.

Most people would walk into Francis' living space and immediately think obsessive compulsive, in a neat freak kind of way. But that wasn't the case at all. He just didn't have much. He didn't need much. "Just the bare necessities" was not Francis' motto, but they were certainly the words he lived by. He didn't need a couch or a coffee table, he never had guests.

He didn't have a TV because the thing made his head pound. He'd had enough of the mindless droning coming from the idiot box while he was a patient under Doctor Singh's care. Other patients, especially that crazy Old Martin, were always trying to entice him to have a seat on the communal couch to watch soap operas and reality TV programs. The casts of the soap operas strove for difficulties in their lives, something that Francis couldn't understand. He'd had enough real life drama, why look for entertainment in the fake problems of actors with painted faces and perfect hair? And the reality programs, they were not his reality. Though he probably wouldn't mind it, when would he ever be stranded on an island? Or vie for the attention of an overly-buxom and clueless bachelorette?

He did like the nature shows, but they were rarely on the hospital's television because the natural violence of chasing down prey, a lion clamping down on the throat of a zebra or wolves pulling down an elk, upset some of the patients too much. He could remember the orderlies spending nearly half an hour trying to coax Cicely Nelson out of the crafts supply closet after she watched a swarm of army ants eviscerate an unlucky sparrow. In Francis' opinion, the animals' efforts to survive were real reality, not trying to live with strangers locked in a house with cameras taping you as you argued over the breakfast table about who was supposed to make pancakes that morning. When the fuck did that ever happen except on purpose? He had thought about asking Terrance to fix him up with cable television so that he could watch nature programs, but he didn't have the time to sit and watch television anyway. He was too busy with his own reality.

His reality at that moment was waiting for Terrance to arrive with his new helper. According to Terry's phone call earlier, his brother wasn't supposed to arrive for another half an hour, but Francis thought it was a good idea to sit at the kitchen table, smoke and drink water while he prepared himself for the invasion. And though his brother was still a half an hour away, Francis had already been sitting there for nearly forty-five minutes. He chain smoked and was careful when taking drags; for the slightest cough grated his ribs, which in turn brought tears to his eyes and deposited each spent butt in the large, white ceramic ashtray taking up the center of the table.

While his hands and lips were busy smoking, his eyes were busy staring at his glass of water. A glass of water always made him think of something that his science teacher, Mister Lewis, had said back in high school. Mister Lewis had said that there is no new water on the planet. All the water we have has always been here and it will always be here, unless people were to send it into space for some reason or unless some ice crystals come to us, hitching rides on meteorites and then evaporate upon entry into Earth's air space. But water isn't always water. Sometimes it is in solid form as ice or in gaseous form in the atmosphere. It melts, it evaporates, it freezes, but it is always the same water.

Francis made it into sort of a game when he stared at the water he was drinking. Was he drinking the same water that someone like Elvis Presley or Johnny Carson or Doris Day had drunk? Was he drinking Napoleon Bonaparte's bathwater, or the sweat that dripped off of plantation slaves? Maybe he was drinking Tyrannosaurus Rex piss, or the water that washed Jesus Christ's feet, or snow that some Tibetan housewife had swept off her stoop. Maybe he was having the same glass of water now that some guy training for the Tour de France had used a month ago. And seeing as the human body is made up primarily of water, maybe he was drinking the body of General Patton, or Sir Arthur Conan Doyle, or his own Great Aunt Lois. *That would make us all cannibals in a sense, wouldn't it?*

"That's pretty gross." Francis answered his thought out loud to the ashtray full of cigarette butts.

Perhaps he was drinking the water that constituted the key ingredient in one of the bottles of that homeless man's whisky. Francis hadn't thought about the man since the policeman had tried to make him talk. He had wanted to cooperate with the officer, but he knew the more he cooperated, the more questions there would be. If he had been a chatterbox, he'd probably still be sitting there with the officer talking about how to proceed with pressing charges against his attacker. Then the court date, or dates, it would go on and on. That's why the policeman himself had had to reach into Francis' back pocket for his wallet in order to learn his name and then physically, but gently, load Francis onto the stretcher that was then placed in the ambulance.

Francis regretted the violence, but he wasn't surprised by it. The condition the dog was in, skinny and starving, immediately let Francis know that he was dealing with a man of sub-humane character. For any person that was capable of such cruelty had no problem with harming another human being. Though he knew the dangers of interacting with such a person, he was still unprepared for the man's brutal charge. His arms were full of pet supplies and it had been ages since another person had used force against him.

The last people to manhandle him were orderlies at the Harper Institute, and they were forceful in order to stop HIM from hurting HIMSELF, they never tried to intentionally harm him as the homeless man had. The only part of the attack that scared Francis was the crazed, more-animal-than-animal look in the man's eyes. The eyes had chilled Francis to the bone and made him hesitant in defending himself. Like a cornered rabbit that sits shuddering in its skin right before the fatal strike from the coyote lands, terrified but resigned to its fate. Even after he had stumbled back into the street and was struck by the front bumper of the taxi laying him out akimbo, the man had kept coming, kicking and swinging while screaming an unbroken string of obscenities. If not for the taxi driver's presence the crazy bastard would have finished him off with his bare hands, maybe by crushing and grinding Francis' head under his heal until it was just a bright red splotch on the blacktop.

Francis' internal revelry concerning wanton violence and the consumption, and re-consumption, of the planet's water came to an abrupt end with a sharp knock on his door. Francis' chest became a little tight, not at his brother's arrival, but at the fact that there was someone besides just his brother on the other side of the door. No one else had entered his apartment since the serviceman from the gas company had done his rounds checking for gas leaks in the neighborhood. Even the delivery kid from the grocery store and the nicotine-stained lady down at the discount smoke shop, with whom he had a special arrangement involving a twenty dollar tip, simply left their deliveries outside the door without knocking as per his strict instructions.

Francis wasn't afraid or ashamed to have people on his turf, for he had nothing to be afraid or ashamed of in the least as far as his apartment was concerned. He just plain, down-to-his-bones didn't like the idea of having people there. The chit-chat, the questions, the looking straight into his face and waiting for him to reply to the most inane of statements. Maybe he could make a rule for his helper, no speaking just listening, and listen closely because having to repeat anything would also be against the rules. But Francis knew he wasn't going to get off that easy.

"Fuck." He grabbed his cane and rose from the table, wincing against the abrasive pain in his ribs and stubbing out his half-smoked cigarette in the process.

"Hi, Francis, this is Susan and Chava Lee from downstairs in 101. They're going to be helping you out until you heal up." Terrance smiled ear to ear.

"This is two people? Why two people, Terry? You said a helper, not helpers."

Susan jumped in. "I'm going to do some cooking and cleaning for you, Mister Tower. Or should I call you Francis? Or Frank, maybe?"

"I don't care. Francis… or Mister Tower; no Frank. I—"

"What time do you usually get up in the morning, Francis?" Susan continued with a grin.

"Uh, six-thirty. Terry, I don't need—"

"Perfect! I finish my shift at the laundry at seven. I'll come straight here and get you fixed up."

"But, I… Terry—"

"I have to hurry off to work now, but I'll see you bright and early tomorrow, Francis." She took the free hand hanging at his side and gave it a quick shake before turning to her daughter, "I'll see you in the morning too, Chava. Dinner is in the fridge. Remember to keep the door locked and don't answer it for anyone. Love you, baby. See you, Terry."

A flabbergasted Francis took a step closer to his brother as Susan headed for the stairs. "Terry? What? You said you were getting me a helper, not… not a STAFF! Not a… a… maid… two people?"

"She's not your maid, Francis." Chava scrunched up her

nose.

"Terry? What, hey! You call me Mister Tower."

"Well, she's not officially your maid. I asked her if she could cook you a meal or two and clean up after you. The cleaning should be pretty minimal." While peaking around Francis at the immaculately bare apartment he added, "She won't be up here for very long."

Francis pointed at Chava. "You! You're the kid from the steps."

"Yeah, the one you never say hi to. I'm Chava. Nice to meet you, Mister Tower. Do you have rattlesnakes up here?"

"Rattlesnakes, what? No, I don't have—"

"Francis? Do you think we could come in for a minute?"

Francis backed up, slowly limping out of the doorway so that Terry and Chava could come in. Terry pointed out the edge of the bed to the girl and took the easy chair for himself. Francis stood looking at them for a few seconds not knowing what to say before going into the kitchen and easing back into the chair, once again leaning the cane up against the table. He took a fresh cigarette from his pack and lit up, not looking at his brother and the kid from the steps.

"Francis, uh, maybe you shouldn't smoke around the girl, huh?"

The smoking brother stared into Terry's face. "Feel free to leave, Terry. And you can take HER with you."

"Okay, man, okay. Don't get nasty." Terry turned to Chava, "He only smokes in here. He doesn't smoke around his pets."

"It's okay, Terry. I don't mind the smoke, really." Her mother, however, would mind it very much. But what she didn't know wouldn't hurt her. Besides, it was three-hundred dollars a week! A little smoke was nothing.

"How convenient for everyone." Francis' mouth was in a tight line as he spoke.

Terry was starting to get angry at his brother's snide comments and stood up from the chair. "Francis. Remember what we talked about. Cut the old codger bullshit," he turned his head quickly to Chava, "Pardon my French," and then back to his fuming brother. "Chava is here to help you, not to act as your personal whipping post. You're better than this, big brother. Act like it."

"Okay, okay. It's just all so, so new." Francis gestured for his brother to sit back down.

"I know it is. But you can do this. How about you give Chava here a tour; give her an idea of what she's going to need to do. How about that?"

"No. Everything has been done for the day. Uh… but in the morning; come with your mom in the morning when she comes to, to… make breakfast. Is that okay, um… Chava?"

"Sure thing. I'll be looking forward to it."

"Okay, then." Francis once again felt like a cornered rabbit.

At that, Terry and Francis got up and headed for the door. "Francis, just sit there and rest. Don't get up."

Chava went out ahead of him. "I'll talk to you tomorrow, big brother. Take it easy, okay?"

"Okay, Terry."

"It'll be fine, Francis." Terry gave his brother an encouraging smile and thumbs up before pulling the door shut behind him.

"Right… fine." Francis moaned to his ashtray and lit another cigarette.

On the other side of the door from where Francis, Terry, and the Lees are talking over the new arrangement; dozens of ears perk up, pivot and vibrate at the sound of unfamiliar voices, as well as the stress detected in the familiar tones of Francis. Noses sniff the air, tongues flit, and heads turn inquisitively. Wings stretch and then re-fold. Scales rasp across wood and electric warming rocks hum under heat lamps. Whimpers and squeaks come from shadowy recesses and nervous grooming is performed. Wheels stop turning and then start up again. Halted

51

meals resume. Smooth heads re-submerge and eyes peer out of the darkness.

V

"A *helper he said, not two! Not a woman AND a kid. He didn't say anything about a woman and a kid, he just said A helper —* "

"*Terrance really dropped the ball this time. I wonder if he even realizes what having those two around will dredge up in me —* "

"*The woman, Susan, the little girl, Chava, seem nice enough. That has nothing to do with anything! They could be a duo of modern-day, crime-fighting saints... But they were a woman and a girl! They could be murderous dope fiends looking for an easy mark, but they are a woman and a girl! That is what Terrance brought here, here where I forget. Try to forget, can't forget... never forget! A woman and a girl...* "

"*Susan Lee standing in my doorway wearing a hotel uniform, a maid, a laundress maybe? Looked like a waitress uniform. Mindy was wearing a waitress uniform the first time I saw her, a pink name tag with* MINDY *and a happy face sticker across the center; working her way through college —* "

"*Melissa would be about Chava's age now. Would we still be calling her Melissa? Maybe Melly? What does it matter? It's all gone now —* "

"*The Lees... The mother cooking and cleaning, the girl helping with the animals; running errands, but that's not all they'd do. That's not ALL that people do. They will talk to me. They will tell me things, things about themselves; things they love, hate, are afraid of, want to accomplish and they'll ask me about things. Why I'm here on the fifth floor, what do I love, hate. What am I afraid of? What do I want to accomplish? Who I am —* "

"*What has Terrance said to them about me? Surely he explained*

SOMETHING *about me to put them at ease; to convince them to 'help' me. To assure them that I wasn't just some whackjob hiding out on the top floor of their building. Did he tell them about Mindy? About Melissa? About what happened? About what I did? What I did to* THEM—"

"*Wait! Let them ask. The Lees aren't Doctor Singh. I have to answer Doctor Singh, try to answer Doctor Singh. The Lees are just helpers working for me, doing what I need them to do. What I tell them to do. They don't have the right to ask me anything. Talk to me about anything, but they will and I'll just say* NOTHING! *I don't have to answer their questions. They are just helpers, workers; hired help—*"

"*They are just a woman and a girl—*"

"*You really dropped the ball this time, Terrance! A bowling ball, and I think it landed on my foot—*"

"What's this?" Francis stared at his plate.

"You've never seen scrambled eggs before?" Susan had a quizzical grin on her lips.

"Yes. But I don't have eggs."

"You do now. Your brother filled me in on what you usually eat; corn flakes and cheeseburgers? That's it? How do you even survive on that?"

"I'm sitting here, aren't I? It can't be too bad for me. I eat to live, not live to eat." Francis crossed his arms over his chest.

Susan rolled her eyes. "I can't argue with that logic. Anyway, your brother gave me some money for groceries before we came up to see you last night. I picked up a few DIFFERENT things on the way here this morning. Terry said you'd be stubborn, but why not just give the food a chance? Who knows, maybe you'll like it."

"I see."

"A thank you wouldn't kill you, you know."

"Terry is paying you."

Susan's face lost some of her grin. "Yes, but that doesn't

mean you can't try to be a little nicer."

He picked up a forkful without looking at her and took a tentative bite. "Thank you for the eggs."

"Eggs are chicken fetuses." Francis muttered while eating.

"And what is ground beef made of, celery?" She smiled at the back of his head. "There, now that wasn't so hard, was it?"

Francis chewed his eggs, not bothering to answer.

On the way up the stairs last night to see Francis, Terry had told her what to expect with Francis in the meals department. He had told her that all she would find in his kitchen would be coffee and the ingredients for cheeseburgers and bowls of corn flakes. Susan had seen the grocery delivery boy a few times before and Terry verified that once a week he had his cheeseburger and corn flake fixings brought over.

Pretty much the only time Francis went to the store himself was when he needed toothpaste, toilet paper, light bulbs, and other non-edible products. But, Susan had seen boxes of produce come in from the farmer's market too. That, according to Terry, was not for Francis, but was intended for his pets. The animals ate very well. Terry wished her luck after she pronounced that she intended to try to get Francis to eat more of a variety of foods, healthier foods especially.

He slipped her a one-hundred dollar bill to help her fulfill that goal, and promised her more cash as it was needed. Susan had intended to ask Terry what had driven Francis to the fifth floor in the first place to live like a hermit on ground beef and corn flakes, but they had reached Francis' door and Terry was knocking, audibly huffing and puffing from the climb up the stairs. Chava stood behind Terry and her mother, not even slightly winded from the exertion of the climb.

Susan stuck to her plan and after finishing her shift at the Paramount Hotel that morning she headed over to the grocery store on Sycamore, right across from the Sycamore Pet

Emporium, to spend the money Terry had given her on different and healthier foods for Francis. The one hundred dollars didn't go very far, but since she didn't have to buy meat she was able to cover the essentials. She left the grocery store with a dozen eggs, orange juice, a nice variety of fresh produce, toppings and dressings to make salads, a bag each of apples and oranges, and a canister of pepper. In addition to the food she also picked up some lemon-scented furniture polish, paper towels, and sponges. From what she saw through the door the night before, the cleaning was going to be easy enough, but the air coming from Francis' living quarters was stale. It didn't smell bad *per se*, but it certainly could use a woman's touch. She made a mental note to pick up a scented candle or two the next time around.

Francis set his fork down next to his plate of half-eaten scrambled eggs and took a drink from the small glass of orange juice. He hadn't had juice since the Harper Institute and the citrus stung his taste buds. Susan heard the clink of the fork on the table and stopped sweeping the floor so she could clear the table and do up the dishes before heading down to 101. She stood across the kitchen from Francis and looked at the plate disapprovingly.

"You didn't like the eggs?" Her hands were firmly planted on the hips of her Paramount uniform.

"No... yes, they were fine."

"What then? Why didn't you finish them?"

"I'm not used to eating eggs. Or drinking juice, but it was fine. Good, I mean."

"Oh... well, I'll cook you only one next time; until you get used to eating them. But at least finish the juice."

"Next time?"

"You didn't think they were a one-time deal did you? Terry asked, and is paying me, to cook for you. I can't very well take his money just for pouring you bowls of corn flakes, can I?"

"I won't say anything if you won't."

Susan grinned. "Was that a joke, Francis?"

"A joke? No, we don't have to tell Terry. You take the money and I eat what I want."

"No deal," Susan felt a little disappointed. "Listen, I made garden salads for you and Chava to have for lunch. They are in the fridge."

"Salad? I don't eat lunch. Or salads."

"Yeah? Why should your pets be the only ones getting any nutrition around here? Don't worry there are bacon bits, shredded cheese, and a choice of dressings in there, too. You can fatten it up as much as you want, but eat the vegetables too."

"Okay, I'll try to. I'll try."

"Hey, I'm going to ask Chava whether or not you ate, so don't think you can get away with just tossing it out."

"I said okay."

"Yeah, yeah, I know how that works. I have a child of my own, you know. Just agree with what I say and then do what you want."

"Susan?" Francis glowered.

"Francis?"

"I don't know what Terry told you, but I'm not a child. I don't have the mind of a child. I'm not retarded or mentally disabled in any way, shape, or form. If this is going to work you're going to have to skip the condescension."

"I didn't say you were a child, or retarded. I'm just telling you what I prepared for lunch; just letting you know what's going on. You don't have to—"

"Wait, let me finish. Let me tell YOU what's going on. This is my apartment. In fact, YOUR apartment is MY apartment. I will eat the eggs, the salads, whatever... IF I feel like it!"

Francis felt himself losing his temper and instantly regretted being so harsh. Where was this machismo yesterday when the homeless man attacked him and he could have used it?

He continued in an apologetic tone, "Don't take me the wrong way. I wouldn't kick you and your daughter out of the building for trying to help me, but I have been alone for a long time, Susan. I'm not used to being told what to do or when to do it. Not since the hospital. And I had enough of that there."

"Okay, Francis. You're absolutely right. I'm sorry for trying to boss you around. It's your apartment, your life, but let me tell you something."

"Yes?" Francis braced himself.

"If you lose your temper with Chava like that, or talk to her like you just talked to me," she paused and scanned the kitchen, "your next visit to a hospital will be so that they can remove a box of corn flakes from your ass."

Susan and Francis stared at each other across the kitchen table for several moments before Francis picked up his coffee cup, took a sip and nodded. "Fair enough."

The long, awkward silence produced by the stalemate was broken by a light knock. Susan picked up her purse and made her way to the door. "That will be Chava. I'll see you tomorrow, Francis."

"Right, tomorrow; see you." Francis sighed.

Susan opened the door to see her daughter standing there sleepy-eyed, but freshly showered and dressed for her first day working for Francis. "Come on in, baby."

The girl bounced into the apartment and threw a small wave in Francis' direction. She got a barely perceptible nod in return. "I'm going down to our place now. You do what Mister Tower asks you to do. There is a salad in the fridge for lunch, okay? Be good and don't give Mister Tower any trouble, and if Mister Tower gives YOU any trouble—"

"There won't be any trouble. I'm not deaf, either!" Francis shot from across the room. His eyes met with Susan's and with that shared look they agreed to an unspoken treaty. Susan nodded approvingly, kissed Chava on the cheek and made her way to the stairs.

Francis looked at her from his seat at the kitchen table. "Come in, then."

The girl hesitated for a second and then stepped into the kitchen. "So, where do I start?"

"Do you like salad?" Francis leaned forward hopefully.

"Love them! You?"

"Damn."

VI

That was nice, even with all the teeth-pulling and head-butting.

If I was to be totally honest with myself, I'd have to admit that it felt kind of good to cook for a man again. I hate to admit that, but it was.

Breakfast time, that's when Harry and I had our best conversations; over coffee and toast talking about everything and nothing, and starting the day together.

With Ron, breakfast time is just 'time to get out' time. Maybe he grabs a bite before leaving, maybe not. Definitely no nice conversations; barely a 'hello' or a 'good morning', but that's okay. It's kind of a relief when he leaves anyway; don't know why I just don't end it. Maybe it is time to.

Francis is not the same as Harry and Ron. No intimacy or lack of intimacy there, just feeding another living person. He's not big on small talk; doesn't even try. He's not shy though; speaks up when he has something to say. I wonder what his story is; too soon to ask.

I don't think he cared for the idea of something different for breakfast. Corn flakes every day?

But he didn't criticize the eggs, not like Ron would if he didn't want them.

Francis wasn't against the eggs; just surprised I think. He almost cleaned off his plate though. He must have at least liked them, or tolerated them. He seems like the kind of guy that tolerates things; never really likes or dislikes, just tolerates.

But then, he doesn't really seem to care what he eats. I don't think he cares about the corn flakes and cheeseburgers, eggs or salads; it's just fuel to him. Like eating is just a chore, something he has to get out of the way.

The rest of the apartment is as simple as his taste buds. Not dusty, but no shine. The bed was made, but not wrinkle-free. Clean bed linen, but no pattern just solid blue. His toiletries; arranged in the order that a person would probably use them. His books shelved neatly; National Geographic magazines stacked straight, nothing hanging on the paneled walls. No photos. Clothes were in neat stacks on his shelf; boxers, socks, pants, shirts… in an order that you would probably put them on. Nothing was on hangers, no closet even; no knickknacks anywhere, no plants. Nothing to complicate day-to-day existence; one of everything needed in a kitchen. Only one coffee cup…

I have to remember to bring a coffee cup for myself tomorrow. I'd sit and have coffee with him. I wonder what he'd say if I just sat down at the table without warning, without asking. Only one kitchen chair…

I shouldn't have argued with him today. I have to remember that he doesn't want us there in his space; just keep my mouth shut and take the money from Terry, but a little talk might do him good. Just shouldn't lose my temper with him. He didn't want to argue, he just doesn't like complications, like conversation or questions it seems. Maybe Chava will pick up on that quicker than I did, but she's just a kid. Not a chance…

Chava stood motionlessly enthralled just past the doorway leading from Francis' living quarters to the much larger section of the fifth floor. Based on her limited interaction with Francis, pretty much all negative thus far, and on what she'd seen of the recluse's living conditions, which were Spartan at best, she was totally unprepared for what she found arranged before her.

She hadn't given it much thought, but she had the vague preconceived idea in her head that Francis housed dozens of animals like mice and hamsters crowded in cages; maybe a bunch of cats and dogs milling around your feet waiting to be fed, the permanent smell of urine and crap stinking up everything in the vicinity. She expected to encounter escaped granules of cat litter crunching under her feet; coats of animal hair and dander clinging to drapes and furniture. Nothing could have been further from the truth. Francis wasn't an animal hoarder, he operated a first-class menagerie.

When the fifth floor had been renovated for Francis' use the plans had called for raising the ceiling another twelve feet, and the walls of the raised portion were constructed of panes of plate glass giving the huge room the appearance of an extremely well-lit botanical garden or maybe an aviary. You could easily grow small trees or allow a flock of birds to fly free in the converted space. In fact, there were several bushy ferns and snaking philodendrons thriving in the ample sunlight and strategically spaced around the room, providing a sort of positive green feng shui feeling.

There was a small spiral staircase in one corner of the room just to Chava's left that allowed access to the roof, or what was left of the roof. The only part of the roof that actually remained was the portion that covered Francis' living quarters, as the rest was a big glass box that served as a ceiling. From where he was standing, looking up and behind him, Chava couldn't make out what Francis had up on the roof, though she could make out what seemed to be the greenery of plants or small trees.

Along the two longest walls of the rectangular space were double racks of cages and glass tanks interspersed with cupboards, sinks, small refrigerators and work tables. At the far end of the room were two floor-to-ceiling enclosures made of chicken wire on wooden frames. In addition to raising the ceiling they must have also reinforced the floor because the center of the room was dominated by a set of four above-ground fish ponds, all in a row down the center giving the impression of a long pool.

As her brain started to catch up with her eyes, Chava's sense of hearing kicked in to add another dimension to this sensory situation. The closest she could initially come to comparing the sounds filling the room to anything she had previously experienced was to the bird house at the zoo. But in addition to the chirping, squawking, singing and calling of birds, there were also non-birdlike tweets, chirps, squeaks, drones, grumblings and barks; some higher in pitch than the birds, many of them lower. These other sounds did away with the zoo's bird house comparison in her mind, and replaced it was the sounds of a jungle, an Amazonian auditory landscape.

Though the room was obviously occupied by a large number of creatures, there was very little smell. She had once visited a classmate and while at the other girl's home her nose was under constant assault by the scents produced by her friend's one cocker spaniel and a pair of gerbils. But Francis' "zoo" was so clean and organized that no harsh odors stood out to assault the olfactory. Just like when you are out camping or hiking in the woods, you know there are lots of animals out there. You know they are pissing and shitting willy-nilly, but the odors do not necessarily dominate the environment. They are more like just a natural segment of the total scene.

And like the bird house at the zoo, or a forest or a jungle, the room was not really suited to human habitation. There were no couches, easy chairs, coffee tables, or televisions. The only conveniences that Chava could spot right away were a clock radio on the nearest work table and a few stools that matched the height of the tables. Everything else in the room was there for the express purpose of caring for the animals. Francis may have spent most of his time in this room taking care of the animals, but it wasn't his space. It belonged to the animals.

"What?"

"I asked if you were going to come in or if you were just going to stand there gawking all day."

"Oh, I... um... yeah, I'm coming in. Mister Tower, this is... it... wow!"

"It's wow?"

"Yeah, I mean. Look at this place. It's wild."

"My friends here would probably disagree, but I do what I can."

"Well, you know what I—"

"I know. The first thing you can do is go up the stairs there and open the window next to the door."

"Which window?"

"It is the only one that opens. There's a latch; you'll see it."

"Okay."

Chava strode to the spiral stairs and headed up its curve. It was only a matter of seconds before she was at the top of the stairs and once she was there she could clearly see the rooftop area. The greenery was from trees and plants as she naturally suspected. There was also a small, wooden bench sitting in front of a large wood-sided box about two and half or three feet deep that took up nearly half of the roof space.

Her gaze lingered on the box for a few moments. *Hmm, I wonder what he keeps in there.*

She had no trouble finding the window, as Francis had said she wouldn't, it was the only one with a latch. She gave it an easy turn and opened it up wide. No sooner had the window swung ajar that Chava stumbled backwards and almost went over the stair railing as a flurry of black, screeching feathers instantly appeared in the opened window.

"What the—!" Whatever else she was going to say was lost in a scream.

"Don't yell. You'll scare her," Francis barked up at the frightened girl.

"It's a big bird, Mister Tower. It's a big, old crow!"

"It's a raven. And HER name is Mavis." At the sound of Francis pronouncing her name, Mavis dipped her head and dived for the table nearest Francis, alighted on the tabletop, pecked a few times at the silver color of Francis' aluminum cane and then croaked up at him, turning her head from side to side looking at him with each of her sparkling eyes.

"Good morning, Mavis, I'm fine, thanks." Francis gave the raven a dog biscuit from a plastic container, "Are you going to stay up there all day?" His eyes never left Mavis as she started working on the biscuit.

"I'm coming... Wow!"

"Wow again."

"Hey, come on, you don't see that every day, you know. She's beautiful; just caught me by surprise, that's all."

Francis seemed to lighten up a little at the compliment bestowed upon his winged friend. "Yes, she really is a beautiful creature." He spoke softly and scratched Mavis on the top of her head, "Aren't you, Mavis?"

He turned his attention back to Chava. "You know the difference between a crow and a raven, don't you?"

"I always thought they were the same thing, just different names. You know, like there are different names of sharks – Great White, Hammerhead, Mako, like that, but they are all sharks."

"Well, they're not the same. Ravens and crows are two totally different birds, as different as canaries and ostriches. They're just both black. Oh, and sharks aren't all the same either." Francis went on, "You see these long feathers on the top of Mavis's head, makes a kind of pointed crown? Crows don't have them. And, did you ever see a crow this big? Mavis is nearly twice the size of the average crow."

"Well, now that you point it out—"Chava reached out to pet Mavis but quickly withdrew her hand after the big bird squawked sharply and nipped at her, "Hey—!"

"Watch it! That beak can cut right into you if she gets you good. You have to let her get to know you. Don't try to touch her unless she comes to you. She'll let you know when it's okay for you to touch her. She's not really tame, just friendlier than most wild birds. Tomorrow morning I'll let you give her the dog biscuit. She might let you pet her after a while."

"Okay, sorry, Mister Tower. Sorry, Mavis."

Francis looked down at the girl out of the corner of his eye. The kid apologized to Mavis, to a bird. The girl's thoughtfulness and willingness to follow the rules pushed Francis to come to the conclusion that she deserved some further explanation, some warning concerning her new job as his helper.

"Hey, Chava; listen, most of the animals in here are pretty much harmless, but you're going to have to be careful with some of them. Don't touch any of them unless I tell you to or unless I'm in here with you, at least until they get used to you. You understand?"

"Yeah, I got it. I promise to be careful and follow your directions, Mister Tower. Can you show me the rest of the animals now?"

"I suppose that's in order. Come on, and pay attention." His tone turned grave, "Your fingers may depend on it."

Chava wasn't certain, but Francis looked like he might have flashed a partial grin at Mavis with that last statement.

Chava spent the next forty-five minutes being introduced to common everyday animals she had seen before; well-known animals she had never seen but had heard of; and odd animals that she never even knew existed.

Leaving Mavis sitting and croaking away happily on the table while busily pecking at her dog biscuit, Chava followed the hobbling Francis to the first of the above-ground enclosures that took up the center of the room. Contrary to what Chava first assumed, only two of the four enclosures contained water, these being the first two that you encountered upon entering the room. At the side of the first of the four enclosures Francis stopped, leaned heavily on his cane and pointed towards the water's surface with the walking aid, "In here, you'll find eight red-eared sliders, or plain, old water turtles, as most people call them. Cleaning this pool is going to be one of the dirtiest jobs I'll need you to do for me. It will take a lot of bending, carrying, and scrubbing. It's not pleasant. You'd think that animals that spent most of their time in the water would be cleaner, huh?"

A large heat lamp was attached to a wooden arm

overhanging a small log in the center of the pool. Three adult, hand-sized turtles lay on the log with all of their feet splayed out like sun worshipers on a tropical beach. The sunbathing turtles cocked their heads slightly up at the two humans when they sidled up to the pool, but otherwise seemed completely unconcerned with them being there. The girl assumed that the red spots on each side of the turtles' heads were the source of their name.

Chava could also see round shapes moving around under the water, the other five sliders she assumed. The turtles looked harmless overall, but they did have sharp-looking, hooked beaks.

"Do they bite?"

"You never know. Reptiles are never really one-hundred percent tame, so don't give them the chance. Especially that big one with the yellow stripes on his feet; see him there all stretched out? His name is Bullet. He is pretty cocky and can be a right bastard when you go to clean the pool. They are much faster than they look, in the water especially, and are unpredictable. But they're harmless as long as you use some common sense. If one does happen to get a hold of you it'll probably take a nice little chunk out of your hand, so don't give them a chance. That reminds me, the first aid box is back at that first table, on the shelf behind Mavis. It's one of them white, plastic jobs with the big red cross on the side." Mavis croaked thoughtfully at the sound of her name.

Francis moved on to the next pool, also filled with water. "In this one is half a dozen Australian pig-nosed turtles. Just like the other turtle pond, this one is a real chore to clean."

Chava could see the bluish-gray carapaces of the turtles gliding around the bottom of the tank. "Why don't these have a heat lamp or a log for sunning like the sliders have?"

"They don't need it. They are the only species of freshwater turtle with true flippers rather than toes. They wouldn't use the log even if they had one in there. It would just take up space. Look back there at Bullet. See his toes? These guys don't have them. But their water is warm. Both pools have submerged water heaters."

"No kidding? Did you name any of them?"

"Nope, no names for these Aussies. You don't really get to see enough of them to get acquainted, just their little pig noses when they come up for air; see, like that," he was pointing towards the center of the pond. Chava could see the perfectly round pair of nostrils of what could only be described as a pig's nose poking up into the air. The nostrils flared once or twice and then submerged. "See? That's all you really ever see unless you fish one out for a closer look or when you clean the tank."

"Well, then, why do you—"

Francis waved her question off and gestured on to the next enclosure. "Let's keep it moving. I still have a lot to tell you."

This brusque behavior reminded Chava that she was here against Francis' wishes. Mister Tower seemed to be enjoying his role as tour guide at first, but Chava saw that all of her questions were starting to annoy the man. "Sorry Mister Tower. I keep interrupting you. I'll try not to ask so many questions. This is just really cool."

"Chava, listen... okay? Don't take it personally. I'm not used to talking or answering a lot of questions. It's not your fault. It's great that you think it's interesting, but I need time to get used to this... this *situation*. Understand?"

"Sure Mister Tower. I know you didn't want me up here in the first place. Or my mom either. I know your brother is forcing us on you."

"You're right on all counts. But, hey, cut the Mister Tower formality. You can call me Francis if you want, okay?"

"Okay, Francis."

"Let's keep going; lots to cover yet."

By the end of Francis' tour Chava was in love with the fifth floor. The third enclosure held a breeding pair of Indian Star

Tortoises named Ozzie and Harriet in a simulated desert habitat complete with sand, cacti, and six large heat lamps.

Chava expected to find another species of turtle or tortoise in the fourth enclosure, but was surprised to find a community of European hedgehogs led by a friendly male named Lucky Max.

Francis didn't take much time showing her the animals on the long right-hand wall for they were all animals that most people were familiar with: mice, rats, guinea pigs, hamsters, gerbils, and rabbits. The only cage Francis took the time to point out special to her along that wall was sitting on the lower of the two racks. The spacious cage held an albino ferret named Felicia.

Francis said that he let Felicia roam about for a while each day, but that she had to be watched constantly because her inquisitive and mischievous nature had more than once caused trouble; she fell in turtle tanks, fought with the hedgehogs, and tried to eat the smaller rodents and birds. She also enjoyed sneaking up on Mavis and pulling feathers out of her glossy keister. The ferret was easy to catch, however, because she was a sucker for red licorice and all you had to do was wave a piece in her direction for her to come running. But Chava was warned not to give her too much of the candy because it turned Felicia's shit red and gave her the runs. According to Francis, Mavis often acted as a lookout when Felicia was out and about and would screech at the top of her avian lungs when the ferret was somewhere she wasn't allowed to be. Francis was positive that Mavis cooperated in this way as a means of getting even with Felicia for plucking her tail feathers. Humans weren't the only animals capable of revenge or ratting others out.

One of the two chicken wire enclosures at the far end of the space turned out to be the source of the chorus of bird calls Chava had heard when she first entered the room. Francis had a wide variety of canaries, finches, parakeets, love birds, doves and other small winged creatures Chava didn't recognize numbering in the dozens within the enclosure.

According to Francis, as long as the different species had

their own nesting areas and more than one feeding station the birds got along just fine. Like people, if you put them all together without separate resources for their own use, they would riot and tear each other apart in the pursuit of dominance and comfort. But as long as they had their own nests, and there were all kinds of nesting boxes, conical-shaped hanging nests, and woven bowl-shaped nests at different heights positioned in the enclosure, the birds got along great. Chava counted no fewer than eight food and water stations positioned around the enclosure, as well as dozens of perches for the birds to sit on while they groomed themselves or each other, or napped. The absence of competition meant the absence of conflict.

The second of the two enclosures was similar in appearance, but very different from the first. In fact, at first Chava thought the second enclosure was vacant. The interior of the enclosure was crisscrossed with tree branches and lengths of rope of different thicknesses. One corner was dominated by a fake, fiberglass log with a big hole in the side. There was a sickly sweet odor that smelled like overly-ripe fruit coming from the enclosure. When Chava asked about the smell, Francis told her that it was the smell of sugar glider urine.

The girl's quizzical expression prompted Francis to enter the enclosure, painfully bending his injured body around the branches until he had moved over to the fake log. He reached in and extracted a small gray creature that looked part squirrel, part rat, and part monkey. "Like the pig-nosed turtles, sugar gliders come from Australia."

The log housed at least fifteen of the small social animals, but Chava would have to come up during night-time hours to really see them in action because they were primarily nocturnal.

They only came out of the log during the day to piss or shit, and once their business was done they darted back into the darkness of the log.

They were called sugar gliders because they liked to lick up sweet juices from fruit and they had extendable, membranous wings for gliding, like flying squirrels. The band of sugar gliders was led by a dominant male named Oliver and Francis assured Chava she could come up and meet him some time in the near future.

As interesting as the other animals were, Chava found that the second long wall of cages and tanks on the other side of the space contained the most fascinating of Francis' creatures. Fascinating and a little disturbing, at least at first. This last wall held animals less often sought after by humans to serve as warm, cuddly companions. There were several different species of snakes, including an eight-foot long boa constrictor named Constance. Her skin was decorated with large brown diamond shaped patches of scales on a field of lighter brown. Despite her size, Constance was harmless unless you were a rodent or a bird. But that didn't mean she didn't bite. Francis made it clear to Chava that if she had to put her hands into Constance's tank for any reason to always move slowly and to always wash her hands first.

"Boa's have extremely poor eyesight, but an excellent sense of smell, as well as a mouthful of barbed teeth. What this uneven combination of senses means is that if your hand smells like mouse she'll strike first and ask questions later." Francis accentuated this point by showing Chava a semi-circle pattern of scars on the top of his hand, "And she was only five feet long when she did this, when I made the mousy hand smell mistake."

In addition to Constance and the smaller snakes, the last of the walls also displayed a three-foot long, bright green iguana named Merlin; bearded dragons, geckos, anoles, more turtles and tortoises of the land-locked variety, big, black emperor scorpions, shambling, fumbling hermit crabs, strutting rhinoceros beetles, bored looking toads and frogs, shy newts and hairy tarantulas.

Chava's eyes widened and she sucked in a breath of air when Francis reached in and withdrew a huge spider from one of the enclosures.

"This is Luis. He is a Mexican red knee tarantula." The big arachnid completely covered Francis' hand. Chava could clearly see Luis' two intimidating fangs hanging from under the creature's head.

Francis held the arachnid out to her. She took a quick step backwards while shaking her head, "Let me get used to the idea."

Francis, not all that surprised at Chava's reluctance, re-deposited the spider in its tank with a humorously over-exaggerated look of disapproval on his face.

"This place is amazing, Francis," Chava squealed out across the room with an encompassing wave of her skinny arms, "Really!"

"Yes," Francis found that for the first time in quite a while he was aware of what he had created on the fifth floor. It took the tour meant for Chava's edification to show him that because he was around the animals every day his fascination had waned, though his devotion to caring for the animals had not lessened to even the slightest degree, "It really is something. I'm going to have some coffee and a smoke now. And you, I need you to go down to the Sycamore Pet Emporium."

"Okay, do you have a list for me?"

"I do. And you have to come back quick. You'll be carrying live cargo."

Chava's eyes brightened at the prospect of being in on the acquisition of a new creature to the collection, "You're getting a new pet?"

"No. I need pinkies." Francis headed towards the door to his living quarters.

"Pink what, Francis?

Mavis paused long enough to let out a low, sympathetic croak and then continued pecking at her dog biscuit.

VII

"*Pinkies are the newborn hairless and sightless young of rodents, usually mice and rats. They're called pinkies because, well, they're pink; no hair yet, as I said.*"

"*Newborn rodents? What do you need baby rodents for?*"

"*The mice and rats and others that I breed here haven't given birth recently, so I have to buy the pinkies. That happens once in a while.*"

"*No, I mean why do you need pinkies at all?*"

"*Isn't it obvious?*"

"*You give them to Constance and the other snakes? You do, don't you?*"

"*Not Constance, she eats full-grown rats and rabbits. But most of the other snakes, yes. And to Luis and the other tarantulas, the scorpions and some of the lizards; even one of the toads. Mavis and the sugar gliders get the dead ones. The snakes and tarantulas and such usually won't touch the dead ones unless they are really hungry. The sugar gliders and Mavis don't mind, as long as they are still somewhat fresh. Actually, Mavis isn't picky at all. Ravens have cast iron stomachs.*"

"CROAK!"

"*It's true, Mavis!*"

"*But—*"

"*Problem?*"

"*Seems kind of cruel. I mean, they're babies.*"

"*Cruel... how so? Everybody has got to eat, right? You like cheeseburgers and hot dogs don't you?*"

"*Well, yeah, but—*"

"*But you have never seen the big, brown eyes of the cow before it is slaughtered, or heard the squealing of the pigs after they smell the blood of the others being killed. To Luis, and the others that eat them, pinkies are just food. There are no cruel intentions on their part. They don't torture or play with them first or get any pleasure, aside from satisfying their hunger, out of killing them. It's just survival, that's what they eat in the wild. Being in captivity doesn't change that. I'd prefer if they liked to eat broccoli and bean sprouts, but that is not the reality of the situation. Surely you've heard of the food chain... nothing much lower on the chain than pinkies.*"

"*But you just serve them up —*"

"*Yes, and so will you if you want to understand these creatures and do this job correctly... so will you.*"

Susan was hurriedly setting the table for dinner already dressed in her Paramount uniform. She was expecting Chava to be home at any second from her first day working for Francis Tower and she wanted to hear all about it.

Her mother's intuition proved correct yet again as she heard Chava's key hit the lock at nearly the same time that she was having the thought. Her daughter walked into the kitchen and had a seat at the table. She looked bushed, but she also had the healthy glow that a solid day of work can bestow upon a young person.

"Hi, Mom! Did you have a good sleep?"

"Yep, eight straight hours; how was your day with Mister Tower?"

"It was good," her downturned eyes and lilting tone contradicted the statement. The work may have done her some good physically, but she seemed stretched a little thin emotionally.

Susan looked at her daughter with a concentrated mother's eye, noting that though compared to the other kids her age she was still a little short, she had grown a little over the past few months. The money from Terrance Tower was going to come in handy when it came time to buy new, longer-legged school clothes.

She leaned against the counter, "You don't sound like you had a good day. What kind of work did he have you do? What kind of animals does he have up there?"

The girl's eyes brightened a bit at the last question. "He has all kinds of stuff... turtles and snakes, birds and a ferret, rats, guinea pigs, spiders and scorpions. Some stuff I never heard of... you ever heard of sugar gliders? And he has a big raven named Mavis that just kind of hangs out with him. She's not a pet, just kind of a mooch."

"Wow! Sounds like quite a zoo. No dogs or cats?"

"No, everything is in tanks and cages. Nothing runs loose except for Mavis and sometimes the ferret, Felicia. He doesn't have any fish either. I asked him about the fish. He said they don't have much personality and so he doesn't have any fun taking care of them. But I don't see what kind of personality a big, hairy spider can have. He has a huge tarantula that he calls Luis. He lets it crawl all over him! It gives me the willies big time."

"Different strokes for different folks, right? Did you have to do much cleaning and stuff?"

"Yeah, but it wasn't hard; just a lot of it. He has a cleaning and feeding schedule on a clipboard, reminds me of a doctor at a hospital walking around with his chart. I just have to follow that and check stuff off as I go. Most tanks and cages are cleaned every two days, except the bigger ones. The turtle ponds get drained and scrubbed once a week. I'm not looking forward to doing that. I have to scrape up bird and sugar glider crap every day. The reptiles and amphibians and bugs in the tanks are pretty easy, they don't crap much or make much of a mess. Anyway, it's not so bad. It wouldn't take so long to do, but he has to talk to every animal, one at a time, while their cages are being cleaned. Like conversations! He answers questions... weirdest thing I ever saw. Maybe he's trying to creep me out on purpose seeing as he doesn't want us up there in the first place. But he's not so bad really."

"Well, if the work and Mister Tower aren't so bad, why do you seem so down in the dumps?"

Chava focused on her hands and wouldn't look up at her mother. "Well, the feeding I guess. Some of it bothers me a little."

"The feeding? The feeding of what to what?" Susan's brows furrowed.

"Francis, he said I can call him Francis, sent me to the Sycamore Pet Emporium for pinkies."

"Pinkies?"

"Yeah, baby mice and rats."

"Baby mice and rats? For what?"

"He gives them to some of the snakes, the spiders, the scorpions, and even one of the toads; a big, bumpy-looking guy named Jethro. I couldn't watch; poor, little squirming things. They can't even see what is going on!" Chava's voice cracked and her eyes were welling up. "And I saw on the feeding schedule that Constance gets a grown-up rat tomorrow!"

"Who's Constance?"

"She's a huge snake! A boa constrictor. It's all just so cruel, mom." She was nearing the point of crying.

"Hey, hey, hey... listen, Chava—"

"I already know what you are going to say, Mom! It's nature, everything eats something, but I don't have to like it, do I?"

"No, you don't. But that's right, everything eats something."

"What makes it worse is that Francis is just so... so... *cold* about it. He doesn't show any kind of emotion at all when he feeds the pinkies to the spiders and stuff."

"Stop and think about it, Chava. Does he look like he enjoys it?"

"Well, no, but he doesn't look like he DOESN'T enjoy it either."

Susan sighed, "Do you remember going to see your dad in the hospital?"

"Sure, I do."

"Do you remember the doctor I talked with about your dad every day that we went there?"

"Yeah, Doctor Wells."

"Right, Doctor Wells. I hated Doctor Wells, sweetheart. For the same reason as you are having trouble with Francis and the pinkies. Doctor Wells showed no emotion, even when he told me that your dad had no chance. When he told me your dad was going to die his face never changed. I got the impression that he just didn't care, but that wasn't true at all. He even came to your dad's funeral. That was the first time I ever saw a doctor go to a patient's funeral."

"So what does it mean, not showing any kind of emotion?" Chava sniffled.

Susan bent down and put her hands on her knees, "Doctor Wells, and Francis, have to do some unpleasant things. Sometimes turning off your emotions is the only way you can get unpleasant things done. Do you see? Francis feeds the pinkies to the other animals almost every day. How could he do that if he let himself feel bad every time? He'd be more of a wreck than he already is. He has to hold on to the fact that it is nature at work, not something he can control. Just like we had to accept the fact that your dad was going to die, that, when it was all said and done, there was no fighting the cancer that ate him up from the inside. Your dad accepted that."

"He did?"

"Yeah, it was scary, but he did. And our last days with him were full of smiles and joking, remember?"

"Yeah, I remember. So Dad was really brave then, huh? Knowing that he was dying, but not letting it get to him?"

"That's right. And Doctor Wells was brave too, having to give me that kind of news. And Francis is brave for doing what he has to do too, even if it seems like a weird kind of brave."

"I suppose," Chava's shoulders slumped, "But I still feel

bad for the pinkies. I peaked in the box on the way back from the pet supply store. For a minute I thought about not going back and just keeping them, but they would have died without their mom anyway."

"I know you feel bad, and that's okay. When you stop feeling sorry for them I'll start to worry," Susan smiled at her daughter and smoothed her hair. "Hey, you ready for dinner?"

"Yes, but no pinkies for me, thanks."

"You're your dad all over," she stood and then turned wistfully towards the stove with thoughts of happier times in her head.

When Terry showed up in the evening to check on his brother and to see how things had gone with Susan and Chava on their first day; Francis was sitting in his easy chair with a glass of water and a cigarette hanging out of the corner of his mouth, his cane on the floor beside the chair, and an older issue of *National Geographic* open on his lap.

He was looking at dog-eared pages featuring photos of skulls; comparing those of carnivores, omnivores and herbivores past and present. Francis' mind was going over the attributes of teeth while he unconsciously used his tongue to explore his own set of chompers.

Other than size, shape and positioning, teeth hadn't really improved all that much over millions of years of evolution, if at all. Francis was considering the evolution of humankind in particular. From stooping to standing upright; to the perfection of the opposable thumb; to an increase in cranial dimension and brain size; to the loss of body hair, but the teeth always stumped him.

Human teeth are incredibly inefficient. Each adult has thirty-some-odd teeth in their head at one time or another, each one representing a potential dental disaster. They chip and break and crack. They become infected where they meet the gums;

food gets caught in the nooks and crannies causing disease and bad breath. New ones grow in crooked; into the bones of the jaw; pushing each other into awkward, painful positions. His own experience with three impacted wisdom teeth was fresh in mind even twenty years after the fact. *Wisdom, my ass. Teeth were designed to go wrong.*

Comparatively, his turtles had the best of possible teeth, or beaks really. Pointed at the front to get the bite started, hard edges to mash up the food and make it suitable for swallowing. How much better would it be to have only two 'teeth'? One on the top and one on the bottom; two hard plates curved to fit the oral cavity. And nerves? Nerves leading to the teeth? What is the point in that? They aren't necessary.

Teeth should have fallen out of the genetic code millennia ago. Just as the human baby toe, according to some in the field of evolutionary genetics, is getting smaller.

Francis' chin was cupped in his hand as he pondered. *Eventually we won't have baby toes because we just don't need the little buggers; they'll merely go the way of full coats of warming body hair, to varied degrees admittedly. So... two teeth plates, fused directly to the bones of the mandibles with no nerve connections; if human evolution had any sense at all, that's the direction it would go in terms of teeth. No muss, no fuss. That's the ticket.*

Francis put the *National Geographic* featuring photos of skulls, past and present, neatly back in its place on the stack of magazines, picked up his cane and painfully heaved himself out of his chair to unlock the door for his brother. Once the door was open he retreated to his chair in the kitchen and left Terry to take care of closing it.

Terry followed his brother into the kitchen after locking the door behind him and leaned against the counter. "How are you feeling, big brother?"

"Like I was hit by a taxi."

"I suppose that was a stupid question. What I mean to ask is, are the pills doing their job?"

"Nah, it wasn't a stupid question, Terry. I'm just real sore. I took one of the pain killers this morning and they do work, but I decided not to take anymore because I don't care for how they make me feel. They make me loopy and drowsy."

"The doctor that treated you at the ER said the pills might have that effect. At least promise me you'll take one before you go to bed, it doesn't matter if you feel loopy while you're sleeping."

"Good point. I will."

The two men were silent with their own thoughts for a few moments before Terry finally asked the question that Francis was waiting for, "How did it go with the Lees today?"

"The Lees... the Lees were...," Francis was nodding his head, "The Lees were fine."

"Oh, yeah?"

"The woman, Susan, made me eggs. They were good; a nice change, but we had a fight."

"What did you do? What did you say to her?" Terry took a deep breath to steady his nerves.

"Don't worry. Nothing serious. We straightened it out. She's a strong woman, Terry. Reminds a little of... of—" Francis blushed, "Chava, she—"

"Wait, Francis. Susan reminds you of Mindy, doesn't she?"

"A little; a little pushy, gets riled up easy. Yes, a little."

"And the girl?"

"The girl... Chava... quite sensitive."

"That's not so bad, though."

"No, she's not bad. She had issues with the pinkies, and she was afraid of Luis and a few of the other animals."

"Well, hell, Francis. Luis scares the bejesus out of me too. And the pinkie thing is kind of morbid. Anyone would have been freaked out the first time. Give her some time."

"Terry?"

"Yeah?"

"You don't have to defend Susan and Chava like that. I'm not some damned Scrooge sitting up here you know. They were fine. But—"

Terry sighed, "I knew there'd be a 'but.' But what? What is it?"

"The questions, they're killing me with the questions, Terry. The questions and the conversing." Francis' shoulders slumped and he hung his head.

"You haven't really talked to anyone in a long time, Francis. The last person you had a conversation with pushed you out in front of a moving car for crying out loud. You're out of practice. You can adjust to the questions, just as Chava can adjust to the pinkies. There is going to have to be a little give and take from both sides."

"I know. But I'd just as soon heal up and have them out of here. The sooner the better; just want to get back to my old routine."

"That won't be for some weeks, or even months considering it's your ribs that are cracked. You know that. Besides, a break in your routine might do you some good. So just stay on an even keel. Can you try to do that? Just try?"

"Yes," Francis muttered through clenched teeth, "Terry?"

"Francis?"

"Susan made me eat a salad for lunch."

"Well, some things are more difficult to get used to than others, aren't they?" Terry smiled.

Terry saw with a thrill, for the first time since Mindy and Melissa died more than seven years ago, Francis' shoulders bounce up and down once in a very brief and completely silent, but obvious, laugh.

VIII

"Yo! Ron! Hey, Ron! Ron! Clean the shit out of your ears, man! I'm talkin' to ya"!

"Knock off your bellowin' for fuck's sake! You're ruinin' my concentration over here."

"Yeah, your concentration on Tanya's ass... fuckin' hound. You been starin' at her can all night."

"So what? What's it to you?"

"Nothin', but you could save some for the rest of us. Ain't you still seein' that hot little piece of chink ass over on Sycamore? The one you always braaaaaggin' about?"

"Yeah, sure. And hey, she's not a chink, she's Korean."

"Gook then, what's the difference?"

"Nothin' really, they're all only good for one thing anyway! No matter where they come from. But don't go callin' her Chinese, or Jap either; she just might stick a chopstick up your ass and break it off."

"Hey, Ron... hey, man... is it true what they say about chink... uh... gook cooze? Does it go sideways?"

"You fuckin' dipshit."

"It does! Doesn't it! Hey, Tanya! Help Ron out! He's lookin' for some up and down cooze! That sideways shit is makin' him dizzy and all disorientaled!"

"Moron! When the fuck was the last time you even saw a pussy, huh? Up and down, side to side or in any shape or form? 'Sides, I don't think I'm goin' back over there anymore. She got all pissed 'cause I said her dead husband looked like a four-eyed Jackie Chan... sensitive cunt. And that fuckin' kid of hers is always hangin' around, givin' me the slant-eyed stink eye... little sawed-off bitch. Nah, I don't think goin' *over there is worth the headaches the two of 'em give me."*

"Geez, Ron, sounds like she ran your ass off. When was it you started lettin' the cooze tell you what's what? Was that the same day your nuts fell off and got kicked under a bus?"

"You know, Susan ain't the only one who can shove a chopstick up your ass, dickhead."

Ron Rhodes parked his black '94 Mustang convertible across the street from 517 Sycamore and looked himself over in the rearview mirror and rubbed his furry, yellow mirror dice for luck. He hadn't been here in over two weeks now, not since the big blow-up with Susan over the dead husband/Jackie Chan remark.

He hadn't called her and she hadn't called him. There is no way that he would ever admit it, but he knew he was out of line with that crack about her husband. But, he figured once she cooled off and felt the itch she'd call him up and he'd swoop in to give her a good scratch. To be honest, though, he didn't really care if she called him up or not. Things were starting to get too emotional, too attached; it was taking all of the fun out of it.

They had been seeing each other for close to a year now since they first met at a Paramount Hotel employee picnic, though he had long since quit his job driving the shuttle bus, and the relationship had always been based on sex, at least as far as he was concerned. But bitches have different ideas.

Now he was starting to see that she expected more from him, for him to act like a real boyfriend or something. He didn't really give a shit about how she felt about their relationship and he saw her as just another notch on the bedpost. He had enjoyed going into *Stew's* and bragging to the guys about the slant-eyed poontang, gooktang he liked to call it, he was getting over on Sycamore. But the bragging rights weren't worth the hassle.

Besides her criticism of his jokes, just like a goddamned wife, she worked nights and they always had to schedule their bedroom mattress wrestling around the kid.

It was obvious to him the kid didn't like him, he was certain of that. Ron didn't really blame the little slope for that. As a kid Ron had watched his own mother go through a whole parade of guys after his dad was out of the picture, even a Mexican and a nigger or two. But just because he understood the kid's point of view it didn't mean he gave a shit about the kid's feelings. *After all, life's a rough ride, kid, get a fucking helmet. You know, just because daddy is worm food, that didn't mean mommy didn't need some lovin' once in a while. You know what I'm talking about?*

The reason Ron decided to drop in on Susan this morning had nothing to do with missing her or their fun in the bedroom, it was because of what that fuckstick said at *Stew's* last night. Fuckstick though the guy is, he was right. What was he doing letting Susan call the shots? Sure, she didn't break things off with him officially, but not calling him for over two weeks surely qualifies as an unspoken, unofficial kissoff, right? *Where does that little gook bitch get off thinking she could get rid of me that easy?* He intended to smooth talk her back into the bedroom, knock off another big piece of that widow ass, and then give her the old "I don't think we should see each other anymore" line.

Watch her get good and steamed. And then, tonight he'd be at *Stew's* hitting on that sweet-assed Tanya and letting the guys know what's what; that his nuts were still attached, alive, and full of bounce and jizz.

Susan was at the sink finishing up the breakfast dishes while Francis sat in his easy chair with a *National Geographic* and smoked. She was a little nervous about this morning's breakfast after throwing Francis for a loop yesterday with the scrambled eggs.

She questioned her motives at the grocery store as she picked out the necessary ingredients to make pancakes. Was she shaking up Francis' morning breakfast routine to help enhance his everyday life and make his convalescence more enjoyable, to give herself something financially constructive to do, or was it more malicious than she realized. If it came right down to it she would probably have to admit that she was messing with Francis a little bit by forcing new meals on him, but the target wasn't Francis in particular.

The target was men in general. In some way she felt that by getting Francis flummoxed in harmless ways she was getting back a little at Harry for dying and at Ron for being such a jerk of a user.

Yes, she was well aware of the fact that Ron saw her just for what he probably viewed as convenient sex. For a while that was fine with her, too, if she was going to be perfectly honest. After Harry died she needed the closeness, even if it was merely sexual in nature. She wasn't anywhere near ready for an intimate relationship when she first met Ron. The loss of Harry was still too fresh; the wounds not even scabbed over, though it had been nearly three years since Harry passed.

Over the last three years without Harry she had been healing more day after day, but the healing process went very slowly at first. Every morning there was renewed agony waking up and realizing all over again that Harry was gone for good. But as time passed the mornings started to get easier, and though she still thought of him regularly and was reminded of him by the most trivial of things on a daily basis, she was healing more quickly all the time. Harry was gone a full two years before she met Ron and he was what she needed at the time after going so long not so much as holding hands with a man.

The last time she seen Ron he made a joke about Harry from his reclined, ruler of the roost position, on HER couch. He pointed up at the photo of him wrapped with the black mourning ribbon and said between sips of beer SHE had bought, "you know, from this angle your dead hubby looks a little like Jackie Chan wearing glasses." The prick had laughed until beer leaked from his nose. What a pig.

What happened next was months in the making. She told Ron that he was a loser and a user; eating her food, sleeping over whenever he felt like it, bouncing up and down on her to satisfy his horniness. And the worst part, though he never yelled at Chava or got physically abusive with her in the least, he treated her daughter like an unwanted cat in the apartment.

He knew she was there but showed her no consideration, recognition, or made any attempts at being even the slightest bit friendly. He never even spoke to Chava directly, but instead spoke through her to Chava as if she was some sort of séance medium: "Hey, Sue baby, ask your kid to head on to bed. Hey, Sue darlin', tell your girl I want to watch the ballgame at seven."

By the time she was finished ranting and raving at him about the Jackie Chan comment Ron was standing on the other side of the apartment door. She slammed it on him and she hadn't heard from him since. Just as well, but she had wanted to end it more maturely. Now, though, she was just glad he was out of her life.

"Mom," Chava's voice coming from behind her almost caused her to drop the coffee cup she had brought up to Francis' for her own use. She hadn't even heard Francis get up to answer the door for her daughter.

"My God, Chava, you scared the kimchi out of me," Susan dropped the cup in the dish drainer. She clasped her hand on the girl's shoulder while she caught her startled breath. "What's up, kiddo?"

Her daughter's worried eyes looked up at her. "Ron is downstairs looking for you."

"Ron?" Susan found him in the lobby of the building checking his hair in the reflection of the window situated next to the wall of mailboxes. *Ever the narcissist,* she fumed. He was dressed up in his best jeans and wearing the navy blue sweatshirt she'd bought him for his birthday a couple of months ago. He was also wearing a big, toothy smile.

She knew what that meant. He was here to make up and was hoping to get a little bedroom action out of it. She actually felt a little bad for him. In those rare moments when he actually talked about his life he let slip a few things about his childhood, and the details weren't pretty.

His father took off when he was around Chava's age, though not until after terrorizing him and his mother for years both physically and mentally. The stress of being a single parent caused his mother to turn to the bottle and she began a new life of heavy drinking interrupted frequently by one-night stands until she finally died of alcohol poisoning in a shabby bachelor's loft down on 6th Avenue.

Ron was a sixteen-year-old high school dropout by that time. She only knew where the woman had died because he had once pointed the building out to her on their way to an afternoon matinee. In the first couple of months of their relationship he sometimes took her out on actual dates, but that stopped once she finally gave in to his sexual advances. Once he got her in the sack all romantic pretenses fell away.

Ron turned at the sound of her voice, "Hey, Susan baby. How you doin'?"

"I'm fine; been a little busy."

"Yeah, your kid said you were cookin' for the weirdo up on the 5th floor."

"Francis isn't weird. He just keeps to himself. But yes, I'm doing some cooking and cleaning for him. And Chava is helping him out with his pets."

"Francis? Not Frank or Frankie? Sounds like a fag. Or maybe he likes kids, better watch out for Chava. There's lots of sickos out there, you know."

"Oh? Now you're interested in Chava? And whether or not Francis is a... a fag... is none of your business. And he's not anyway." She couldn't believe she was having this conversation and that jerk just stood there grinning as if his hurtful remarks and insults were somehow charming.

"Well then, maybe you're doing some other kind of cookin' up there for him, eh? You're not steppin' out on me already, are you Susan baby?"

"This is why you came by? To start a fight? To make fun of people that you don't know? To say nasty things about me?"

Ron changed his tune when he saw that he was quickly defeating his own mission for being there. He lowered his voice and stepped closer to her, "Nah, baby, I'm sorry. I didn't mean to talk like a horse's ass, really! I was just missin' you, that's all. Then I find out you're spending time with another guy. I just got jealous. I'm sorry, baby."

"Not that it's any of your business, but I'm not WITH anyone. Chava and I started helping Francis out a couple of days ago because he got hurt. Some crazy homeless guy pushed him out in front of a car. He's banged up pretty bad."

"That was this guy? Holy shit! McPhee was in *Stew's* telling everyone with ears about how he got away with some shit like that. Said he broke out of the hospital 'cause the doctors thought he might have rabies or something. Said he was in there 'cause a couple of guys picked a fight with him on the street and the cops were trying to blame him for starting it. I didn't pay much attention. That McPhee's a real fuckstick, always talking shit. Hey, I can kick his ass if you want."

"It was one man, and it wasn't a fight. He attacked Francis. And no, I don't want you to kick anyone's ass, Ron. And, actually, I don't think I want to see you around here anymore."

There. I said it. Now she only hoped that he was mature enough to accept it and leave the building peaceably. She realized that dumping him with no other people around was probably a bad idea, but she didn't want to have to deal with him trying to charm his way into her apartment. She could yell, but who would come? The residents who weren't out working were elderly and could only call the cops, IF they even heard her cries for help.

Ron's lip quavered and his eyes narrowed. His expression was like a foiled cat that unexpectedly let a mouse escape seconds before chowing down. *She's dumping me? Right here?*

That's not the way this was supposed to play out. She was supposed to be glad to see him, be open to his still unspoken suggestion to go inside. Then he was going to drop her like a hot potato while she was still laying there in her birthday suit. She wasn't supposed to dump HIM.

"Uh... what's that, Susan? Are you sayin' you're dumpin' me?"

"Come on, Ron. Nobody is dumping nobody. You knew this wouldn't last. I'm sorry, but it's true. We had some fun for a while; can't we just call it quits and end it nice and friendly?"

Now she was going to pity him? Apologize to him? Ask him to fuck off and be friendly about it? "Listen, bitch—" his voice started to rise just as a mailman came in with his sagging mailbag slung over his shoulder.

The mailman was a mild-mannered, black guy, well-liked by everyone in the neighborhood. Even the dogs liked him. And Susan, as well as the entire neighborhood, knew him by name.

The mailman looked back and forth between the two, "Missus Lee? Is everything okay here?"

"Yeah, Marshall, everything is fine," Susan fidgeted from side to side, hoping that Marshall didn't believe her. It went through her mind how strange that was, the order of emotions... embarrassed and then afraid. Wouldn't it make more sense to just tell Marshall that she was afraid of Ron?

"Yeah, Marshall. Everything is fine. Why don't you just ease on down the road?" Ron jerked his thumb over his shoulder.

"Excuse me, sir?"

"You heard me Tyrone, I said make like Michael Jackson and beat it."

Susan's initial embarrassment leap-frogged over fear and turned into instant anger. "Ron! Get the hell out of this building and don't ever come back here! You piece of shit!"

Both men's eyes widened at the small woman's outburst, but their eyes quickly found one another again in order to continue their stare down.

"Yeah, Ron is it? Maybe you are the one who should go," Marshall's measured tone hugged the edges of patience.

"How about YOU go, Amos, and I'll stay here until I'm ready to leave. And if you don't like that idea, maybe I could just kick your ass. What's your choice... bro?"

Marshall took a step closer to Ron and smiled, "I'd think I'd like for you to kick my ass... bro. Then you can get YOUR ass raped for a year or two in the federal pen for assaulting a government employee on the job. Or you can go now. So, what's your choice... Billy Bob?"

Ron hadn't expected such a level-headed defense from the other man. He knew there was no way out of this with his pride intact, so he just turned to Susan, "Fuck you, you slant-eyed whore. I was finished with you anyway!"

He spat, walked to the door, and swung it open. "Oh," he turned to face Marshall, "Fuck you too, Sambo." He left the door open behind him and crossed the street to his Mustang.

Susan looked at Marshall after Ron's huffy exit, "Marshall, I'm so sorry about that. But I have to admit, I'm also glad you showed up when you did. I've never seen him like that. I knew he could be a jerk, but... my God."

"You don't have to apologize, Missus Lee. I've run into worse than that bozo. What about you? Are you going to be okay? That guy doesn't seem very stable. If you want to talk to the police about this, I'll be happy to tell them what I saw and heard."

"No... no, I don't think that will be necessary, but thanks, Marshall." Watching Ron speed away caused her stomach to tighten. She was going to have to work on believing her own words.

IX

"Sorry I haven't been by to check in on you. I've been busy with work; you know how it gets."

"That's okay."

"How are you feeling? Susan said you slipped in the tub."

"I'm fine. But I think the fall aggravated my rib injuries. I had to take two painkillers yesterday."

"You want to go back in and let the docs check you out? Maybe get another X-ray?"

"No. When you pull a scab too soon it just scabs back over and the healing starts again. No new injuries, just strongly reminded of the ones I have. When did Susan tell you about my fall?"

"Before I came up here to see you, I stopped by to pay them for the week."

"Okay."

"Now I'll ask you what I asked them. It's been a week, is this arrangement working out so far?"

"How so?"

"Well, are they being a help to you?"

"I can take care of myself."

"Francis—"

"Fine, Terry. Yes. They are. She is feeding me well. And the kid is a quick learner, okay? They've been a big help, you don't have to rub it in that you were right!"

"Good, but you don't have to be snippy about it. What happened here the other day with Susan's ex-boyfriend? Chava started to tell me something about an incident but Susan walked in and stopped her before she could get it out. She acted like it was a secret or something."

"Her ex-boyfriend? I didn't know she had a boyfriend at all. I assumed she was married."

"She was. Her husband died."

"Oh, that's news to me."

"You know, Francis. It bugs you when people ask you questions. Maybe YOU could talk to them. Ask them some questions; get involved with them, with their lives. Get to know them. They are very nice people, you know. And they like you, despite your efforts to make them feel otherwise."

"I don't want to—"

"Yes… yes… I know. You don't want to get involved."

"You know this, but you still push me. Why?"

"A couple of reasons, big brother; first of all, if YOU ask them questions about THEM you can keep the topic of conversation off of you, right? And secondly, you think of them as friends now don't you? I mean, they are up here with you every day."

"Not my choice. According to you, they are a necessity."

"I know, but after you are healed up are you just going to ignore them when you see them in the lobby or on the street? Just pretend you don't know them? Friendships can grow out of situational necessity, you know. Remember how I met Lorraine? She had a flat tire and I stopped to help her out? You know that story."

"Well, yeah—"

"Come on, Francis. You're anti-social, but you're not a cold, rude asshole. I knew you before all of this, remember? You used to have tons of friends. You were a popular, likable guy!"

"That was back when I deserved it. Before I kill—"

"If you finish that sentence I'm calling Doctor Singh to have you re-committed. You understand me?"

"Stop threatening me with that shit! That's twice in one week. I don't appreciate being constantly reminded that I have no power over my own life."

"Stop making me threaten you, and you know damned good and well that it's not about power. Francis, listen, just try to initiate some conversation with the Lees, on your turf and terms. This is your chance to rejoin the human race, man. A chance for you to stop just… just

existing and get back to living."

"That's pretty much the opposite of what I want, Terry."

"Is it really, Francis?"

Of course, Terry was right, Francis conceded. Susan and Chava did represent a chance for him to re-enter the human arena. But it was easier said than done. After three years in the hospital with Doctor Singh, surrounded by medical staff and other disturbed people, some of them straight-up whack jobs, followed by four years living alone up here on the fifth floor with his animals. What was he supposed to do?

Did Terry just expect him to walk up to some random smiling face on the street and say, "Hi, my name is Francis. I'm a middle-aged, suicidal recluse. Want to go for a cup of coffee and then maybe a movie? I'm trying to rejoin the human race."

Terry knew better than that. No, all Terry was asking him to do was to be friendly with the living, breathing people at hand; Susan and Chava. Was Terry overlooking the fact that Susan and Chava might remind him of Mindy and Melissa? Surely Terry didn't overlook something so blaringly obvious.

There was a pretty good chance that the reason Terry chose Susan and Chava was simply because of the convenience. They lived in the same building. Chava had nothing better to do than be a pinkie-toting lackey and Susan's schedule fit well with his meal times. It was probably as simple as that. Terry was a busy guy, always something on his plate; the family business, his own wife and kids, and taking care of his damaged brother.

I knew I was a burden to a point, but could I be weighing that heavily on Terry's shoulders? Is Terry looking for help bearing that burden? I already ended the lives of those I loved best. Am I over-complicating the life of the person I've known longest? Am I driving away my very last connection to my old life?

If only he could bring himself to ask Terry these questions. What was stopping him? He didn't usually ask people questions because he didn't want to know, he didn't want to get involved, but he and Terry, they were brothers, they were already involved; long before Terry was a singular case, the one person he actually cared about, not that he showed it very well it was true. But he needed to know what Terry thought, what his motives were in choosing the Lees. He was just afraid of what those motives might be. He was afraid of the possibility that his brother might be trying to pawn them off as replacements for Mindy and Melissa in some way. Surely Terry didn't think it would be that simple.

But maybe I can make it easier on Terry by trying to do what he asks of me. Francis snubbed out his cigarette in the ashtray.

The Lees weren't that bad; Susan's cooking and extra feminine touches around the apartment did make his life more pleasant, though he didn't know how to express that openly. She put a small woven throw rug in front of his easy chair yesterday; made it quite homey. Just this morning she asked about bringing up some scented candles to take care of the stale air. He had never even noticed the air in his apartment was stale. He wanted to veto the candles offhandedly, but then he envisioned the years of chain-smoking and burger grease smoke and gave in to her suggestion.

Chava's questions were always about the work she was doing for him with the animals, never really of a personal nature. She was actually a pretty good kid. Maybe it would be okay if he asked them a few things about themselves. Inquired a little. And if it was too uncomfortable, he could always retreat back into his usual mode of restricted interaction.

Okay, Terry. I'll try it for you.

Ron was sitting at his usual ass-worn stool at the end of the long scratch-riddled bar at *Stew's*. The bar couldn't really be classified as a dive, not yet anyway. Sid had purchased the bar shortly after Stew had died years before, but the name remained unchanged so as not to drive off the regulars. He kept the bar well-stocked and the worst of the riff-raff out on the weekends.

It was on the weekends that suburban types came down for a pathetic go with the karaoke machine and to get bleary-eyed on vodka gimlets and martinis, and other drinks Ron never considered giving the time of day. But the weekdays belonged to the regulars, guys like Ron who ordered beers and rounds of whisky or, when they were feeling more exotic, tequila shots. Sid made a lot of dough on the weekends off the crooning alligator-shirt-and-loafer crowd, but the steady stream of regulars kept the place lucrative and stable.

In addition to the queer karaoke machine, the bar had a vintage jukebox, two pool tables in the rear of the establishment, some ancient pinball machines, a few booths, and the sweet-assed Tanya schlepping the booze. It was a comfortable, working-man's bar. But it also attracted some of the less desirable individuals and at that moment in time Ron qualified as one of those undesirables.

He had been sitting at the bar knocking back shots of Jack and chasing them with beers for about seven hours. He didn't move much, just his hands for lifting the drinks, throwing back his head to accommodate the alcohol, pointing his fingers first at Sid and then his empties to signal for refills, and hourly strolls to the men's john; each jaunt becoming more unsteady than the last. Luckily he had the quickest route to the urinal etched into his brain so deeply that no amount of alcohol could erase it.

While Ron wasn't showing much movement on the outside, he was bucking and weaving on the inside. The longer he sat there the more pissed off he was becoming. Pissed off at Susan for dumping him before he could dump her; pissed off because his plan to knock off a piece of gook ass fell through; pissed off at the way her brat gave him the slant-eyed stink eye when they ran into each other in the apartment building lobby; pissed off at the confrontation with the nigger mailman. By the time that nigger mailman walked in, he was about to just throw some insults at the little bitch, maybe a good shot or two about her dead hubby and her pussy kid, and then leave willingly and of his own accord; get in the last word. Flip her the bird, jump in the Mustang and get on with his life; plenty of fish in the sea and all that jazz. But the nigger stood there and watched him get the short end of the stick. He saw Susan come out on top. He could have lived with getting dumped, hell it wasn't the first time and probably wouldn't be the last. But to get the heave-ho in front of a witness, in front of another man; a black man, it was a pride thing, and that bruising of the machismo is what had him sitting on the stool abusing his liver all that day. He didn't give a rat's ass about Susan really, but as the entire history of mankind can attest to, the bruising of one's pride calls for getting even, calls for revenge.

Ron looked down at the end of the bar where Sid was standing with a bar towel draped over one shoulder, smoking a Camel and totaling the night's receipts. "Hey, Sid. Where can I find Lawrence McPhee? Wait; tell me when I come back." He then backed unsteadily off the stool and stumbled along his course to the john.

Terrance Tower couldn't get comfortable. Lorraine lay beside him sleeping quietly. Terry had always appreciated that about his wife, never a snore or a snort in her sleep. She might smack her lips once in a while after a particularly good meal, but that was it. He wished he could have returned the favor. Poor Lorraine had rolled him over on his side hundreds, if not thousands, of times in an effort to silence his slumbering concerts of snores, snorts, moans, groans, and lip-smacks.

She never complained about it, just joked over breakfast about the fact that he made noises like cattle mating when he slept. The kids got a kick out their parents comically prodding at one another in that fashion. His oldest, Amy, was getting prettier every day, but she also had a brain to match her beauty. She was in the seventh grade, had perfect attendance and had never received a grade lower than a 'B'. His boy Terry, Jr. was in the fifth grade and never got an 'F', though he didn't get the grades that his sister got. And the kid was a natural on the guitar and showed a lot of interest in science, biology in particular. They were good kids. He had a loving wife, a thriving business; a great life. *Francis...*

During these episodes of self-congratulatory revelry his thoughts always turned to Francis without fail. He loved his older brother, and he was all that Francis had. They had a younger sister, Lily, but she had married a British exchange student she met in university and they now worked together at an architectural firm in Switzerland. Their father, the founder of Tower Properties, had died from complications following open heart surgery nearly fifteen years ago. Their mother suffered a series of strokes over a period of three years and eventually succumbed to a final one that took her peacefully in her sleep a couple of years before Francis went into the hospital. They were not close to their extended family, though they did have some aunts, uncles and cousins spread out around the country.

No, Terry was all that Francis had. Before the terrible accident that killed Mindy and Melissa, the two families had been very close. Melissa, Amy, and Terry, Jr. played together, spent the night at each other's homes. Lorraine and Mindy were like sisters, cooking all the holiday meals together; the real brains behind the parenting. Terry smiled as he remembered how they used to go in halves on a babysitter so the two couples could go out to dinner and a movie together, sometimes a concert, sometimes even dancing.

Those were great times... and then the fucking accident. Terry really missed his sister-in-law and niece. They were beautiful people gone far too soon. It was a hard time and Francis wasn't the only one to suffer. But Francis was the one carrying around all the guilt; so much guilt that he didn't want to live without Mindy and Melissa.

After the accident Francis couldn't even attempt to focus on work. He spent all of his time at home sitting at the kitchen table.

Terry would stop by daily on his way home to check on his brother, who was ALWAYS sitting at the kitchen table smoking and looking at family photos. Sometimes Terry found him straining to look at the photos in the dark because Francis couldn't be bothered to switch on the light after the sun went down.

At first Terry took the more-than-willing Lorraine and the two kids with him on these visits, but Francis showed no interest in them; wouldn't talk to them, or even look their way. Though his wife and kids wanted to continue going with him for the visits, Terry finally stopped taking them along for their own sake. He was afraid the deep depression Francis was mired in would become contagious. His family had suffered enough already.

Terry had always been thankful he had made the decision not to take his family with him to see Francis anymore because they were spared the sight of his first brutal suicide attempt. His brother had stopped answering the door, so Terry had taken to letting himself in with the spare key he'd had made. His brother wasn't at his usual place in the kitchen, chain smoking and pining over lost times represented in the photos; which instantly set off a frantic alarm in Terry.

A quick search of the two-story home led Terry to the basement where he found his brother in nothing but boxer shorts and propped up against the clothes dryer with blood seeping from both wrists and one of his thighs. Terry immediately wrapped and bound his unconscious brother's wounds and called 911. Luckily, when Francis had slashed at the femoral artery in his thigh with the box knife he had only nicked the major artery, so he hadn't bled out. In addition, the chilly concrete floor of the basement had slowed the bleeding some. Still, according to the paramedics another half an hour and he would have been gone. If Francis had attempted to kill himself in a warm bath, or even on a warmer floor, Terry would have been too late to save him.

Terry didn't give his brother a second chance to get it right.

Francis went straight from the ER to the Harper Institute where he was given over to the care of Doctor Singh. Lorraine and the kids insisted on visiting Francis with him in the institute, but the drugs turned Francis into a drooling statue and Francis' refusal to acknowledge them in any way was too hurtful. After only a handful of visits Terry put an end to them; though Lorraine did accompany him from time to time, usually around the holidays.

The kids would send crayon-drawn pictures to their Uncle Francis, but he wouldn't even look at them and the drawings were never anywhere to be seen on the following visit. Whether they were thrown out by the staff or by Francis' own hand Terry never thought to ask. The kids finally gave up on making gifts for their uncle, and Terry didn't blame them a bit. Youth is for happy times and life, not for half-comatose uncles who won't even look at you. But Terry was proud of the way his kids stuck by their uncle for as long as they did. He considered it a testament to the strength he had always felt in his family.

Once the right mix of medications was worked out and Doctor Singh had had some time to work with him, Francis came around bit by bit. He wouldn't initiate conversations or ask questions of anyone, even with Terry, but he'd respond in limited, impatient sentences. He took on a reluctant existence. He couldn't be trusted to be left alone with sharp objects or anything long enough to hang himself. During his time in the institute he had tried to kill himself using a syringe, a fork, a curtain, a curtain cord, a wire clothes hanger, another patient's hospital gown, and a piece of safety glass he chipped away with repeated blows by his own fists. He even tried bashing his head in by ramming it repeatedly into a cinderblock wall, but that landed him in a padded room. So he never tried that again; no possibility of trying again in the padded rooms. When he was thwarted in his attempts he was always calm and never offered any resistance when seized by the staff; in fact, he always wore a patient "you got me this time, but just wait until next time" expression on his face.

Then, at the next opportunity, he was at it again with

anything resembling a blade, or a point, or anything that could act as a makeshift rope.

What really brought Francis around, if that expression can really apply, was the Pets 'N Patients program. Francis really took to the animals. According to Doctor Singh, the guilt felt by Francis over the deaths of Mindy and Melissa was alleviated by the tasks involved with caring for the animals. His brother's attempts at suicide were a method of trying to assuage his guilt; caring for other living creatures also served to assuage these feelings. But Francis could not show the same care for humans, other people. The association between his dead wife and daughter was too great. Singh said that basically Francis was afraid of caring about people. The loss of his family overwhelmed him and the risk of experiencing such a loss again was terrifying.

Thus, Francis had switched from having a powerful urge to kill himself to having an equally powerful urge to NOT kill himself for the sake of the creatures under his care. Putting himself in the position to care for other people, though, would also put him in the position of caring, which would once again lead to fear and the desire to kill himself. Terry had a tough time getting his mind around this, but as Doctor Singh always said, "The human mind is a sticky wicket."

The animals proved to be a suitable substitute for socializing with other people. They needed constant care, but asked no questions. This desire to take care of the animals in order to preserve his own life, this is what prompted Doctor Singh to release Francis back out into the world. The doctor didn't offer Terry a one-hundred percent guarantee of success, but they agreed that it was worth a shot. In fact, besides a lifetime of drugs and observation, it was their only shot at re-introducing Francis to the world outside the Harper Institute. And it was successful, to a certain extent. After a few months on the fifth floor at 517 Sycamore, Terry took Lorraine and the kids over to see Francis. The kids had all but forgotten what Francis looked like. Three years is a long time for a kid after all, but they were excited about being reunited with their Uncle Francis. Francis didn't even attempt to say hello and he had even forgotten their names, or so it seemed. Amy cried and Terry, Jr. just looked angry. So Terry had decided to not subject them to Francis any further.

For some time Terry had considered that maybe he was being too easy on Francis, letting him bask in his own protective routine, his shell. The day Francis got hit by the taxi and acted so stubborn concerning the possibility of outside help; that was the straw that broke the camel's back. Terry needed help. He wasn't going to abandon Francis, that was certain, but Terry alone couldn't draw Francis out. The meek kid sitting there on the steps, she looked like she needed someone too. The decision to ask Susan to do some cooking and cleaning for Francis was on the fly. It just seemed like a good idea at the time; a situation where everyone would win.

The Lees could make some money, the kid would have something to do, and Francis would be forced to interact with someone besides Terry and his animals. And it seemed to be working. Francis was still putting up a fight, but the threat to put him back in the institute was holding strong because he wasn't going to risk leaving his animals. Francis even seemed to be warming up a bit to the Lees. It was only after the fact that Terry saw the correlation between Susan and Chava and Mindy and Melissa, a parallel Terry was sure that Francis had noticed from the start. But would that help or hurt? They would all have to ride it out and see. He just hoped he wasn't doing more damage in the process. *Francis...*

Terry took his eyes off the bedroom's dark ceiling, rolled over and kissed the sleeping Lorraine on her cheek, then rolled back over and closed his eyes. In a matter of minutes he was snoring contently and dreaming of a time when Francis was Francis.

X

"Thank you, Susan."

"Sorry?"

"I said thank you for the breakfast. I don't remember the last time I had maple-smoked bacon. It was very nice. The eggs were very nice too."

"Oh. Well, I'm glad you enjoyed it."

"Your hair looks very nice today."

"What?"

"Your hair. I said it looks very nice."

"My hair? Uh... thank you, Francis."

"I like the new rug... in front of the chair. It is also very nice."

"Francis?"

"Yes?"

"What are you doing?"

"Doing? I'm not sure I know what you mean."

"I've been coming up here for over two weeks. Aside from the... um... little disagreement we had on the first day, this is the most you've said about anything. Why is everything very nice all of a sudden?"

"Well, it isn't all of a sudden. Not really. I should have said something sooner. You and Chava... it has been very ni—, really good having the two of you around."

"Are you feeling okay, Francis? Do you need a pill?"

"No, I am fine. I can compliment you if I want, right? That's what people do, right?"

"Well, yes, I suppose—"

"We're people, right? Two adult people."

"Listen, Francis, I'm glad you like the food and the rug and my hair, but I just got out of a relationship and I don't think, well, you've been alone a long time and—"

"Huh? No, no! You misunderstand me, Susan. I'm simply trying to express my appreciation for what you and Chava have done, are doing; that is all. I'm trying to... I'm being... um... friendly and interactive."

"Oh. Well, then in that case, you're welcome, Francis. Would you like a refill on that coffee?"

"Yes, I would. Your coffee is very nice."

"You're weird, Francis."

"Weird, weird or friendly weird?"

Francis was seated on a stool at one of the work tables refilling the food dishes for the rodents. He had several large, white, plastic containers containing alfalfa pellets, sunflower seeds, corn kernels, sesame seeds, and less easily identifiable nuggets of vegetarian foodstuffs arranged and opened up before him. To the side was a stack of empty plastic food dishes of various sizes drip drying after being scrubbed clean of rodent droppings by Chava.

Francis worked quick and sure, dipping a small scoop into containers and creating different food mixtures for the rats, mice, rabbits, hamsters, gerbils, and guinea pigs. Chava offered to do this chore, but according to Francis different animals needed different mixes and the specific, singular formulas were all in his head. But he had appreciated the offer. It showed initiative.

While Francis mixed the food, Chava was going from cage to cage; refilling water bottles and changing the litter and wood shavings. She actually enjoyed this task because, though she was handling urine and rodent feces, the cedar aroma from the shavings was very pleasant. The litter and shavings were changed like clockwork, every two to three days, so it really wasn't all that gross anyway. The animals probably could have used the materials for another week or more, but Francis was fanatical about cleanliness and the avoidance of odors less pleasant than that put off by the cedar shavings.

Most of the rodents were very friendly or took absolutely no notice of Chava's hands invading their living spaces. The hamsters and mice just retreated to their hidey-holes and peaked out with whiskers twitching. The rats, where Chava expected some trouble, simply gave her curious sniffs and waited patiently in their corners for her to finish what she was doing. The guinea pigs were nervous by nature and would dart from corner to corner squealing and making a ruckus, but they were calm enough if she tried to pet one. The rabbits were fat, lazy things and Chava had to physically move some in order to clean under them. The gerbils were the least accommodating; instead of hiding out or getting out of the way they always got in the way, and some of them took curious nips at her fingers, though with no real intention to do any harm.

Working together, Chava and Francis had the rodent cages cleaned and water bottles and food dishes refilled in a little less than two hours. The final part of this task was to check the small blocks of wood that were given to the animals for chewing. According to Francis, the buck teeth of the rodents never stopped growing so they needed something to chew on in order to keep these incisors worn down to a comfortable and serviceable length. If the animals had nothing to chew on the teeth would continue to grow until they couldn't eat, or even close their mouths. They'd eventually starve to death. If a rodent was heard chewing on the bars of their cage, it was a safe bet that their block of wood had grown too small to easily chew on.

Francis had several cages that stood empty except for when a female was pregnant and needed to be separated. The pregnant rodents were placed in these birthing cages to insure the expectant mothers' cage mates didn't make snacks of the newborn young; a cannibalistic practice that Chava was previously unaware of. The resulting pinkies born in the birthing cages were used to feed the tarantulas, snakes and other creatures who appreciated, and counted on, a live, warm meal.

Francis was careful to avoid population explosions and the males and females of any species did not share a cage unless there were no pregnant females. They were allowed to share cages on a staggered schedule in order to provide a non-stop supply of pinkies, but sometimes the pairings did not produce as expected. So, once in a while pinkies had to be bought from the Sycamore Pet Emporium.

Some pinkies were left with their mothers and allowed to reach maturity, but the majority of these lucky few were destined to serve as meals for Constance and some of the other larger snakes. Through the selective breeding practices and the use of pinkies as food, the rodent population was strictly controlled.

After the last refilled food dish was replaced, the last empty water bottle was filled, and the last wooden block deposited for chewing; Chava placed the large trash bag of used litter in the 50-gallon can with the hinged lid standing next to the first work table.

Her last task of each day was to take the trash down to the dumpster located in the alley next to the apartment building. If the litter and shavings weren't so light, carrying it down five flights of stairs would have been too much for a girl her size, but the trash was thankfully always on the light side.

She stood back to examine a job well done. All of the animals had long since resumed their interrupted activities. The guinea pigs and the rabbits were at the food dishes, but the mice, rats, gerbils, and hamsters were mostly busy on their exercise wheels.

"Look at those stupid things; running and going nowhere."

"Not so stupid. They're just getting some exercise."

"They have to know by now that they're not making any progress."

"Have you ever been in a gym?"

"Sure, we play basketball and stuff in the school gym." Chava looked at Francis, her face scrunched up with barely concealed surprise that he had asked her a question. He usually gave instructions for doing the chores or offered information about the animals that he thought Chava should know, but he never really asked her anything.

"No, I mean a gym where people go to work out; adults for the most part."

"Oh, sure. Yeah, I've been in one."

"What were the people doing?"

"They were exercising, of course."

"How were they exercising?"

"You know. The usual kind of stuff. Lifting weights, using weight machines, swimming in the pool... that kind of stuff."

"And?" Francis leaned in closer to her.

"And what?"

"What else were they doing? What other stuff?"

"Um... well, bike machines and treadmills, too."

"Uh-huh. Rowing machines and stair machines, did they have those?"

"Yeah, I suppose so. Yeah, they were using those, too."

"Kind of stupid don't you think?"

"They were exercising. What is so stupid about that?"

"Were they getting anywhere?"

"No, but it's different, don't you think?"

"Yes, it is different. These animals here, they are locked in cages, so they run on wheels. Do you think a rat living in a sewer would stop to run on an exercise wheel if he happened to come across one? The people at the gym, were they locked in?"

"No, I guess they weren't."

"And they PAY to get nowhere. So, who's stupid?"

Francis and Chava had two stools pulled up to the work

table eating their lunch and listening to the oldies station on the radio. Buddy Holly was singing about if we knew Peggy Sue while the duo ate chicken salad sandwiches and dill pickles.

Francis had told Chava not to ever change the radio station because the animals didn't like most music recorded after the early '70s. Heavy Metal, Rap, Hip-Hop, and current Pop were strictly off limits, but they were particularly fond of George Jones, Telemann, Vivaldi, Doo-wop, and '60s Motown; especially singers and groups like Diana Ross and the Supremes, Marvin Gaye, Aretha Franklin, the Jackson Five, the Shirelles, Martha and the Vandellas, and Gladys Knight and the Pips. For some strange reason, Luis became more active when The Archies were on the radio. Stevie Wonder especially got the birds to singing and the rodent wheels to turning. Constance even uncoiled and climbed around more on the branches in her tank when Stevie was belting out a tune.

The sandwiches were gone, nothing but crumbs to mark their passing, and the two were working on the remainder of their pickles when Francis turned toward her, "What happened to your father?"

"My dad?" Chava stared open mouthed at Francis, "Why do you ask—"

"Terrance told me your father died. How?"

Such a direct inquiry made Chava forget about her pickle. Her voice was weak, "Um... cancer. He died from cancer."

"When?"

"When I was ten. About three years ago."

The girl is thirteen? I thought she was younger. Francis looked at her, crunching on his pickle. "That must have been rough on you and your mother."

"Yeah."

"What kind of cancer?"

"Um... pan... pancri... uh—"

"Pancreatic?"

"Yeah, that's the one," Chava returned her attention to the half-eaten dill.

"That's very painful from what I've heard."

"He didn't show it. He was laughing and joking the last time I saw him. He died the next day."

"That's too bad. I don't think most people have that ability. The ability to laugh and joke when they know they are about to die, I mean. It sounds like he was a very strong man."

"He was. I really miss him."

"I bet you do. Cancer is very interesting."

"Huh? Cancer is interesting?" Francis' words halted Chava's pickle-chewing.

"Well, rather, the human view of cancer is interesting I should say. The word 'cancer' has such evil connotations."

"That's because it is evil."

"I suppose so, from a certain point of view."

"What? There is no supposing to it or other points of view. It kills people!"

"As do cars and dogs and falls in the tub."

"That's not the same thing and you know it!" Chava clenched her jaw. *How could a person defend cancer for crying out loud?*

"It's simple cell division; over-active cell division, beyond the normal limits. There is no evil there; disease is just another form of life."

"But diseases kill—"

"I'm not saying it produces a desired outcome; anything pleasant. Hurricanes are natural, but people don't usually welcome them."

"Then what are you saying? Why is it you think cancer is so interesting?"

"Well, the formation of a fetus after impregnation. That is also cell division."

"Fetus?"

"Yeah, babies. When a baby is made."

"Babies aren't cancer!"

"I didn't say they were. But babies are transformed cells. It then grows, takes over the womb. Babies aren't cancer, but they are parasites. They survive by living off of the mother. Cancer and babies, they both represent cell growth. But one is desirable, one is undesirable. That is what is interesting to me, mankind's childish habit of labeling one thing good and one thing bad. When the things they are labeling aren't all that different at the core."

Chava's anger at Francis lost momentum when she realized he was not trying to bait her, but was merely attempting to make conversation. *But what kind of conversation is this? Cancer was bad. Babies were good. Everyone knows that.*

"I see what you are saying, but I don't think I'd put cancer and babies together. It just doesn't seem right."

"Okay. How about babies and murder?"

"What are you—" Chava's mouth hung open in disbelief.

"I think making a baby is murder. Planning to make a baby is premeditated murder." Francis' tone was steady and level, very matter-of-fact.

"How do you figure that?" Chava's mind digested his statement. She was more filled with interest than with anger now.

"Easily if you look at the end results of both actions. What do you and me, the rats over there, Mavis, everyone you know or have seen, all the fish in the sea... what do we all have in common?"

"We're all alive?"

"Yes, and?"

"We eat and drink and sleep and—"

"Yeah, yeah, but what's on the other end of life?"

"Death?"

"Right."

"We all die? That's what we have in common? What does that have to do with babies and murder?"

"Okay, if every living thing is destined to die, which is something every rational person knows, then why make more life? Every time a man and a woman make a baby, aren't they sentencing that baby to an eventual death?"

"I see what you mean, but they don't want the baby to die. It's... uh... it is... oh, what is the word for killing someone accidentally?"

"You mean manslaughter?"

"Yeah, at the worst it's manslaughter."

"Nope. Manslaughter isn't intentional. If that taxi driver hadn't seen me in time and kept driving, and ran over my head or something, killing me; that might have been manslaughter. Or better yet, the guy that pushed me in the street could have said it was an accident that he pushed me in front of the vehicle... that could have been manslaughter if it killed me. Your mom and dad knew that by combining an egg with sperm, by providing the means for life to take hold, by making you, that you would one day have to face death. That is intentional. It is premeditated murder."

"My parents aren't murderers!"

"Not by our definition of murder, but the facts remain the same. By creating life, you are also creating death."

"That's nuts."

"It might sounds nuts, but think it through. Don't get hung up on the words and definitions and such." Francis finished off his pickle and wiped his hands on a paper towel, "Can you put these dishes in the sink, please? Then we'll get started on the bird and sugar glider cages."

"Um... yeah, sure," Chava stacked the two plates and started for Francis' living quarters.

"But, hey," Francis added, "It's still too bad about your father."

XI

Sons of bitches and whores...

For my entire life I've been ill-used by sons of bitches and whores! Not to mention the bitches who squeezed out the sons of bitches...

Do they think I enjoy living out here? Sleeping on benches, asking for handouts, not showering for months at a time; it's not my fault...

I was one of them! I had a house, I had a career. It was sucking the life out of me, but I had it! Wife, kids; the whole shebang...

Fucking wife! It started with her. Always yakking and bitching about the drinking, the gambling; the girls on the side...

I'm a man for fuck's sake! That's what we do, but the controlling cunt couldn't see that...

She couldn't even see it when I had the ice pick to her throat! I should've carried out the threat. I might as well have lost everything over murdering the whore seeing as just the threat was enough! I should have made her pay in full...

Still can't believe everyone sided with her! Like, I'm the first one ever to smack a mouthy bitch around. I know for a fact I'm not...

Took my house, took my money, took the kids; worthless little brats that they were, but they were still mine! I made the little fuckers; paid for everything from hospital bills to fucking Christmas presents...

Made me move into that shitty efficiency with the fucking kitchenette; dry cum in the orange carpet...

Then the guys at the firm! Some friends they were. What happened to alcoholism being a disease? Where did that theory run off to once I started drinking too much? Like they were a bunch of fucking teetotalers? Didn't they see hitting old Mister Burghess with the golf club was a cry for help, but they didn't fucking help. A forced resignation they called it; pack up and get the fuck out was more like it...

Put me on the streets! It's their fault. Fucking missions invite you in; leave your booze at the door or else there is no bed for you. Fucking do-gooders and their rules; wouldn't mind giving that fucking priest another knock to the nose. Irish prick; just like my dear, old dad. You know he's a boozer, but he says I can't keep MY bottle...

They'll all pay someday...

All I had was that mangy-ass dog, then that fucker turns my own dog on me! Feeds the dog but won't spare a buck for another person. Who the fuck does he think he is...

Fucking cabbie and the cops blame me of course...

Worthless fucking mutt; don't even have the dog now. Couldn't catch him again after they sprung me; fucking cheeseburger bastard. Haven't seen the dog since he picked that fight, but when I do; push him in front of a bus next time! No dog to help him next time...

I need a fucking drink; wonder if Sid down at Stew's would float me a drink or two. He'd done it a couple of times, but he probably won't; not after that scuffle I had with the waitress last time. Hot ass on that Tanya; bitch couldn't take a compliment...

Bet if I was wearing a slick suit and flashing cash or singing My Way on that queer karaoke machine it would have been a different story! Fucking sons of bitches and whores...

They'll all pay someday...

Susan hadn't spoken to him all morning and he was starting to feel a little anxious without her regular off-and-running chit-chat. In addition, she had forgone her home-cooking and had plopped a bowl of cold cornflakes down in front of him after he sat down at the kitchen table. He didn't really mind the silence or the corn flakes, it all felt like old times, but he knew the source of these reversions were his fault somehow and he was uncomfortable knowing that he was to blame.

Should he say something? Try to find out what was wrong? Try to find out if it was indeed his fault? But what could he have done? He only saw her in the mornings for about an hour and a half, and yesterday was the first time he'd said anything of length since she started working for him more than two weeks ago. See, this was why he preferred to stay out of things.

He rubbed his temples. *Why is mankind destined to suffer?*

"Susan?"

"Francis?"

Wow, chilly. Penguins would feel at home in my kitchen right now. "Is something bothering you, Susan?"

"Yes, Francis. As a matter of fact, something is bothering me; bothering me very much."

"May I ask what is bothering you, Susan?" Francis felt his stomach tightening up.

Susan turned from the sink and looked down at the seated Francis. "Are you telling me that you really don't know? You have no idea why I'm angry at you?"

"You're angry with me?"

"Yes, Francis. I am angry at you." Her voice rose sharply.

"I have to be honest with you, Susan."

"Please do, Francis."

"I have absolutely no idea why you are angry at me."

Susan's slack-jawed expression let Francis know immediately that he was missing something obvious. But isn't that always the way with people? The slightest action or word perpetrated innocently and without malice can offend another to the bone. And what may royally tick one person off might make another person laugh uproariously. It was all just too confusing to deal with. And what made it worse, the offended seemed to always feel the need for the offender to own up to the offense, even if the offender didn't know what the offendee was offended about. It was all very offensive.

"Honestly, Susan. I don't know."

"Chava told me that the two of you had an interesting conversation yesterday!" Her voice wobbled through clenched teeth.

"Well, yes. We talked at some length over our lunch break. It was very nice."

"It was very nice, huh? Well, I don't think it's very nice when my daughter comes home and tells me that she will never get married and have kids because she doesn't want to be a murderer, Francis."

"Oh, we... that was—"

"Babies are parasites, Francis?"

"You see... I was—"

"Cancer and babies are the same things, Francis?"

"No, it was—"

"What the fuck is wrong with you, Francis?"

"You don't understand, Susan. I was—"

"You're right, Francis. I don't understand. I don't understand how an adult can fill a kid's head full of such bullshit."

"Actually, it wasn't bullshit I was going for. It was—"

"What right do you think you have to say things like that to my daughter? I know you have issues, but Terry said you weren't dangerous," her face was becoming more crimson with each word, "But I'm starting to doubt his assurances."

"Please, may I finish a sentence?"

"Yes, finish a sentence, Francis. Please finish a sentence. Tell me in a full sentence why you would say such things to my daughter."

Francis took a drag off his cigarette, exhaled and then took a deep smokeless breath before he continued in a calm, steady tone, "You see, I was merely demonstrating to Chava that there is more than one way to look at something, everything, actually. It was a mental exercise, that's all. I don't necessarily subscribe to the views I presented. I just—"

"She's thirteen, Francis! She isn't old enough for other ways of looking at things like that; of crackpot theories and opinions. In her mind, cancer is BAD and babies are GOOD. Parents are NOT murderers and diseases are NOT misunderstood forms of life!"

"Susan," he raised his hands helplessly, "You're right, I didn't consider the girl's age. We just started talking and my mouth got away from me."

She took a deep breath. "I believe you, Francis, and I don't really think you meant any harm by it, but the things you said were inappropriate, especially to a kid."

"I know that now, after hearing you say them, but I was just trying to converse more. I was trying to be, friendly. You see?"

"Yes, I see. Like you were being friendly by complimenting the food and my hair yesterday, right?"

"Exactly."

"That's great, it really is, Francis. But you need to keep it light, if you don't mind… okay?"

"Okay, I will."

"If Chava comes home confused and ranting about AIDS being our friend or the evils of puppies or something equally batty; well, we won't be able to work for you anymore. Do you understand that?"

"Yes, I understand, Susan."

"And?" She stared at him.

"And?"

"And don't you have anything else to say?" Her eyebrows were arched as high as they could go.

"Um… sorry?"

"Okay! Shake on it?" She extended her small, laundry-calloused hand, apparently satisfied.

"Right," he looked at her hand for a moment before giving her a small shake.

"Susan?"

"Francis?"

"I've never seen you so orange before."

"What? Orange? What is orange?"

"When you got angry. You turned bright orange."

"What the hell are you talking about?"

"Yellow and red make orange."

She smiled brightly at him. "Hey weirdo, do you want me to make another pot of coffee before I leave?"

"Yes, please." A relieved Francis eagerly lit a new cigarette from the pack on the table.

Okay, now how did that NOT offend her? People...

"Is today the day? Do you think you are ready to feed Luis?"

"Well... no, no I'm not. I don't think I can do it yet." She had watched Francis feed the pinkies to Luis, the other tarantulas, the snakes, the scorpions, and the geckos numerous times already, but it always made her cringe and wince. The thought of putting one of the weak, blind, squirming babies in the cage was too horrible to imagine actually doing herself. The way Luis hungrily watched, rubbing his hairy mandibles together, like some kind of mad scientist looking over his next victim. Luis never hurried; he just kind of meandered over to the pinkies and looked them over before finally sinking his fangs into their plump little bellies. The pinkies didn't seem to suffer for long and squirmed for only seconds.

None of the animals played with the pinkies or caused any undue suffering that Chava could see. The scorpions gave them quick stabs that left them immediately paralyzed, the geckos and snakes swallowed quickly, head first. Chava had given dead pinkies to Mavis and left them in the sugar glider feeding trays, but she still needed time to hand the live ones over for execution. Francis said that Chava still looked at the pinkies like they were babies instead of food, and Francis was completely correct in saying so.

She hadn't fed Constance or the other snakes that took mature rodents either. She probably could have done that. It seemed different somehow. The grown rodents seemed like they'd be able to present some sort of defense, however pointless, against their attackers; which was silly of her to consider, but the pinkies were one-hundred percent defenseless.

Chava assumed Francis never asked her to feed Constance or the others because of her reluctance with the pinkies. Or maybe Francis thought she should master the more unwholesome tasks first. Perhaps he was just waiting for Chava to offer to do it on her own. She wished Francis would just tell her what he was thinking and save her the trouble of wondering.

To be honest, though Chava did not enjoy the fact that an animal was being killed, watching Constance eat was a thrill. Francis always placed the rat or small rabbit at the opposite end of the tank from where the snake was coiled. He did this, not to make Constance move or to give the offered victim a fighting chance, but to avoid being bitten by mistake again.

Constance had no poison or fangs, but Chava had seen the inside of her mouth when she yawned or had her jaws disjointed to swallow her food, and she saw that her mouth was full of needle-sharp, curved barbs. A bite from that big, toothy mouth would sting like the dickens. Sting nothing, it would hurt like hell!

After dropping the hapless rodent in the tank they would stand back and watch. Francis said he didn't watch because he enjoyed watching the rodents die, but because if the rodent made a few rounds of the tank and Constance showed no interest, Francis had to extract the ignored meal. Normally, Constance didn't even have to move, the pea-brained rodents would actually wander over to within striking distance. Sometimes they even climbed on her before she struck.

And the strike… my God! Even though it was expected, it never failed to cause Chava to jump, and even Francis blinked when the strike occurred. The human eye can't follow it close enough to completely describe it. One second the snake is motionless, and less than a second later it is coiled around the victim, barbed teeth hooked into its hide. As the animal exhaled Constance's grip tightened, snapping ribs in the process. In a matter of seconds the animal was dead. Sometimes the pressure from the serpent's muscular embrace was so great that the poor

117

creature's eyes would almost pop out of their sockets. It was so gruesome and brutal, but also so efficient; so undeniably natural, so strangely elegant.

Francis took Constance out of her tank once in a while to hold her; after thoroughly washing his hands of rodent odors, of course, and never immediately after she had eaten. During one of these instances he had let Chava hold her as well. The powerful creature had put her face up level to hers. She was scared shitless, but the snake just looked at her eye to eye; reptile to mammal, flicking her tongue out every few seconds to smell her, lightly grazing her skin with the forked tip of her tongue.

Francis said that as long as Chava didn't threaten her in any way, she would be as friendly as pie on Sunday. He also said that most animals wouldn't attack simply for the hell of it. It was almost always defensive or because they were hungry. And Chava was too big for her to eat. If she were an infant, it might be a different story. Chava shuddered at the thought of that and was thankful Francis didn't go into detail or offer any true-life examples.

Pretty much the only animal that attacks, hurts, or kills for no good reason; or simply for the fun of it, are humans. He said Chava had only to watch the evening news or pick up any newspaper and they would support that statement with ample grotesque examples. From what Chava had seen so far of the world, even without the assistance of news anchors and the printed word, she had to agree with Francis on that one.

Chava's eyes had wandered over to Constance's tank where she was resting peacefully on her heated stones. There was a perceivable bulge in her abdomen from the meal she'd had a few days before. It took her a while to digest a meal, so she only ate one every week or one and a half weeks, depending on the size of her dinner. Francis could easily tell by the snake's behavior when she might be ready to eat again. While she was watching Constance digest, Francis was busy putting pinkies in tanks for the spiders, scorpions, Jethro the toad, and the bigger geckos.

Chava heard the top of a tank being removed and turned

her attention to Francis' movements and noticed that though the man spoke of the pinkies coldly, as merely meals, he never plopped the pinkies down helter-skelter. He always sat them down gently next to a heat rock or on some soft shavings as if he was offering the helpless creatures final acts of comforting kindness before their destined end. To Chava it only verified what her mother had told her; Francis fed the pinkies to the other animals because it was necessary, not because he enjoyed it. Chava felt a subtle softening of her feelings towards the strange man.

For more than two weeks now she had been cleaning, feeding, and taking out the garbage, with only yesterday's disturbing conversation about cancer, babies, and murder to show that Francis thought of anything other than taking care of his pets. But now Chava was starting to see there was more to this fifth floor recluse; more than just a grouchy hermit who wouldn't say 'hi' on the stairs. He was a man who thought and felt. Sure, some of his thoughts were pretty far out there, stuff that you could only think of if you were to spend months or years in seclusion over-thinking every little thought. His feelings were guarded, but they leaked out around the edges of his defenses; such as in the way that he gently handled the doomed pinkies and how he said it was too bad about her dad.

There was no doubt Francis was a strange egg, and that egg might become more scrambled over time if he continued to live up here alone, but he was a person. And from where Chava was standing, he was a good person; a good and decent person worth knowing and caring about. For the first time since Terry made their acquaintance, Chava considered what sort of relationship she and her mother could have with Francis once his ribs and leg were fully healed, which probably wouldn't be too awfully long from now; unless he had more repeats of his fall in the tub.

Francis was wincing a bit less when he turned or got up from chairs and he was starting to leave his cane behind when he didn't have far to walk. Her time as Francis' helper couldn't last for more than another couple of weeks, three or four at the most. But she didn't want to stop coming up and helping with the animals and Francis wasn't the type to invite her to do so, at least not in this stage of their friendship. So, the ball was in her court. How could she keep Francis in her life? How could she solidify a friendship which, at the moment, was no stronger than a pinkie under the fangs of a tarantula?

XII

"Hello? Hello? Is anyone there?"

"Hi, Lorraine."

"Uh... hi... may I ask who is calling, please?"

"It's Francis Tower."

"Francis!?"

"Yes. Hello Lorraine."

"My God, Francis! I didn't recognize your voice!"

"Yes, it has been a while."

"A while? I haven't seen you in nearly two years! I haven't heard your voice since... since I don't know when! Are you okay? Do you need to talk to Terry?"

"No... no, I'm fine, Lorraine. I just wanted to say hi and ask about the kids... um —"

"Amy and Terry, Jr.?"

"Yes, Amy and Little Terry. Are they well?"

"Sure, they're great. Growing like weeds. We don't call Little Terry 'Little' Terry anymore, you know how kids are; just Terry or Terry, Jr. now. But, tell me, Francis. How are you doing? Terry told us all about your accident, we've been worried about you."

"I'm doing fine. A little sore still, but getting a little better every day. I have some people helping me out."

"I heard, Terry told me about the Lees."

"Yes, Susan and Chava. They are very helpful and very nice."

"Well, that's great, Francis. Really! We'd all like to see you, you know. When you are ready... when you feel up to it."

"That's kind of why I'm calling, Lorraine. Have you been to see Mindy and Melissa? At the cemetery, I mean."

"*Yes, of course, we visit the cemetery on their birthdays and on the anniversary of their... well, you know.*"

"*I understand.*"

"*How about you, Francis? Have you been to the cemetery lately?*"

"*No. I've never been.*"

"*Oh... well, that's okay, Francis.*"

"*No... no, it isn't. I was wondering—*"

"*Wondering what, Francis?*"

"*Do you think we could go? I don't drive anymore and, well—*"

"*You don't want to go alone?*"

"*That is a big part of it too, but mostly, well, I don't know where they are, Lorraine. I don't know where my wife and daughter are.*"

Terrance and his kids were sitting in the living room watching sit-coms and snacking on popcorn from a large, plastic bowl. Terrance and Amy took up each end of the sofa while Terry, Jr. sat on the floor with his back against the sofa between their two pairs of legs. The popcorn bowl occupied the center of the sofa within reach of the trio. With the dexterity that only a pre-teen boy could exhibit, Terry Jr. was reaching up and behind his head and grabbing popcorn without losing a single, fluffy kernel in the space between the bowl and his busily munching mouth.

He must have eyes in his fingertips. Terrance smiled at the thought as Lorraine came rushing into the living room. He could tell by her body language that something unusual was going on, even before she spoke to confirm it.

"Terry!"

"Yeah, hon? What's up?" He kept one eye still honed in on what was happening in the land of make believe.

"You're not going to believe who I just got off the phone with," she placed her hands on Terrance's shoulders.

"You're not going to make me guess, are you?"

"Moooom… we're trying to watch!" Amy's voice was shrill.

"Yeah, Mom; come on," Terry, Jr. flung his hands up in the air.

"It was Fran-cis," she over-pronounced the syllables in her brother-in-law's name.

Terrance quickly grabbed the remote control and turned off the canned laughter coming from the television, and jumped up to face his wife.

"Hey! Dad!" the two young Towers exclaimed in unison, "Come on!"

"Quiet, you two," he shot at them. "Francis? He called."

Amy rolled her eyes. "Big whoop, crazy Uncle Francis dialed a number."

"What was that? How would you like to be grounded for the rest of the year?"

"Come on, Dad. I was just joking!"

"You know damned full well that your Uncle Francis isn't a subject for jokes. There was a time when you two were happy to see him. You're not little kids; you know what he's been through! You've SEEN for yourselves what that accident did to him. Why don't you try acting your age? You—"

Lorraine put her hand on his shoulder to stop his emotions from running away, as they often did when the subject of his brother came up, "Terry… Terry, she didn't mean anything by it… take it easy, Hon."

Terrance looked at his family's faces, their expressions a mixture of shame and apologetic concern. "I'm sorry, guys. Amy, I'm sorry. I'm just sensitive when it comes to my brother, your uncle, that's all." He took a deep breath and ran his fingers through his hair while Lorraine rubbed his neck.

"No, I'm sorry, Dad," Amy spoke softly, "I was acting like a stupid little kid."

"Mom?" Terry, Jr. spoke up breaking the tension, "What did Uncle Francis say?"

"Well, he asked about you two; he apologized for not seeing us for so long… and…," she looked at Terrance, "he asked if we'd take him to see Mindy and Melissa."

"He wants to go to the cemetery?" Terrance was looking right through Lorraine as if having trouble comprehending this news.

"Yes. He doesn't want to go alone and… he doesn't know where they are buried."

"That's right. He never asked, so I never told him."

"What?" Amy choked, "He doesn't know where Aunt Mindy and Melissa are buried?"

Terrance looked at his daughter, his eyes starting to well up, "No, he doesn't. You two were still little, so you probably don't remember very well, but he wasn't at the funeral."

"Why not, Dad?" Terry, Jr. stared up at him, "He didn't get hurt too bad in the accident I thought."

"He didn't, not physically. When I went to pick him up for the funeral, he wouldn't budge from his hospital bed, or even talk to me. He just stared at me, like he didn't know who I was. I don't think he even knew what was going on. Either that or he was shutting everything out. It was a few weeks after the funeral before we were able to take him home. Then, well, you all know what happened next."

"I told him I'd tell you that he wants to go to the cemetery, and that the two of you could work out a day for us to go. I was thinking we could all go. Maybe he'd like to see the kids. He did ask about them."

"No kidding? Okay, that's fine then. I'll go over tomorrow and talk to him. Want to watch a DVD or something?" He turned to his kids, trying to lighten the mood, but plainly revealing on his face that he wasn't really in favor of his own suggestion.

"Not really." Terry, Jr., got up and went to his room. Amy and Lorraine shortly followed suit and left Terrance sitting in the living room. Strange that only moments ago the room was cozy, filled with easy chuckles prompted by prime time comedy programming.

As so often happens, past tragedies and the memories of

happier times come back to haunt the living. It would be nice if life could be like a sit-com. A problem arises, but not a problem that will tear your family apart or send members of your family into hiding. Only enough of an obstacle to cause a little confusion, something you can laugh at later over a bowl of popcorn in the comfort of your living room surrounded by your loved ones. But in real life problems are not solved in twenty to twenty-two minutes plus commercials and present no consequences later, but instead drag on for years and years, from generation to generation, spawning other problems and heartache along the way. Last, but not least, real life woes don't come with a laugh track.

That was weird. He hadn't made a phone call since... who the hell knows. Not since he'd been living at 517 Sycamore anyway, and not during the entire time he was in the Harper Institute. The staff at the institute always made the calls for him, or brought him the phone. The only person he even had to call was Terry, and Terry always preempted his every need knowing how much Francis hated using the telephone. His telephone, a heavy, old model, had sat on the end table all this time, one of the best dust collectors in the room, ringing only once in a while, and it was always Terry.

The only reason he even knew Terry's number was because his brother had left his card with his work and home numbers under the phone in the case of an emergency. Up until tonight he had never even felt the urge to use the phone. But sitting in his easy chair reading about the Galapagos Islands, he had a sudden thought concerning Mindy and Melissa.

He wasn't quite sure where the Galapagos Islands were, somewhere off the coast of South America, but which side? And that got him to thinking about places he knew the names of, but not their geographic locations like Timbuktu, or the Garden of Eden, or the far end of rainbows, or his dead family. He didn't know where they were. He didn't go to the funeral seven years ago, he wasn't even aware of a funeral being held. It was only much later that Terry had tried to tell him about the memorial service before Francis put his hands over his ears as a desperate signal for Terry to stop talking about it. Terry had never brought it up again and Francis had never thought to ask.

For some reason, tonight he thought about it. A thought triggered by a collection of desolate rock islands inhabited by marine iguanas, giant tortoises, and hundreds of species of finches. He wondered what Doctor Singh would say about this. He'd probably call it a breakthrough of some kind. A personal revelation, a giant step in the healing process and maybe it was. The interaction with Susan and Chava Lee had awakened something in him. Not a sudden desire to run down the street embracing all of mankind, but a sort of regrouping; a kind of merging, a connecting of the past with the present. A need to see where he stood with those he used to be close to. Terry had been his faithful watchdog; seeing to his needs, making sure he was okay. But Terry's family, he had shut them out. After all the good times, all the closeness, and family sharing they'd experienced. Would they even want him back? He'd seen the kids about four years before, soon after he'd first moved here from the institute. The visit didn't go well. But they had tried. He was the one who hadn't tried, who had fallen short of the family bond. They had stuck by him, even when he lacked adhesiveness.

The sound of Lorraine's voice on the telephone made him feel so hopeful, that at first he couldn't talk; and he was hesitant and brief with her on the phone once he did finally find his voice. But it was still a conversation of sorts. She sounded happy to hear his voice. He could probably call her again tomorrow and she would talk to him some more; fill him in a little bit on the last seven years. Maybe he could even say hello to Amy and Little Terry; Terry, Jr. rather.

It was possible. Susan and Chava had made that possible. It was such a simple thing they did. They came into his home, cooked for him, cleaned for him, and talked to him; every day activities that people do all of the time without thinking. People do them all the time... people.

They treated me like other people. Like a person. Not like a loon who had cut and stabbed at himself. Not like a loon who had tried to hang himself with belts and curtain cords. Not like a loon who had killed his... not like a loon.

It was the first time he had made a telephone call since Mindy and Melissa died. What else hadn't he done in seven years? He hadn't been to a movie or a restaurant. He hadn't traveled outside the city. He hadn't ordered a pizza or been to a park. He hadn't laughed out loud, at least to the best of his knowledge. He wasn't sure about when he was on the medication. Maybe he laughed like a lunatic then.

When Mindy and Melissa died, he died. But he wasn't dead. He enjoyed Susan's eggs and talking to Chava while they cleaned the animal cages. He looked forward to his brother's visits now, which he only begrudgingly tolerated before. He had enjoyed talking to Lorraine on the telephone, however briefly.

Is that what being a person is, interacting with other people and doing people things, and liking it? He had made a phone call. He could do the other things again too. It had never registered in his mind that he was still able to do these things. He had been totally occupied with the single act of surviving biologically to the point that nothing else mattered. The only thing that had mattered for so long was to not spill his own blood or cut off his own air supply. But things were mattering again. Breakfast with Susan mattered and working with Chava mattered. Terry and his family mattered because he mattered to them. He wasn't dead because to them he was alive.

Susan sat in the laundry break room deep in the bowels of the Paramount Hotel drinking a bottle of chilled water and looking forward to the end of her shift. The steam from the industrial-sized linen irons had her feeling overheated and a little dizzy. She was sweating freely and the skin on her hands was dried, cracking and sore.

At least the hot, steady work in the laundry had taken her mind off what she thought she may have seen today. The downtime in the break room brought it all back in a rush. When she had left 517 Sycamore to come to work she could have sworn she'd seen Ron's black Mustang in her rearview mirror, but when she turned her head to look behind her it was no longer there. She thought the confrontation in the lobby of the apartment building may have rattled her a little more than she originally thought; that she was just unconsciously on the lookout for more trouble. However, during the drive she thought she had glimpsed the car once more in the mirror, though again it wasn't there when she turned her head to look more closely.

She had never thought of Ron as the stalker type. He was overly macho and confident about himself, sure. But he had never seemed to care enough to evolve into anything dangerous. In fact, the incident the other day was the first time she had ever even seen him lose his temper since she'd known him. Was it possible that he cared for her more than he had let on while they were dating? Did breaking up with him set free some hidden monster of jealousy or possessiveness that he had never previously displayed; something potentially hazardous to her and her daughter's safety? After all, it is not uncommon for people considered to be harmless to crack and commit vicious acts at the drop of a dime. It happened every day. Was Ron cracking?

I'm just being paranoid. There are thousands, no, tens of thousands of black cars in this city and probably thousands of black Mustangs. But how many of those cars had furry, yellow dice hanging down from the rearview mirror in the center of the windshield?

XIII

"Hello? Doctor Singh? This is Terrance Tower, Francis Tower's brother."

"Of course, Terrance, how are you? It's been a long time. How is Francis doing?"

"That's why I'm calling; there have been some... um... developments."

"Oh? What sort of developments? Francis isn't exhibiting renewed suicidal behavior is he? You remember the symptoms I went over with you, right? Loss of control over one's emotions, drastic changes in eating habits—"

"Yes, I remember, but no, it's quite the opposite."

"Oh? How so? Please explain."

"Well, you got the message I sent you about Francis' accident... the cracked ribs and all?"

"Yes, I did. Thank you for helping keep our records current. I trust he is healing nicely."

"Well, he's healing up, and I hired a woman and her daughter, they live in his building, I hired them to help Francis out."

"I see. And how is that going?"

"He was resistant at first and he had some rough spots with the Lees, especially the mother."

"The Lees being the woman and the girl?"

"Correct."

"He had some trouble with them... go on."

"Now, he's... well, he likes them. All of a sudden, he has two friends."

"That's wonderful, Mister Tower."

"There is more. He called our house the other night; he made a call for the first time since before the accident that lead to his problem. He called and talked to Lorraine, my wife."

"That must have been quite a surprise after all this time."

"Yes, it was."

"Then what is it exactly that is disturbing you about this behavior?"

"He wants us to take him to see his wife and daughter's graves. You see, he's never been to the cemetery."

"And you are going to take him?"

"Of course! I mean, I couldn't say no. But I wanted to talk to you about it first; see if there is anything you can tell me about what to expect. At the grave site I mean."

"Well, first of all, this is a very positive development, Terry. But you can expect a show of emotion on Francis' part, at the graves, I mean. He is taking steps on his own, which is remarkable, to deal with the deaths of his family, as well as the guilt that he feels about the way they died."

"Okay, great! Then all of this is a good thing."

'Yes, but you should know that these steps he is taking aren't necessarily thought through on his part. He's sort of going with the flow, following his emotions. It is possible that he could regret the steps he is taking, though that doesn't mean that he shouldn't take them. The emotional pain that he is leading himself to is a necessary component in his recovery."

"What do you mean?"

"Well, you said that his actions have changed dramatically."

"Yes, and quickly... over just a few weeks."

"Then it is possible that he may be biting off more than he can chew, at least all at once. If it proves to be too much, too fast, he could possibly regress. These changes, these re-entries into society, they are usually very gradual. From what you've told me, these changes have taken place quickly."

"Yes, like I said over the course of a few weeks. Is it possible that by going too fast that he might try to commit suicide again?"

"It is possible, but I don't believe it is all that probable. I would *venture to say that he would hide himself more deeply within the routine he has created with his animals if anything."*

"Or?"

"Or he might handle it just fine. Continue to adjust and eventually lead a normal life."

"So, basically, we just…"

"…have to wait and see, yes. I'm afraid so, Terry. I'm afraid that it is going to mean flap and fly or crash and burn for Francis, but it wouldn't be a good idea for you to try to stop him from trying."

Francis had given Chava her own key to the fifth floor apartment a few days ago in case he was in the bathroom or tending to the animals and didn't hear her knocking on the door. She usually arrived around the time Susan was leaving and Francis was still sitting at the kitchen table smoking and drinking coffee, but Francis said that there were always unexpected scenarios to contend with and that after working for several weeks it surely wouldn't be long before Chava arrived late one morning.

The girl had protested that statement saying that she lived in the same building, how could she possibly be late for work? She finished off his protest by promising never to be late for work. Francis had just cracked a grin and told her to take the key anyway.

Chava didn't know whether Francis unintentionally planted the idea to be late in her head or whether Francis was just psychic, but Chava had woken up later than usual this morning and she was nearly an hour past her usual time of arrival upstairs. Francis had told her to always shower before coming up because humans can carry cold and flu viruses that could be passed on to other species, so Chava had showered in record time, threw on some clothes and flew up the stairs to Francis' apartment.

She didn't bother brushing her hair or eating breakfast, but that was okay. She figured going hungry until lunch time could serve as punishment for failing to live up to her promise not to be late.

When Chava opened Francis' door, she saw her mother coming out of the bathroom with an armful of Francis' dirty laundry. Her mom was still here, so maybe she wasn't as late as she thought she was, but Francis wasn't at his usual place at the kitchen table.

"Hi Mom, sorry I'm late. Is Francis mad?" She gasped as she tried to catch his breath after the sprint from the first floor.

"Hi, hon," Susan smiled, "No, he's not mad. He told me to tell you when you got here that 'he told you so'. What's he talking about?"

"It's nothing, just a Francis-style joke. He didn't start without me did he? We're draining the turtle ponds today. His ribs are lots better but he shouldn't be lifting the heavy buckets yet."

Susan looked at her daughter, impressed by her concern and amazed at how grownup she seemed at that moment. "He didn't start on anything. He's having coffee up on the roof. I took it up to him a few minutes before you got here."

"Oh, okay."

"You know, that was the first time I've been past that door? It's amazing back there! He said that you could give me a tour and show me the animals some time."

"Sure! I—"

"Here, hon. Take this bagel," Susan reached for a plate on the counter, "He's waiting on you. He said for you to come up on the roof when you got here."

"Okay. Wait, you were on the roof?"

"Yeah."

"I've only been to the top of the stairs, to open the window for Mavis. What's he got up there?"

"It's kind of strange, to tell you the truth. He has a cemetery up there."

"A what?"

Chava went through the door that separated Francis' living quarters from his pets and made an immediate left towards the spiral staircase. She was up the stairs in seconds with her bagel on the plate in one hand and a glass of orange juice in the other.

She had been up here every morning to open the window for Mavis the raven, but she'd never gone through the door of paned glass to the roof. Through the glass she could see Francis sitting on a wooden bench with a smoking cigarette in one hand while he scratched Felicia, who was in his lap, on the belly. Mavis was perched on the back of the bench looking over Francis' shoulder, intensely interested in the belly scratching. Four or five feet of rooftop stretched between the bench and the large wooden box that took up most of the space.

Chava tapped on the glass with the edge of her plate causing the heads of man, ferret, and raven to turn towards her. Francis signaled to her with a small movement of his smoking hand to come on out. The door was unlatched so a gentle nudge with the toe of her shoe opened up the glass door to the roof.

Chava could see why Francis had decided to take his coffee on the roof this morning. It was a gorgeous day; warm and breezy, the sun just high enough to offer warmth, but not enough to blind you if you looked in its general direction as it rose amongst the taller buildings.

"Good morning, Francis. Good morning, Mavis, Felicia."

Mavis croaked in response and Francis nodded in return, but Felicia had already gone back to the luxury of the belly scratch and couldn't be bothered. She was laying on her back, legs akimbo and her eyes half-closed. A half-eaten piece of strawberry licorice lay at Francis' feet.

"Have a seat, Chava."

Mavis sidled a few steps closer to Francis to allow her room to sit. "Sorry I'm late, Francis. It won't happen again!"

"Hah! Don't worry about it. I've just been enjoying the

morning with my friends here." He was still scratching Felicia. If the albino stretched her legs out anymore they were going to pop out of their sockets. Even her fluffy white tail looked about three inches longer.

"I stayed up too late watching a movie last night, so I didn't hear my alarm clock go off this morning."

"Really, it's okay. What kind of movie were you watching? I haven't watched a movie in years."

"It was a horror movie. A pretty scary one too; gave me some creepy nightmares."

"I used to like horror movies quite a bit; especially the old ones, the black and white ones."

"I never would have thought that. Why don't you watch them anymore?"

"I don't even have a TV, Chava. Besides, they aren't as scary as they used to be. You become desensitized as you get older. Enjoy the thrills while you can. But I still think about them sometimes."

"About your favorites you mean? The ones you used to like?"

"Yeah, but I also made a game out of comparing the monsters in movies to people."

"Famous people? Like how Bela Lugosi really did look like a vampire? Like that?"

"No; just comparing monsters to different kinds of people. Go ahead, name some monsters, I'll show you what I mean."

This is new. Francis' conversations had become much more normal lately, more about everyday topics. Now he wanted to talk about movie monsters? "Okay, how about vampires then?"

"I look at vampires like they are the world's rich and powerful."

"Because they control people?"

"Yeah and because they suck the life out of others. Especially the weak and naïve. And they have no conscience whatsoever. Give me another one."

"Okay. How about Frankenstein?"

"Frankenstein's monster, you mean. They are the world's heavies."

"Heavies?"

"Yeah, the guys who do the dirty work for those in control. Like soldiers and your everyday working stiffs. Keep going."

"I do tons of dirty work around here; you calling me a heavy?"

"Right. You're my ninety-five pound heavy. Name another one."

"Zombies?"

"That's easy. Look over the wall there; you will see dozens of zombies walking around down there. Everyday people going about their routines dressed in suits and carrying briefcases with blank looks on their faces; not even always aware of where they are or what they are doing. Sometimes the zombies and Frankenstein's monsters are hard to tell apart, sometimes they are exactly alike. Be careful that you don't turn into one of them."

"Werewolves?"

"The misunderstood. People, who for some reason or another, exist on the fringes of society. The insane, artists... people who have a different view of things from the majority, from the zombies," Francis took a drag off his cigarette, set Felicia gently on her feet next to the licorice and picked up his coffee from the arm of the bench.

"The Creature from the Black Lagoon?"

"You know, I never came up with a parallel for that one," he smiled, smoke wafting around his head, "Just a plain, old fish head."

"Which one are you? Which monster do you think you're most like?"

"Good question. Which would you compare me to?" Francis stared intently at her. "How you see yourself isn't usually the way others see you. I doubt zombies see themselves as zombies, you know."

"Okay, you're a... werewolf. Definitely a werewolf."

"Oh?" Francis didn't really look surprised, "Why's that?"

"Like you said, on the fringe of society. You don't suck the life out of people or do dirty work for others, unless you count feeding pinkies to tarantulas or cleaning up bird poop. You're definitely not a zombie. And you're not a fish head."

"Guess you're right," Francis shook his head in agreement. "I'll tell you what's really interesting about those old monster movies. Interesting to me anyway."

"What's that?" Chava smiled and leaned closer to him. She was enjoying this conversation with the recluse. He was so odd and looked at things from perspectives she never began to consider. To her, monsters were just monsters, meant to frighten for entertainment. To Francis, however, there was a bigger meaning to everything and she really got a kick out of his explanations.

"Okay, get this, Dracula and Frankenstein's monster, what do they have in common? Besides being monsters, of course."

"They are black and white movies?"

"Come on, not the movies themselves, but the characters. What do the characters have in common?"

The girl's nose and eyebrows knotted up into a frown as she considered this question. "Well," she began after some long seconds of thinking, "they're both European and they both live in castles... uh... and they're both dead. Or at least dead-ish."

"Sure, every European lives in a castle, right?" Francis jokingly mocked. "You're getting warm with the dead-ish observation."

"Uh... they can live forever?"

"Right. They are immortal. That's exactly right."

"So?"

"So? So... what? That's it. They are immortal. People have been watching vampire and Frankenstein movies since they first started making movies. And they read books about them even before that. Before that, at least with vampires, it was stories around the campfire. Human beings have long been obsessed with living forever. Heck, that's even one of the attractions of going to heaven if you stop and think about it."

"So is that why women are so crazy about makeup? Trying to look younger?"

"Maybe so, some of them do look monstrous." Francis grimaced.

"What about werewolves?"

"They are a different story; The Creature from the Black Lagoon, too. Some people are obsessed with the primal side of man."

"Primal?"

"The primitive side... the animal side... our basic animal nature."

"So they want to be animals?"

"Sure, why not? Animals are, for the most part, free of guilt and worry; the things that make being human so rough sometimes. There is even a medical condition... a mental condition, rather, called lycanthropy in which people actually believe they transform into wolves. Not so much physically, but in mind and spirit."

"Huh," the girl exhaled, staring out over the animal cemetery.

"Yeah... huh," Francis agreed. "It's quite ironic. People want to live forever but they are uncomfortable in their own skins."

The two sat quietly for a few moments giving their conversation some thought while watching Mavis groom herself and Felicia chew on her licorice before Francis finally resumed the conversation.

"Anyway, what kind of monster was in the movie you watched last night?"

"Ghosts."

"Ah, ghosts. Not really monsters, but scary none-the-less."

"Yeah, they scare me the most I think."

"Me, too. Why do you think they are so scary?"

"Well, you can always see the others coming. You know they are going to jump out of the dark or something, but ghosts pop up out of the middle of tables and through doors or out of the drain in the bathtub. You never know."

"And what about you? Why do you think they are the scariest?"

"For the same reasons as you, but mostly because I believe ghosts are real I think. They are actually based on real beings."

"You're kidding me. You believe in ghosts?"

"Yes, but not like the ones you see in the movies, or most of the movies anyway."

"What do you mean? There aren't different kinds of ghosts are there? Ghosts are just spirits, right? Spirits that haven't gone on to heaven, or hell, right? They hang around causing trouble for the living."

"That's what most people think of as ghosts, but I'm not a big believer in the concepts of spirits and heaven and hell."

"Then what are they? If they're not spirits, I mean?"

"Well, you know that living organisms, like you and Mavis and so on, they produce electrical charges."

"We do?"

"Sure, little electrical charges are constantly firing through your nerves. And this energy is actually strong enough to power a light bulb. We vary in how much we produce, but we all produce energy."

"I didn't know that, but what does it have to do with ghosts?"

"Energy doesn't just disappear. It goes on forever. Even when something dies other organisms feed off of it, the energy gets passed on. Who's to say that some of that energy isn't just released, you know? Just out there floating around until it dissipates. Like a bolt of lightning, but slower. I think that what we perceive as ghosts are merely units of, I don't know... I'll call it organic energy."

"Yeah, but what about ghost shapes; people-shaped ghosts? Energy doesn't have a shape."

"The energy in a thunderstorm doesn't have a shape until it makes a lightning bolt. It's a natural event. Maybe when something dies, the death acts as a catalyst that gives the energy a shape. The shape it would be most familiar with, the shape of its previous host."

"That's pretty far out there, Francis."

"I didn't say it was a fact, just thinking is all," the man shrugged his shoulders.

Chava wasn't satisfied. "Okay, how about when ghosts make trouble for the living?"

"I'm not sure that they do. I don't know, maybe carpet shocks and static cling are the ghosts of dead enemies getting revenge," Francis smiled.

Chava chuckled at Francis' dry humor before finally asking, "Francis? Speaking of creepiness, why is there a cemetery on your roof?" She nodded her head in the direction of the two dozen or so small graves in the large, soil-filled box.

"You didn't think my pets lived forever did you?"

"But why did you keep them?"

"I didn't keep them. I buried them."

"Yeah, but—"

"They were my friends, Chava. I wanted to keep them close. Don't worry. I seal them in glass jars before I bury them. And I wrap duct tape around the jars so that somewhere down the road, when I'm dead and gone and out causing static cling, people won't freak out when they dig them up."

"Why is that one in the corner the only one with flowers on it? What makes it so special?"

"That's Little Demon," Francis sighed.

"What was he... or she... a tarantula or something?"

"No, Little Demon was a very fuzzy and very friendly hamster. He was my first pet; he made it possible for me to leave the institute. He was the first pet I had here. You could say he saved my life in a way."

"That explains the flowers."

"It's the least that I can do for a friend."

"Why did you name a fuzzy, little hamster something like Little Demon? Kind of a weird name for a hamster."

"I guess so, but the first time I saw him he was running like crazy on a wheel, like he was trying to get away from something. At that time I was trying to get away from some things myself. Personal demons you could say. So, I named him Little Demon. That's nothing too mysterious, right?"

"Francis?" Chava's voice became low and serious.

"Yes?"

"Why were you in the Harper Institute?"

Francis said nothing and stared at Little Demon's grave. Mavis and Felicia sensed his discomfort. The bird nuzzled his ear and the ferret rubbed up against his leg.

Chava immediately regretted asking Francis the question, "Sorry, Francis. That was too personal, never mind. Forget I asked it."

Francis turned and looked at her, "Yes, it is personal. But that's okay. I just don't want to talk about that. Not today. It's too pretty outside today. Okay?"

"Sure… sure… hey! We should probably get to work, right? Those turtle tanks won't drain themselves," Chava blurted in an attempt to erase the tension she felt she had created.

"Right and Bullet gets crabby if his water gets too dirty." Francis smiled, letting her off the hook.

XIV

"Why Chava, Susan?"

"Why Chava what, Francis?"

"How did a Korean couple come to name their daughter after a Russian Jew?"

"Oh! Ha! Well, no big mystery there. Her father and I really loved The Fiddler on the Roof. *We watched it every time it was on TV. My favorite song is the one Tevya sings about his daughter, Chava... his little bird. So, when we had a girl... she was so beautiful, so precious and tiny... she was our little bird. Our own Chava."*

"Yeah, I can see that. I like that story. Uh, Susan?"

"Francis?"

"I've been meaning to ask you something, how is it Chava has so much free time to spend up here working for me?"

"You know I work nights and I sleep a big part of the day, and it is summer vacation. She'd just be sitting around bored and watching the boob tube waiting for me to get up."

"Yes, but aside from the money Terry is paying you guys, isn't this pretty much ruining her summer vacation? Why doesn't she ever go anywhere with other kids? She's never even mentioned her friends. She does have friends doesn't she?"

"I suppose in school she does, but it's hard for her."

"How so?"

"There aren't any other Korean-American, and not even many Asian-American, kids in her school. She's kinda' small for her age, you've probably noticed that. And she's a girl; hell, almost a young woman and she hasn't... uh... developed at the same rate as the other girls in her class, if you catch my drift. She gets her little crushes on

one of the nicer boys sometimes. They aren't mean to her, but they don't really see her, either. She's embarrassed by how she looks."

"Yeah, don't tell her I said so, but I thought she was around eleven when I first saw her. You mentioned the nicer boys. Are some of them mean to her? She gets picked on? Bullied and such?"

"That is part of it, but it's more than that and it's not only the boys."

"What else would turn a kid into a homebody besides being bullied?"

"Well, there are some kids who call her names, and it seems to really bother her."

"Racial slurs?"

"Yes, that's part of it, but not just simple, stupid things like that. They call her things like the Orphan. And they ask her mean things like, 'What? Ran out of dogs and cats so you ate your dad?' Stupid shit like that."

"When you're Chava's age I suppose that's worse than getting physically bullied."

"Yeah. And it's not just how some of the kids behave."

"What? Don't tell me adults at her school say stuff like that to her, too?"

"No, of course they don't. It's the pity and special treatment they show her. The teachers and the principal, they dote on her a little because she's small and her dad died. It isn't their intention, but they treat her a little like a pet. That just makes the teasing from the kids worse. It seems like the more the school staff tries to shield her the more the bullies try to get at her."

"They're like piranha, they smell a little blood in the water and can't resist going for it."

Yeah... uh... You know, Francis. You and Chava really aren't all that different. You have both shut yourselves away over things that aren't your fault. Maybe that's why she likes you so much."

"She likes me? Seriously? And I wouldn't encourage pointing out any similarities between the two of us if I were you."

"Are you kidding me? She can't wait to come here in the morning! It's always Francis this and Francis that and Francis said *once she gets home. And what's wrong with comparing her to you?"*

"Well, I'm not exactly the best role model to wish on a kid. You don't want her to grow up to be an oddball."

"She's well aware that you are an oddball, *your words not mine, but she told me that you are interestingly weird. Frankly, I'm getting a little tired of hearing about you.*

"Hah! I can't argue with the weird part."

"Neither can I. Do you want another pancake? There is some batter left."

"No, I'm stuffed. How about you make yourself some and sit a while. Have some coffee while we wait for Chava."

"Uh... okay, but you only have the one chair."

Lawrence McPhee was sitting in a booth at *Stew's* nursing the one beer he'd collected enough change on the street that day to buy. He preferred to sit at the bar next to the waitress station so he could get a good look at Tanya, but Sid had banished him to a booth due to the cloud of body odor he emitted and because he couldn't keep his hands to himself.

Sid didn't want to refuse service to a paying customer, even one as unpleasant as McPhee, but the long, wooden bar was like the high roller's room in a casino, not just anyone could get in; especially homeless guys who hadn't showered or shaved since before their last birthday. Just bad for business.

Even though that horse's ass Sid wouldn't let him sit at the bar, his eyes were glued to the action in that part of the establishment. Being a Tuesday there wasn't much going on, but there were a few tasty ladies in skirts sitting there with their dates. McPhee watched like a hawk when the ladies turned to get off their stools for trips to the restroom because if he watched real close he could catch a glimpse of their underwear. Lucky for him the women weren't there together, so the "all women to the powder room" pack mentality didn't send them scurrying and dismounting their stools all at once, so he was able to give his full attention to each one individually when nature called.

McPhee was zeroed in on the redhead in the black, leather miniskirt who was starting to squirm a little on her stool. She was going to be making a trip to the john any second now. As he watched in anticipation a shadow fell across his table and he heard his name. "McPhee? Lawrence McPhee?"

McPhee reluctantly tore his eyes away from the black miniskirt and looked up at a clean-cut dude in his late 30s that he'd seen around *Stew's* a few times but never had the displeasure of speaking to. "Who are you and what do you want? I'm busy."

"Yeah, you look it," the clean-cut dude's voice was ripe with sarcasm, "I'm Ron. Ron Rhodes."

"Okay, Ron Ron Rhodes. Now answer the second part of the question. What the fuck do you want?" McPhee's lecherous gaze having since returned to the ladies at the bar.

"Take it easy, man. I just want to talk to you, that's all."

"Maybe I don't want to talk to you. Did you stop and consider that?"

"I did. But I didn't think you'd say no to a couple of rounds. On me."

McPhee broke out in a toothy grin that immediately upset Ron's stomach. McPhee, through good genetics or luck, had all of his teeth, unlike most street people. They were scummy looking, kind of green, that was for sure, but there they were big and straight.

"Now you're talking, Ron Rhodes, my friend. Have a seat," McPhee waved towards the bench seat across from him," Just slide that stuff on over and make yourself some room there."

Ron flashed the peace sign at Sid signaling for two fresh beers and then looked down at the greasy-looking duffel bag on the seat. He didn't want to touch the nasty looking bag for fear of typhoid or fleas, but McPhee wasn't making a move to clear it out of the way for him. Ron unconsciously took a deep breath and slid the bag over. It felt nearly as greasy as it looked.

"What do you have in there?" Ron pointed at the bag.

"Pretty much everything I own," McPhee's friendly tone was gone as fast as it had come, "Why?"

"Nothing, just curious, that's all." Tanya saved him the uncomfortable task of thinking of something else apologetic to say by arriving with their beers balanced on her tray.

"Thanks, sweetness," Ron offered her a smile and a ten-dollar bill, "Keep the change." Tanya gave him her come-hither smile, but was obviously working on ignoring McPhee as much as she could.

Ron and McPhee watched her smile, take the bill, and saunter off to her next stop.

McPhee whistled. "That gal sure has a sweet ass."

"That she does, Larry. That she does." Ron agreed nodding.

"Leave it at McPhee, or Lawrence. My friends call me Larry."

"Okay, sorry, McPhee. Would you mind if we could cut the badass routine now? I'd like to get to the point of this conversation."

"Fine. It's about goddamned time."

McPhee could see for the first time since the conversation began that Ron Rhodes wasn't just another dandy in for a drink. He looked like a guy that knew how to handle himself, even if his haircut did him look like a fucking poof. "What can I do for you, Rhodes?"

"You were in here a while back bragging about knocking a guy out in the street and getting away with it."

"Hell yeah, the fucker tried to steal my dog. So I showed him that I wasn't someone he could push around."

"Not what I heard. I heard you jumped the guy and then your dog jumped you. It turns out that animals find you just as unpleasant as people do, huh?"

"What's your fucking point, smart ass?"

"My point is, do you know 517 Sycamore?"

"It's an apartment building. So?"

"So, that's where the guy who got you bit and hassled by the cops lives. He owns the building."

"Go on." McPhee leaned in towards Ron, becoming increasingly interested in what the other man had to say.

"I thought that might interest you. The guy's name is Francis Tower."

"Fucker looked like a Francis, or maybe a Teddy, or a Gaylord. What's the beef between me and that faggot got to do with you anyway?"

"Well, I just thought that maybe you would be interested in a little plan on evening things up. I mean, you're not going to just roll over and let him get away with that shit, right?"

"Maybe, maybe not, but you didn't answer my question. What's this got to do with you?"

"Tower got a little banged up by that taxi you pushed him in front of. Now he's got a woman and a kid working for him, helping him out until he's back on his feet. The woman is my ex. The kid is my ex's daughter."

McPhee was amused by this information. "So, some little bitch throws you over for this Francis piss-ant and you want me to get rid of him for you, is that it? Maybe he's not a faggot after all. Sounds like love to me."

"Listen, scumbag, I just figured that seeing as people we both have beefs with are spending a lot of time together, getting good and chummy, we might have a mutual interest in fucking with them. Two heads are better than one."

"Who said I have a beef with Tower? He could have pressed charges, but he didn't. Why would I want to get even, I should probably send him flowers or something for being such a stand-up, forgiving kinda' guy."

"I did a little checking up on you, McPhee. A real riches to rags story. Then along comes a guy like Francis, a real fruitcake by the way, who humiliates you out on the street. Did you know that spic cop and the nigger cabbie were all set to testify if he chose to press charges? The only reason you are sitting here having this beer and freely smelling like a dumpster is because Tower didn't think YOU were worth fucking around with. You weren't worth his precious time."

"You think you're real smart, don't you pretty boy? Real clever, huh? Get the ranting street trash all riled up and let him do your dirty work, huh? You think I haven't done some checking of my own? I know who Francis Tower is! Saint Fucking Francis with all his cute, little animals up there on the fifth floor. You're not telling me anything I didn't know except for the fact that you were banging the chink cleaning lady he has working for him."

"Korean, she's a gook, not a chink," Ron corrected taken aback by how strongly he had underestimated McPhee.

"What the fuck's the difference? They all eat with sticks and have slanted eyes. The point is I already plan on evening things up with that fucking Tower character."

Ron was surprised at the bum's possession of information. He might be living on the streets and smelled like a bus station toilet, but he hadn't lost any of his old businessman's sharpness. "I see. Then I guess there is no point in us talking about this."

"Hold on, pretty boy. There might be something to the two heads are better than one logic. Buy me another beer, or four, and we can talk about it."

"Okay, then," Ron shot two fingers towards the ever-vigilant Sid again. "Any ideas off the top of your head?"

"I think sending them a message would be a good first step."

Ron could see the proverbial light bulb switch on over the man's matted hair. "A message, what do you mean? Just exactly what kind of a message do you have in mind?"

"You got a strong stomach, pretty boy?"

Chava stood in the middle of the sugar glider enclosure with a dozen furry marsupials crawling up and down her arms and legs; going in and out of her pockets and sitting on her head. The little creatures only paused their explorations for seconds at a time before they were on the move again. They were like little battery operated toys on uppers. They lay asleep in their log all day on chargers and when the sun went down they leapt into action. They left the dark recess of the log in twos and threes, stopping to take a crap and a piss and then started jumping around; branch to branch, up the wire walls of the enclosure and taking turns on the four exercise wheels mounted on the thicker branches, and then finally to the food dishes. They'd have a piece of corn, a chunk of apple, maybe a dead pinkie, and then they were off again to do their acrobatic rounds.

It never failed to amaze Chava how tame and friendly the little omnivores were. The very first time they encountered the girl, they showed absolutely no fear. Their leader, Oliver, took a special liking to her and enjoyed digging around for lint in her pockets or resting on her neck with his long, svelte tail curled around Chava's ear.

"What's this thing on Oliver's head, Francis? It looks like a scab or something."

Francis was sitting on a stool outside the enclosure watching the sugar gliders use Chava for a jungle gym. "That's a scent gland. All the males have them on their heads. You ever notice that Oliver always rubs you with his head, but the other males don't? And he's the only one that spends any real length of time sitting on you? As far as they are concerned, you belong to Oliver. That's also why you smell a little like sugar glider pee." Francis chuckled at her.

"Is that the same like when dogs pee on fire hydrants?"

"Yep, exactly the same. Most animals mark territory or their possessions in some way. That includes people."

"Huh? People don't go around peeing on stuff to show they own it."

"They don't? Well, okay, they don't usually pee on stuff, but they do other things with the same intent. Watch people when you are outside. If you see a couple walking down the street, the man will usually hold the woman's hand or put his arm around her if another guy, or group of guys, is near. He's showing that she belongs to him. They don't even think about it, it's just a natural behavior."

"I never thought of that," Chava pried a sugar glider's tiny claws out of her scalp.

"Sure. How about personalized license plates and monogrammed pajamas. And don't forget fences."

"Fences?"

"Yeah, fences and walls are an age-old, basic method of marking territory, been around since mankind first settled down to live in one place. You don't just jump fences and go in peoples' yards do you?"

Chava thought for a second and scratched Oliver under his pointy little chin, "I guess you're right. 'Cause they're off limits."

"There you go. The other sugar glider males don't get in your pocket because it would be like jumping a fence."

Chava raised an eyebrow and smiled. "Hey, I saw a homeless guy peeing on the side of our building the other day. Was he marking it?"

Francis caught the joke and ran with it. "Nah, that was another basic instinct. When you gotta' go, you gotta' go."

XV

"Are you sure you want to go through with this?"

"Why do you ask?"

"Well, it has been over seven years since they died. Why do you want to go to the cemetery all of a sudden?"

"All of a sudden? You just said it yourself, Terry, it has been over seven years. My wife and daughter have been dead for over seven years and I've never been to their graves. I don't even know where their graves are for fuck's sake."

"Okay, Francis. Take it easy. I'm just making sure. I worry about you taking on too much all at once, that's all."

"Sorry, Terry. I'm not cussing at you. I'm cussing at myself. What kind of man doesn't know where his dead family is buried? I should have visited them long before now. I should have gone to the funeral in the first place. What kind of man doesn't go to the funeral for his own family?"

"A man who has been traumatized; a man who experienced something so horrible, that he had to retreat deep within himself to escape the horror. Reality was too much for you. No one judges you for trying to escape that amount of pain."

"You know, you sound like Doctor Singh."

"Maybe he rubbed off on me a little, but it's true, isn't it?"

"That's what I'm told."

"I'm just saying there is no hurry. Take all the time you need. You've been doing so well lately."

"I was in the Harper Institute for three years trying to find a way to join Mindy and Melissa. I've been up here on the fifth floor of this building taking on the responsibility of these animals in order to keep

from killing myself. But I'm starting to peak out, Terry. I miss living, man. Susan and Chava, they've shown me what I've been missing."

"They aren't Mindy and Melissa, Francis."

"I know that! I never said they were! I am not trying to replace my family, Terry. I'm just saying that I see now that I don't have to live like this."

"So you don't blame yourself anymore for what happened?"

"No, I am responsible for that. I killed them, Terry. I'll always have to wrestle with that fact. But I don't have to wrestle with it in the dark by myself."

"Now who sounds like Doctor Singh?"

"Smartass. I need to visit their graves, Terry. Can't you see how big of a step that is if I intend to get on with things, with my life? I need to follow this lead, who knows when I'll have another chance to escape out of the dark?"

"I do see it. I just hope you're ready for it."

"I am."

"Okay, big brother. You're the boss. Then how about Saturday afternoon? Me, Lorraine, and the kids will swing by and pick you up. I'll ask Lorraine to pack a picnic and we'll make a day of it. If we approach this a little more festively, like a family reunion or something, maybe it won't go as hard for you as it might otherwise. The cemetery is grassy with plenty of shade. It is actually very nice for a cemetery. What do you think?"

"It is a family reunion of sorts, Terry. So that sounds perfect."

Francis was faced with something he hadn't felt even once since the death of his wife and daughter. This long-absent, and slightly uncomfortable, feeling was genuine concern for another person. Sure, he had felt concern for Terrance's troubles with dealing with a suicidal, reclusive brother, but the concern for his brother was based on his own shame and inadequacies in facing life. The concern he was feeling for Chava Lee stood alone with no connections to his own problems, based solely on the

151

problems the girl was dealt; in particular the girl's subjugation to the cruel, wickedness of her adolescent peers.

Francis remembered back to when he was Chava's age. He had scads of friends, and they ran together like a pack of overly-exuberant, but friendly, dogs. There were about half a dozen boys in their core group, and though Francis can't say he was ever truly the leader of the group, he was always on equal standing with them and never experienced more than the friendly ribbing that they all gave out to one another every time a chance presented itself.

Boys being boys was all it was, no cruel intentions intended, though he's sure they probably went too far from time to time. Terry as a younger sibling-in-training fell under the protective umbrella of his older brother's standing in the pre-teen community and ran in the equally rambunctious, and no less friendly, group of younger boys that tailed their older brothers from one point of childish mischief and tomfoolery to another.

But Chava Lee didn't run in a pack. And she didn't have a younger brother or sister to tail after her. It was just her and her mom, and now Francis. Francis was acutely aware of the fact that he was probably the girl's only real friend, and that was using the term loosely, outside of the ragtag group of outcasts she was probably mixed in with while school was in session.

Francis could remember a similar group from his own school days. It consisted mostly of minorities like Chava, the kids that were way too smart for their ages, and kids with some sort of disability or singular physical trait, like Simon Brewster, the boy with the cleft palate. The misfits formed an uneasy alliance, because even in a supposedly peaceful school setting there is always strength in numbers. Unlike Francis' pack of friends, however, the band of misfits dissolved and scattered once school let out and didn't normally regroup until school started up once again the next day.

Francis and his friends weren't normally the type of boys to pick on these outcasts, but there were other groups roaming the halls of education; some of these groups were mean-spirited bands of bullies. He had distinct memories of the outcasts being shut up in lockers, pushed into the restrooms of the opposite gender, having their pants pulled down around their ankles on the playground, having the choice parts of their lunches snatched, and sometimes just getting pummeled mercilessly without warning or the slightest provocation. Francis and his friends even stuck up for the outcasts on occasion when the numbers were in their favor, but they never truly befriended them. It was fine to stick up for Simon Brewster when the bullies had him cornered and forced him to whistle through his cleft palate, but it was another thing to let Simon into the group. However, Francis could now see the fine line between indifference and cruelty in that practice.

It had been years since he had even thought of his old school friends. He had no idea where they were or which ones were even still alive. He didn't know if the old group would approve, but he was going to take an outcast into the pack and make her a full member. He and Chava would be their own pack of two and the bullies had better watch their asses.

Chava was standing stock-still and staring down into the red-eared slider pond. She was getting herself geared up to do the weekly draining and scrubbing of the pond when something going on under the water caught her attention. After a few moments of trying to figure out what was going on she motioned for Francis. "Hey! Francis! What's going on here?"

Francis had been sprinkling vitamin supplements on the chopped vegetables and fruits for the various lizards. The lizards would sometimes eat only the bits of vegetables and fruit that they particularly liked and leave the rest, which could result in vitamin deficiencies that weakened their bones. Merlin, the three-foot male iguana was notorious for this. The big, emerald-green lizard was a sucker for bananas and it was always a battle for Francis to get him to eat anything else. Bananas were nothing more than a snack with very little value for the overall health of a full-grown iguana. It would be like a human trying to survive on marshmallows. Francis looked up when he heard Chava's call, grabbed his cane and headed over to the turtle pond. He could walk fine without the cane now, the bruising in his thigh was nearly gone and only a dull ache remained, but his balance was still off. The cane had become a precaution rather than a necessity.

"What are you hollering about?"

"Look at Bullet," Chava pointed down at the water, "What's he doing?"

Francis smiled when he saw what was happening. "Oh, he's just trying to impress one of the ladies."

Bullet and the target of his energetic attentions were both submerged in the pond facing each other. The female was mostly just sitting there with her head half-pulled into her shell, but Bullet was frantically busy. The big male had both of his front feet fully extended out in front of him with the tops of the feet turned facing one another. Every few seconds Bullet would gyrate and vibrate his toes in a waving motion. He looked like a kid trying to dig a hole in the sand while the sand was trying to cave back in on the hole. The female slider looked mostly unimpressed and quite bored, but who could tell what goes on in a turtle's head? For all she knew the other turtle could have thought Bullet was doing the sexiest dance she'd ever seen and was just pretending to be unimpressed. Could turtles be coy?

"Is it working?"

"Well, she's not nipping at him. That's a good sign. If he was annoying her she'd be trying to chase him off by biting at his toes. Like a woman hanging up on a guy or slapping a guy when he gets too fresh on the dance floor."

"You always do that. You like to compare what your animals do to what people do, don't you?"

"Yeah, I guess that's true. But that's only because it's so easy to do. Us and the animals, on a basic level, we are not all that different. There are natural parallels between our behaviors and it doesn't take a genius to notice them."

"I'm starting to see that."

"Oh, yeah? Give me one of your observations, genius."

"I don't know... well, like the sugar gliders."

"Okay? What about the sugar gliders then?"

"Well, Oliver is the leader. That is obvious. He gets first pick at the food. First pick of spots to mark with that gross little ... what did you call it... gland? He's the only one that gets in my pockets."

"Right, but where is the human parallel?"

"Well, like a good leader, he doesn't abuse his, um... power, I guess you could call it. He always leaves plenty of the food for the others, and he doesn't get mean when one of the others stays too long on my shoulder; just kind of nudges them away."

"What would happen if he didn't act like that?"

"You mean, if he DID eat all the good food and acted mean with the others?"

"Yeah."

"I suppose the others would get enough of it after a while and one of the others would take over as leader, right? Maybe they'd gang up on him and one of the other's would take his spot?"

"That's exactly right. In fact, that has happened before with these guys. Oliver wasn't always the leader. You know Martin, the sugar glider with the piece of an ear missing?" Francis hadn't forgotten his fellow patient, Old Martin, when it came time to name the sugar gliders. The fact that Martin's namesake had turned out to be unlikable was just a happy coincidence.

"Sure, he's the one that kind of sticks to himself all of the time."

"Right, well, he used to be the dominant male, the leader, but he abused his position, his power, like you said. Oliver stepped up, took that chunk out of his ear during the coupe."

"I can't see Oliver doing something like that."

"Well, he's nice enough to Martin now though, but

155

desperate times called for desperate measures. So Oliver got just mean enough, long enough, to take over. Oliver will even groom Martin now, but I don't think Martin has ever fully forgiven him.

If you watch closely you might notice that Martin always knows where Oliver is, he never lets him out of his sight. It's almost like he's looking for his chance to regain the power he abused and lost, but I doubt he'll ever get the chance. The others like Oliver too much."

"If you had to have a leader, I suppose it would be nice to have a guy like Oliver to follow."

"Hey, Chava?" Francis' voice grew thoughtful.

"Yeah?"

"You don't have many friends, do you?"

Chava stood up straighter and her face took on a defensive glare, "Why do you ask that? We were talking about sugar gliders. What does that have to do with me? I have plenty of friends."

"Who? You never talk about anyone from your school, the neighborhood, or from anywhere else for that matter."

"Well, I do have friends. Gillian Lester and Phillip Liu and... um... Tracy Nielson. They're my friends!"

"School has been out for the summer for over a month, since a couple of days before my accident. You've been up here with me pretty much every day. Why haven't you seen these friends of yours?"

"You know how it is. Everyone is busy during summer vacation, including me. In fact, I need to drain this pond right now. So why don't we quit talking and get to work?"

"Okay, okay, but first... say the first word that pops into your head when I say these names, alright?"

"What? Why?"

"Can you just go along with me for a minute?"

"Fine."

"Okay, first name... Phillip Liu."

"Chinese."

"Second name... Gillian Lester."

"Chess champ."

"Good, third name... Tracy Nielson."

"Wheelchair."

"Chava?" Francis was thinking back to the group of outcasts from his own childhood. The group that consisted of minority kids, kids with disabilities, and kids who were too bright, or not bright enough.

"What?" Her visage had lost all of its bluster.

"Are they REALLY your friends?"

"Just at school, but they are nice."

"I'm sure they are, and I'm not saying that you shouldn't be friends with them. But the other kids pick on you, don't they?"

"A little."

"Just a little?"

"Most of the other kids are okay, but there are some real jerks at school too. Like Martin. They think they can boss everybody around, make them do what they say. Maybe I should bite a chunk out of one of their ears, huh?" She made a show of chomping her teeth together.

"Well, I wouldn't resort to drawing blood or cannibalism. That's no way for a person to gain popularity. It'll just make the other kids afraid of you if you go nuts in the gym and bite some other kid on the ear."

"Of course I'm not going to bite anybody, but then what should I do? I look different. I'm short, even shorter than Phillip Liu and he's a year younger than me! If I didn't have long hair lots of the kids probably wouldn't even know I'm a girl, and my dad is... my dad's dead. How am I supposed to fit in? That's a lot of stuff for people to make fun off."

"You think being short, or looking different than most of the kids, or losing your dad makes you less of a person than the rest of the kids?"

"No, but... But it's not what I think that causes the problem, is it?"

"That's a very logical observation and I'm glad you don't blame yourself for how your classmates behave. However, those

157

things are only part of who you are, Chava. You're a good kid. Funny. Smart. A damned hard worker. Ignore the bullies as best you can, and you can be friends with all the other kids. When you have everybody else on your side, the bullies won't stand a chance. Strength in numbers you could say."

"I understand that, but it's easier said than done."

"Yeah, I know. But it's something to think about anyway."

"At least I have one friend to see outside of school, right?" Chava beamed up at Francis.

"Don't get mushy, yeah, we're pals. But I think I can do you one better. I have a nephew and a niece, Terry, Jr. and Amy.

"Terry's kids?"

"Right. They're around your age. You want to meet them?"

"Sure, I guess so. But do you think they'd like me?"

"Why wouldn't they?"

"I don't know... I...," Chava looked off towards the sugar glider enclosure and thought of Oliver and Martin, "Yeah, why shouldn't they?"

"Great. This Saturday we'll knock off early. We have a picnic to go to."

The skinny, mange-covered dog was living the ultimate canine nightmare. He had lived a miserable life in the service of McPhee, tied to the nearest tree, hydrant or fence post; unfed for days at a time, drinking from any available water source no matter how foul and given very little in the way of attention or affection, unless it was to be yelled or kicked at to stop whining when he was hungry or an occasional theatrical pat on the head to gain sympathy for his master from the pedestrians passing by on the sidewalk.

As bad as all that was, he missed his previous life with McPhee. Any dog born into servitude grows to love their master, no matter how harsh or cruel they may be. It may not be a real love, but more of a mixture of fear and hatred tempered by the understanding that one's life is in the hands of a tyrant, like a dirt-poor peasant liberated by a murderous dictator, you have to go along to get along.

Now he no longer even had McPhee. He had committed the greatest sin a dog could commit; he had turned on his master. When the strange man fed him the meat, it had been at least two days since he had tasted food of any kind. The strange man had mercy on him and his ever-shrinking stomach, and McPhee attacked him. McPhee had lashed out at the only real kindness that had ever been directed towards the dog, or at least the only real kindness in the animal's memory. So in an outraged defense of this kindness the dog had turned on his master and in the process freed himself from his tether. The dog ran away, leaving McPhee bleeding and cursing, and never looked back.

He now spent his days combing the alleys and abandoned lots in search of edible garbage and rats, if he could catch them. He avoided human contact because in his dog's mind, he was a traitor of the worst sort. However, he always perked his ears up at the sound of a human voice for he knew that if he heard the voice of McPhee he would hazard approaching the betrayed master, ears flat in supplication and head bent low, and he would squirm and grovel in the dust for a second chance, a second chance to be the abused servant of the tyrant, his cruel, beloved McPhee.

XVI

"Well, you all heard right. I invited the girl to the picnic. Do you have any thoughts on this you'd like to express?"

"Okay… okay… simmer down… that's just jealousy talking. I know you all better than that."

"What are you squawking about, Mavis? Don't act like you don't like the kid! You've been taking biscuits and pinkies from her for weeks now. You know, it wouldn't hurt you to let her scratch you on the head once in a while. She's been nothing but nice to you and, to be honest, I'm a little ashamed of your standoffish behavior."

"You like her well enough, right Felicia? I know she's free and easy with the licorice. Don't think I haven't noticed all of the red dumps you've been taking."

"I know you don't mind the kid, Bullet. She's drained your pool how many times now? Six? Seven? And you haven't tried to take a bite out of her yet, you old softy. You put on a good tough-guy show, but there is a little heart of gold beating inside that shell of yours."

"And you snobby pig-noses, I've seen you come up for air when she walks by your pool whether you need it or not. You're not fooling anybody."

"I know if Oliver and the other gliders were awake they'd back up my decision to ask her along. They were all over her the first time she met them. Even Martin gets close enough for a sniff, that grouchy old bastard."

"You don't think I haven't noticed how you birds avoid shitting on her shoes when she's in your enclosure? You don't even show me that kind of consideration! Is that because she so thoughtfully divides up the fresh bean sprouts and romaine lettuce? She makes sure *everyone gets their fair share of the goodies. What's not to like about that?"*

"Luis, I know you are a little put off by the fact she still hasn't built up the nerve to hold you! You know perfectly well that eight hairy legs and your fangs don't exactly inspire cuddling. Remember how cautious I was with you when I first brought you home. In spite of her fear of you, doesn't she always go for pinkies when we're out? She would never neglect you no matter how distastefully she views your meal preferences, you know that."

"Thanks, Constance. I knew you'd be the cool head of reason. She's a good kid and you can smell that as well as I can. I could see your attitude towards her warm up after she got over her squeamishness and fed you that rat a while back. She also found that nice spot between your eyes that you like to have rubbed didn't she? I saw you eating it up."

"Merlin? Hey, look at me you little banana-eating dragon! Don't tell me you don't appreciate the way she scrubs your heat rocks down. You know you've never had them so clean!"

As for you beetles; I know you don't care one way or the other, but I've seen how she gives you only the juiciest pieces of fruit. If you were capable of gratitude, I'm sure you'd show it."

"You guys don't have to be jealous, you know. You know how much you mean to me. I need you even more than you need me. I need you all to remember that. If I could fly with Mavis, or swim with Bullet, share a meal with Luis, or rest in Constance's coils it would be a different story! I'd do any of those things in a heartbeat. But I can't. I don't live in a tank or a cage. I live out here, where the people are. I'm a person. I need them, too, and I want them to need me. After all this time I want people to need me again."

"What? Is it too soon to visit Mindy and Melissa's graves? That's a weak argument. Are you kidding? It's been over seven years! It's high time I went. I should have gone a long time ago. I put fresh flowers on Little Demon's grave every week, but I've never been to the graves of my own family. Take it easy! My human family, you know what I mean!"

"How am I going to act when I get there? You know, that's a

pretty good question, but, they're gravestones; it's not like I'll actually SEE them."

"So what if I do cry? What of it? That's the thing to do if it feels right. You rodents, how do you feel when your newborn are taken away? You know where they are going. I've seen you parakeets stand watch over your dead until I take them out of the enclosure. Why do you do that? You guys are no strangers to emotions, so why can't I show some?"

"Besides, you've seen me cry before. Remember when Little Demon and the others died? You saw me... ah, I see. YOU won't be there to see me cry at the cemetery, is that it? Out of all the creatures in this room, the green beast of envy is the only one I don't care about."

"I do have a life outside of this room as a matter of fact. The girl's mom, she cooks and cleans my apartment. I talk to her every morning. She does for me what I do for you."

"And I have to warn you, it's only the beginning. I'm going to start doing things again! Outside things with Terrance and his family... MY FAMILY—"

"Hey! Hey! Take it easy! That doesn't change anything between us; I'm still here for you."

"But everybody needs somebody! Somebody like them, don't you see?"

Over the past week or so, Francis and Susan's routine had changed. Previously, Susan would arrive after her shift at the laundry, cook breakfast for Francis, and do the necessary housecleaning. Pleasantries were exchanged and the only hanging out that Susan did was lean against the kitchen counter for a cup of coffee once her work was done, and that only after she had finally brought a coffee cup of her own.

By that time, Francis was finished with his morning chain smoking and was out in the pet area waiting for Chava. Now, though, after Francis invested in a second kitchen chair, Susan sat with Francis over coffee until Chava arrived. The pleasantries had evolved into actual conversations. Once in a while she even bummed a cigarette, but was always sure to crush it out if Chava arrived before she was finished smoking it. Their conversations had evolved to include Francis' comments on Chava's work with the animals and Susan's suggestions for other meals and ways to cozy up Francis' living quarters. Topics of the week's conversations had included the weather, music, the animals, Chava's likes and dislikes, and Susan's job at the hotel laundry. Light, casual chat for the most part.

But today Susan had something heavier on her mind. It was Thursday and it had been two days since Chava had told her Francis had invited her along on a picnic with himself, Terry, and Terry's family. Susan had no objections to Chava going on the picnic and spending time with people other than she or Francis; or to her getting to hang out with a couple of kids who were around her own age. In fact, Susan was happy about that and figured it would do her lone wolf daughter some good.

Then Terry had stopped by, unaware that Susan already knew about the picnic plans, to clear Chava's attendance at the picnic with her; Francis had never thought to do so. Terry told her they were going to have the picnic at a cemetery. That struck Susan as a bit odd, but it was more logical after Terry told her they were visiting the graves of Francis' wife and daughter.

It wasn't until Terry mentioned that this would be the first time Francis had visited the graves that she grew concerned. Her concern was Francis could possibly have some sort of emotional meltdown at the cemetery, something that can be disturbing for a kid, especially for a kid that had already seen someone she loved wither away and die.

"Francis?"

"Yes, Susan?"

"Chava is looking forward to the picnic with you guys on Saturday."

"Yes, it should be a nice day for it. It's too bad you have to work the night before. We'll try to save you some chicken and potato salad."

"Yeah, thanks. Well, I wanted to ask you about something; something about where you are planning on having the picnic."

"Sure," Francis set down his cup of coffee and took out a smoke, "What is it?"

Susan had grown to recognize this reaction. Whenever Francis was nervous about something he tended to smoke even more than he already did; one after another, sometimes when he was especially nervous he had two burning at once. She had opened the window once to air the place out during one of his nervous smoking binges, but that raven kept trying to come in and there was no getting rid of her, so she gave it up and learned to ignore the blue cloud building in the room.

"Well, Terry told me this will be your first visit to your wife and daughter's graves. Is that right?"

"Yes, that's right."

"Don't you think that it might not be a good idea to have anyone there, other than family, I mean? You haven't really known Chava all that long."

"You're afraid of how I'm going to react once I see their resting places for the first time aren't you?"

"Yes, to be honest. These sort of things can be very emotional, even traumatic. You don't think it's going to be, but when you get there; when it's solid and real, right there in front of you. When I saw my husband's grave for the first time I bawled my eyes out. I regretted having Chava with me that first time. She watched me like a hawk for weeks after that visit. I think she thought I was breaking down on her, that she was losing another parent. There were times I wasn't sure about it myself"

"I see."

"And, you see, you've never really talked about Mindy and Melissa with her, or me for that matter. Or what happened to them. The only reason I even know their names is because Terry told me. Keeping that kind of stuff in… it can be hard to control once it starts to leak out. Seeing those stones; that might just be the reef that cracks up your boat."

"Nice metaphor. You are afraid I might get too emotional, maybe scare Chava. Scare her like you did by breaking up at her dad's grave."

"Not exactly; not just emotional, it's different with you. More serious with you because you were in a... um... well, you know."

"In an institution? A mental health facility? The looney bin? A cracker box? The booby hatch?"

"Come on—"

"Yes, Susan. I was in a hospital. I was suicidal. I tried to kill myself numerous times, more than numerous times. It was all I wanted... all I thought about. Got close more than once. But, guess what, I'm not suicidal anymore."

"I know that, Francis. If I thought there was still a danger of that, I wouldn't let Chava work up here with you."

"Then what?" Francis huffed, lighting another smoke.

"Well, all these years; you've distanced yourself from what happened to you and your family. What is going to happen with you once the evidence... the end results... of that tragedy is right up in your face?"

"To begin with, nothing happened to ME. I am responsible for the deaths of my wife and daughter. It happened to THEM. I should have died with them or instead of them. But I didn't. My punishment is to live with the knowledge that I killed them."

Susan looked at him and gaped. "You don't actually believe that God would punish you for something that you did by accident? Whatever it is you think you did, I should say."

"Who's punishing me?" Francis stared at her, his brow furrowed and eyes narrowing.

"God. You think God is punishing you?"

"Don't be ridiculous. I never gave that fairy tale a first thought."

"Fairy tale? You don't believe in God?"

"Of course not! You do?"

"Yes, I do."

"Oh, let me guess. Harry is sitting on a cloud up in Heaven

165

watching over you and Chava, right?"

"Yes, that's right. I don't appreciate the sarcasm. And I don't appreciate being talked down to."

"Sorry, no sarcasm intended. But let me tell you what I think. I think Mindy and Melissa and Harry are encased in boxes, rotting away like Little Demon and the other animals up on my roof! Blissfully unaware of any pain they ever suffered in life and that they lack the capacity to give a shit about what is going on amongst the living because they're DEAD. I—"

Stinging pain erupted across Francis' face as Susan's right hand whipped out and struck him flat and solid across the jaw.

"You crazy, fucking... fuck—"

Francis looked at her kindly, wiggled his jaw a couple of times. "Let me say one more thing, seeing as you are already in upset and offended mode," his voice dropped to almost a whisper, "If there is a God, he can go fuck himself. What do you, we, owe him for our pain? Is killing your husband with disease or taking my family away in a twisted mass of metal and flesh how a truly benevolent God should act? Is that a being that you would wish to WORSHIP?"

"Oh, and I'm not crazy!" He turned his attention back to his coffee and lit yet another cigarette.

After sitting quietly for several minutes, Susan finally found the nerve to look at him, her eyes wet with unshed tears. "How can... how can you say things like that? Even if you believe them, how can you say those kinds of things to another person?"

"Susan, listen; I've lost a lot of things over the time I've spent alone. I'm sorry for you that tact is one of those things. My views of... of God... my beliefs and disbeliefs... they are mine, and I shouldn't have flung them at you like that. It was cold and callous of me to do that."

"I don't—" Susan started, but Francis put his free non-smoking hand on top of the nearest of hers.

"Please, don't say you think Chava shouldn't come on the picnic with us. I would never say anything so harsh and blunt in front of her, really. And I swear that I'll be fine at the cemetery.

You don't have to worry. And if I'm not fine, if I have some kind of meltdown, as you said, well, Terry will be there too, remember? And his wife and kids will be there. It's going to be a good day, a day of positivity; the start of a new time. Please, Susan. I want to share that day with one of the only two friends that I have."

"If Chava didn't like you and your animals so much—"

He rushed to interrupt her, "I wish you wouldn't finish that sentence. Getting to know you and Chava has done more for me than anything the doctors could ever do in the hospital. I was restrained in the hospital, physically sometimes; and I've been restraining myself up here with the responsibility of taking care of my animals, but I don't feel the need for restraints anymore. I wouldn't jeopardize what you and Chava's friendship has done for me so carelessly. You have to believe me when I say that."

"I do. For some reason I do."

Francis grinned conspiratorially, "Hey, you want a smoke before Chava gets here? I think you still have a few minutes."

"Yeah, I could use one, thanks." She took the offered cigarette and placed it between her trembling lips.

Francis reached up and gingerly rubbed his tenderized jaw, "You ever hit your Harry like that? You pack quite a punch for your size, sister."

"No, I never had to. Harry never pissed me off like you do. Pass me the lighter, fruitcake."

"Holy crap! Are they doing what I think they are doing?" Chava's eyes widened in the face of nature at work.

"Who are you talking about? And what do you think they're doing?" Francis limped over to see what she was staring at. The girl was staring at one of the rabbit cages, "Oh, yeah. They are doing what you think they are doing. Doing it like rabbits." Francis chuckled, "How did you think it worked? Did you think the stork brought baby rabbits or something?"

"No! I'm not a baby, you know. This is just the first time I've seen this... happening."

"You never saw two dogs with their butts stuck together or playing piggyback in the park? Nothing like that?"

"Butts stuck together... piggyback? No. What are you talking about?"

"Oh, boy," Francis screwed his face up in mock exasperation, "You have so much to learn about the world, kid."

"I guess so! They aren't very shy about it, are they?"

"Hah! It's not like rabbits can get a room down at the Motor Lodge for an hour or two, now is it?"

"Huh? What do you mean?"

"Never mind, ask me about it again in another five or six years. Come on, let's give them their privacy." The two walked over and sat at their stools for their lunch of tuna fish sandwiches and apple juice. Francis switched on the oldies station to hear Sam Cooke singing about Cupid drawing back his bow. *How appropriate,* Francis smiled as he unwrapped his sandwich.

"Hey, Francis?" Chava was holding her own sandwich but hadn't taken a bite yet. It seemed like she wanted no obstacles blocking the clarity of what she was about to ask.

"Yes?"

"When I got here this morning my mom's eyes were a little red. Was she crying?"

"Yes. She was. We had a little argument, but we worked it out okay. Everything is fine now."

"Francis," the girl's tone sounding much more serious than her age should be capable of allowing.

"Yes?" Francis looked at her with his full attention.

"Don't make my mom cry, Francis."

"Well, I'll do my best. But people cry sometimes, Chava. I didn't try to make her cry."

"Try harder. Don't make her cry."

"I'll try harder."

The two spent the next several minutes chewing tuna fish

and thinking about the more-serious-than-usual exchange that had just passed between them. It was Chava who finally broke the silence with another question.

"Francis?"

"Yes?"

"Do you like my mom?"

"Yes. Of course I do. You already know that."

"I mean... do you LIKE my mom?" Chava looked uncomfortable with having to elaborate on her question.

"Ah, I see. You mean LIKE, like... holding hands, moonlit walks on the beach, and whispering sweet nothings kind of like."

"Yes, do you?"

"No."

"Well, why not? Don't you think she's pretty?" Chava huffed, slightly offended.

"Yes, she's very pretty."

"So what's the problem then?"

"There is no problem, Chava. I just don't see your mother like that. Pretty isn't enough, you know. You wouldn't want me to date your mom just because I think she's pretty would you? Besides, just over a month ago I was... was... well, you know how I was. You can't expect me to be looking for a girlfriend or something." Francis' face flushed a little red from the subject of conversation.

"I know, but—"

"But what?"

"Well, my mom broke up with that Ron guy, thank goodness. I just don't want her to start dating another jerk like that. I want her to find somebody nice. That's all."

"Not a big fan of Ron, huh?"

"He was a dick."

"Hey!"

"Sorry, but he was... is."

"Well, he's history now, so you don't have to think or worry about him anymore. And young ladies shouldn't use that kind of language—"

"My mom is really nice and pretty and smart, why would she date somebody like him? A jerk like that doesn't deserve my mom."

"Don't know. Your mom and I never really talk about her personal life, boyfriends and such. Maybe she was lonely after your dad died. People get lonely and need somebody. Maybe he wasn't always such a di... less than pleasant fellow. People change, you know. And people change their minds about each other, too. It's all very grown-up and complicated. Don't warp your brain trying to figure it out."

"I guess. It just bugs me that's all."

"Don't worry about your mom though. She's a smart lady, like you said. She won't make the same mistake twice."

They finished their tuna sandwiches and were working on finishing their glasses of apple juice. Francis wouldn't say it out loud, especially to Chava, but he had to admit that he did think Susan was a very good woman, very attractive as well, and he did consider maybe asking her out sometime in the future. But he was far from being ready for anything like that and it was more of a pleasant musing than anything.

He didn't think it would be fair to Susan, or any woman for that matter, to get involved with a train wreck like him. He was carrying way too much baggage. Until he was able to shed some of that weight, he wouldn't be much good to anybody. This wasn't self-deprecation or self-loathing, but was just the reality of the current situation. For the present, Susan's friendship was more than Francis could ask for and he was happy enough having her in that capacity.

Francis continued on the same topic of Ron Rhodes, "Does your mom know you didn't like Ron?"

"Well, I never told her so. But she must have known. Me and Ron didn't really talk, ever. In fact, he usually just acted like I wasn't there at all. Like I was a piece of furniture he had to walk around or something. That's how it felt anyway."

"So he never hit you or yelled at you or anything?"

"Nah, nothing like that, but I could tell he didn't like me or even like me being around. Like I said, it was like I was in his way or something. If he wanted me to know something he'd just say it to my mom when I was in the room. You know what I mean? Like he'd say stuff to my mom like, 'Hey, Susan. Don't you think it would be nice if we had a little privacy?' or 'Don't you think it's time for the kid to go do her homework?' He didn't even call me by my name. He always called me 'the girl' or 'the kid' or 'your daughter' and stuff like that."

"Your mom never said anything about it to him?"

"No, at least she didn't say anything about it in front of me. I did hear them arguing a few times. And I know I heard her say my name while they were arguing. So I think she must have said something about it to him. I don't know for sure. I never asked her."

"Why not? You should have asked her."

"I know, but..." It was obvious Chava didn't want to finish the train of thought she had set rolling down the tracks.

"Were you afraid of what she might say?"

"I suppose. I knew he didn't like me, but who really wants to hear out loud that somebody doesn't like you? Even if that somebody is just a jerk like Ron Rhodes."

Francis drained the last of his apple juice and set the glass on the table before looking her in the eyes and smiling wide, "You know, Chava, you were right."

"Right about what?"

"Ron Rhodes is a dick."

Gary R. Gowers

XVII

"Hey! There he is! Over by that dumpster right inside the alley; stay back a little. We don't wanna' spook him. If he runs off who knows when we'll be able to spot him again?"

"Do you think this is a good idea? I mean, you don't think we're taking things a little too far?"

"Don't go chicken shit on me now, pretty boy. YOU are the one who came to ME, remember?"

"Yeah, but this just seems like we're going over the top."

"You wanna' get back at that little bitch or not? I'm telling you, this will send that faggot Tower and the gook a message they won't soon forget!"

"Okay, okay. I just didn't think we were going to be this gruesome, that's all. And what if the cops find out?"

"Gruesome? You candy-ass, all you have to do is drive the car. I'll take care of the rest. And so what if they do call the cops, what can they tell them? Wait! He sees us! You shut up now. Here, dog! Over here Doggy boy!"

"What makes you think he will even come to you? He bit the shit out you the last time he saw you, why wouldn't he do it again? It's obvious he didn't like you much, can't say that I blame him, either."

"Very funny, Rhodes. You're a regular Don Rickles."

"Don who?"

"Never mind, shit-for-brains. Don't you worry, he'll come to me. He's been living out here on his own for over a month. Anything familiar is going to look good to him. You don't know nothin' about nothin' do you? Here Doggy boy! Come and get it, buddy! I have a treat for you Doggy boy! You like hamburgers so much you mangy, *ungrateful fuck, I got some hamburger for you! There, he smells it. Here he comes."*

"I can't believe he's actually coming to you."

"I told you he would. There is no way he can resist the combination of a familiar voice and the smell of raw meat."

"What did you put in it?"

"Rat poison... lots of it... enough to drop a horse."

"You sure he'll eat it? He won't taste that shit in there? Or smell it?"

"That mutt is so hungry he won't be able to stop himself, even if he did taste or smell it. When something is desperate enough or hungry enough, it'll kill itself just to hold on to its worthless life a little bit longer, even if it kills them in the end. Just you watch, Rhodes. See? See that pause? He smelled it, but there he goes! He's wolfin' it down anyway. There you go Doggy boy, eat it all up like a good little fucker."

"Jesus, that's cold, man."

"Fuck him! He's got it coming, turning on me like he did. That poison is goin' to start doin' its stuff in a couple of minutes, Rhodes. Better go get the tarp, we don't wanna' give that classy ride of yours fleas, now do we?

Francis had been pacing his apartment since Chava left. When he heard the key hit his lock he almost knocked her over opening the door. "Did the Pet Emporium have my order?"

"Yeah... boy, this stuff is pricey. What is it?" Chava stumbled back a step before handing him a white bag bearing the Sycamore Pet Emporium's grinning dog logo.

Francis took off as soon as he had the bag in hand, leaving Chava to close the door behind her as she entered.

"It's a vitamin supplement; a super supplement, rather. You can put it on their food and in their water. He won't get around ingesting this stuff. Obstinate little dragon."

"What's wrong with the supplements you already use?"

"Nothing, except Merlin here needs some extra help. He's

being stubborn because I won't give him anymore bananas, so he's not eating much at all. Look at how pale he looks. He should have shed that old skin by now. And he's definitely developing a slight brittle bone condition."

"He's a little pale, yeah, but he looks good otherwise. Look at how fat his legs are," she pointed at the iguana's thick stubby legs.

"That's exactly it. Thickening of the limbs is a sure sign of bone trouble. The animal's flesh will beef up to protect the weakening bones. Unfortunately, if the condition worsens the muscles around his backbone can't beef up enough and the vertebrae will eventually collapse under the new weight of the animal's limbs. Understand?"

"You mean that the bigger muscles on his legs meant to protect his bones will eventually kill him by breaking his back?"

"That's right. Gravity and Merlin's addiction to bananas are the enemies here. But we're not going to let that happen. I'll force feed the little jerk his vitamins before I'll let that happen. I doubt I'll have to do that, though. This is the same stuff zoos use when they have stubborn reptiles like Merlin here to deal with. It's potent enough that I can put it on his worthless bananas and it will still do him some good and, like I said, I'm also going to dose his water with it."

During his explanation Francis was busily dicing up a banana and sprinkling the new vitamin supplements on the fruit. After placing the dish of medicated bananas in front of the iguana he removed Merlin's water dish, washed it out and refilled it with new water treated with supplement. After replacing the water dish the two of them stood back and watched with satisfaction as Merlin started gobbling down the diced bananas. Happy that the reptile was fooled into eating the vitamin-laced food, Francis lifted the lid of the tank up to put it in place. Just after setting it down on top of the tank Francis winced and grabbed at his side with both hands.

"Francis? You okay?"

"Yeah. Drag that stool over here, will you?" His voice was

forced from between clenched teeth.

Chava grabbed a stool and set it down next to her friend, "What's wrong? You want me to call Terry... or an ambulance?"

"No, it's okay. Hah! I could probably use a dose of that supplement myself. My ribs are still barking a little, especially when I lift anything more than shoulder-high."

"Well, let me do the lifting then. Geez, that's why I'm up here, you know? What would Terry say if you hurt yourself even more doing the stuff that I'm supposed to be doing?"

"Okay, Mom, lay off," Francis smiled, "Hey, Chava. Want some advice?"

"What?"

"Never break, or even crack, a rib."

"I'll try not to. You sure you're okay?"

"Let me sit for a minute. We can sit here and make sure Merlin eats his medicine. Drag yourself a seat over."

Chava pulled up another stool next to Francis and took a seat, "I hope you'll be okay for the picnic tomorrow. I'll do all the feeding in the morning before Terry comes to pick us up, okay?"

"Deal. It's already feeling better."

The two sat and watched Merlin finish up his bananas. The big lizard then crawled over and took a good, long drink of the fortified water before returning to his heat rock and shutting his eyes for his fifth or sixth siesta of the day.

"He sure has an easy life."

"Yeah, but it's a trade-off."

"What do you mean?"

"He gets everything he needs; food, medical care, warm rocks, but no freedom. Just lives in this tank."

"Yeah, but he doesn't know what he's missing, right?

"Maybe, but the negative side is still there. Anything positive; there is always a negative somewhere. It's just the way it is."

"I guess." Chava rested her chin on her fists.

"Yeah... hey, did you ever hear the story about the farmer,

the farmer's son, and the horse?"

"A farmer story? Not that I remember."

"Want to hear it?"

"Sure."

"Well, there was this farmer. He w—"

"Where did he live?"

"It doesn't matter; Pakistan, Iowa, China... you pick."

"China."

"Fine, then. China it is. There was this Chinese farmer. He was really poor, the only things he had of any value were his one son and a horse. His land wasn't that good, but with his son and the horse he was able to make enough money to support the place."

"Didn't he have a wife, too?"

"He's got a son, so it's assumed. Just listen."

"Okay."

"Well, one day the horse got out of the rickety, old corral and ran off into the woods. The farmer was pretty upset and his neighbors came over to comfort the guy. They went on and on about how unfair luck was to him and all of that. The farmer was sad that his horse ran away, but all he would say to his neighbors was 'Who knows what's good or what's bad'."

Chava frowned. "His horse ran away, that's bad for him."

"You'd think so from the get-go, but the story goes on. Well, a couple of days later his horse comes back, and the horse isn't alone. While the horse was out in the woods it met another horse, and when he came back to the farm the other horse came with it, straight into the rickety corral. The farmer was happy about this, of course. All of his neighbors came over again and went on and on about how luck was smiling on the farmer."

Francis shifted in his seat before continuing. "Again, though the farmer was happy to have his horse back, all he would say was 'Who knows what's good or what's bad'. The day after the horses came home the farmer's son, a young know-it-all like somebody I know, decided that he wanted to ride the new horse. But the horse was a little wild from living on its own and, well, when the farmer's son got on the new horse's back it jumped and bucked like crazy and sent the son flying off. The kid broke his leg. This upset the farmer for a couple of reasons; first, because now he didn't have anyone to help him work the farm and second because he cared for his son a great deal."

Chava shook her head. "So the horse wasn't good luck after all!"

"Well, hold on. So the son breaks his leg falling off the horse. Here come the neighbors again moaning and groaning for the old farmer, saying how unfair luck was being to him. But the farmer just said—"

"Who knows what's good or what's bad?"

"That's right. Anyhow, a couple of days after the son broke his leg a warlord came marching through the farmland—"

"What's a warlord?"

"Ah... it's a guy, usually a rich guy, who builds up his own army and takes over a territory—"

"Okay, keep going."

"Thank you. As I was saying, a warlord came marching through the farmland to... uh... oh, yeah... he was looking for young men to force into joining his army. When they stopped at the old farmer's place the only young man they found was the farmer's son with a broken leg, but he was useless to them, so they marched on. Again the neighbors came over, this time moaning and groaning for themselves because all of their sons had been taken and forced into the warlord's army. But they also pointed out how luck had smiled again on the old farmer."

Francis stopped talking and looked at Chava, but with no signs of continuing the story.

"And?"

"And what? That's it."

"So what's the point of the story?"

"What do you think it is?"

"Uh... could it be you never know what is good or what is bad? Or is it that good things can come from bad things and vice versa?"

"Sure. Both. Take your pick. They both work. You could also say that something that is good for one person might not be good for another person."

"Yeah... but I don't think things work like that in real life, do they?"

"Sure they do. Why not? Would we have become friends if that guy hadn't pushed me out in the street? That hurt, and still hurts, like hell, but something good came of it."

"Okay. That's the good. Doesn't that mean that something bad is going to happen next?"

"Well, that's called waiting for the other shoe to drop."

"But what if you don't want the other shoe to drop."

"That's just too bad. Shoes drop all the time. There's no stopping the shoes."

"Hey, Lorraine, did you remember to pick up a jar of sweet pickles for Francis... the little, sweet baby pickles?" Terry was peering into their pantry.

Terry, Lorraine, Amy and Terry, Jr. were in the kitchen of their home doing the last-minute preparations for the following day's picnic with Francis and Chava Lee at the cemetery. They were going all out; they had fried chicken, roast beef and honey-glazed ham for sandwiches, white and wheat bread, blocks of cheddar and Monterey cheese as well as American sandwich slices, fresh tomatoes, onions and lettuce for the sandwiches, celery sticks filled with peanut butter and creamed cheese, carrot sticks and sweet mustard dressing to dip them in, potato salad, coleslaw, barbequed baked beans with brown sugar, pitchers of lemonade and iced tea, cans of cola, bottles of fruit juice, bottled water, five different flavors of potato chips and pretzels, and all of the condiments one could ever need or ask for at a picnic. They were going to strap on a king-sized feed bag.

"Yes, they're in the fridge next to the cold cuts." Lorraine's eyes never looked up from her cutting board.

"Remember how Francis used to go for the sweet pickles? He always loved them. Even when we were kids. Our mom used to yell at him about eating too many because he always gave himself a stomachache. He even got the runs from them a few times, but that was because sometimes he drank the juice after the jar was empty."

"Terry, that's gross. What's with males and the toilet humor?"

"Seriously, Dad, every other word out of Terry's mouth is crap or poop or fart. What's with you guys?" Amy added.

"Hah! Crap!" Terry, Jr. chimed in so not to be left out of the conversation.

"Okay, come on, that's enough. I won't be able to eat any of this stuff if you guys keep it up." Lorraine set the knife on the cutting board and glared at her husband.

"Right," Terrance coughed, "Hey, you guys looking forward to seeing your Uncle Francis again?"

Both of Terry's kids nodded their heads affirmatively, but they were visibly lacking in enthusiasm.

"Dad," Amy started, "It's been a long time. What do we even say to him?"

"Whatever you want, Amy. It's going to be awkward for him too. It'll be okay, you'll see. It won't take long for the three of you to remember how much fun you used to have together."

"Who's this kid he's bringing with him?" Terry Jr. looked up at his father.

"I told you... Chava Lee. She's the girl from the building that has been helping your uncle out with his animals. She's a really good kid, you'll like her. She's thirteen, just a little younger than you two."

"Kinda' weird, ain't it? A kid hanging out with a grown-up so much? I would never do it." Terry Jr. shrugged his shoulders.

"'Ain't' ain't a word, dummy!"

"Right," Lorraine put her hand on Amy's shoulder, "And don't call your brother a dummy."

"But it is kinda' weird, ISN"T it?" Amy backed up her

179

brother.

"No, guys, it's not weird. They're neighbors and friends, and Chava works for your uncle, as does her mother. There is nothing weird about that!" Terry's face was starting to flush red, "Why don't you go over there and help your mom cut up the carrots and celery. When did you kids become so mean and judgmental? And another thing, she lost her dad to cancer not so long ago... so keep that in mind when you two are talking to her! I'm not sure, but it might be a sensitive topic for her."

"We don't mean anything by it, Dad. We're just nervous about seeing Uncle Francis again. I'm sure we'll get along great with her... right, Terry?" Amy hung her head.

"Yeah, right, another girl to deal with, though... sheesh." Terry, Jr. chimed in.

Lorraine could tell her husband was getting a little aggravated with their offspring by the way he was chewing on his lower lip. "If you think you're nervous, imagine how your uncle must be feeling. Just think about that! Think about how nervous he must have been after all of these years to call us up and ask about going to see your aunt and cousin's graves. Now let it go and help me finish getting this ready. The more we get done tonight the less we'll have to rush to get done tomorrow morning!"

"Yep... Francis used to get the runs all the time from eating too many sweet pickles. That goofball," Terry mumbled to himself as he went down the picnic checklist again from the top.

XVIII

"What do you think, Mavis? Am I full of shit?"

"Croak!"

"Good comes from bad, bad comes from good. But what I didn't tell Chava is that the good and the bad do not usually come to you in equal amounts, if that sort of thing can even be measured. I'm sure her dad had some decent Jell-O while he was dying in the hospital... which is good, but that doesn't really make up for dying of a painful disease. I doubt there is no amount of good that can possibly overshadow losing a parent at that young of an age. If only we were all poor, Chinese farmers with little problems like half-wild horses and warlords, huh?"

"Croak!"

"And if my little story is correct, if the cycle of good and bad holds true, I'm about due for the next bad patch. Getting pushed into the street and getting banged up was bad. Terry's insistence on me having helpers who have now turned into my friends, thus helping me inch back into the groove of interactive life was good. Is going on this picnic going to herald the next episode of bad?"

"Croak?"

"So what if it does? What is the worst that can happen? I might break down at the graves; the guilt might rise up stronger than ever and get the best of me in front of my brother and his family, in front of Chava. I might retreat; run back here to the fifth floor and extend my animal collection to include Japanese fighting fish and chinchillas; cut off all interaction again. I'm probably healed up well enough to handle things up here on my own again."

"Croak!"

"How long would it be before good comes back around again? Another seven years? I thought for sure that nothing would ever diminish the pain I feel over the loss of Mindy and Melissa. Will seeing the end result of my carelessness; my selfishness, send me back to square one? The crazy-ass condition I was in seven years ago? After tomorrow, will the animals continue to be enough to keep the blade from my veins? The noose from around my neck?

"Croak. Croak!!"

"Terry asked me if I'm really ready for this several times since I asked to go to the cemetery. Does he see something in me that I'm too close to notice? Should I trust his reluctance?"

"Crooooaaaak?"

"No. I know myself better than he knows me! I'm the one who has spent day after day for years examining myself; listening non-stop to every thought streaming through my head. There have been major changes in the stream since I got banged up, an entire redirection of the river of thoughts and emotions. Instead of trying to take a boat ride down my stream of thoughts towards its end I'm now paddling upstream; trying to regain distance, regain time... regain my life."

"Croaak!"

"I was going with the flow, crashing through the rapids without oars or a rudder the entire time I was at the Harper Institute. Only the animals were my anchor, Little Demon was my first desperate grab at the jagged rocks on the bed of the stream; the only thing keeping me from rushing headlong over the falls."

"But now Chava and Susan, they're my oars; giving me the means to move back from the brink. And Terry and his family, they can be my rudder. Our past together can help me steer my way clear. Everyone has these oars and rudder, these instruments of control and self-preservation, but not everyone uses them. The people who lack this equipment, as I did, they are the ones doomed to crash up on the rocks."

"But I've pulled up my anchor. It's sitting in the floor of the boat. It's traveling with me now. It served its purpose. It saved my life, but now I'm pulling on the oars and steering with the rudder; saving my own life. Tomorrow, if bad takes its turn in the cycle, I'll drop anchor once again and hope that it snags on the bottom."

"Is being snagged on the bottom, anchored in place, is that better than taking the plunge over the falls and losing oneself forever in the blinding foam? It was, but I don't know if it would be better to do it again. Is it the best of the bad? Is existence without really living better than nothing at all?"

"Croak."

"Right, tomorrow I'll keep a firm grip on the oars; trust in my rudder to steer me. And maybe, someday, after enough effort, enough huffing and puffing against the shoving, obstinate current of the stream, maybe I'll be able to plant my feet on dry land once again. And once I've done that, I can proceed towards the falls on foot at the same pace as everyone else and in good company."

"Okay, enough about that. I need to tend to the others. And besides, I think I've run out of boat metaphors."

"Croak!"

"Smartass bird."

Ron Rhodes sat in an old, tattered lawn chair in his garage with a quickly-warming bottle of beer and stared at his freshly washed and waxed black Mustang. His mind was still reeling from, and trying to process, what had transpired over the last few nights. When he approached Lawrence McPhee about forming a partnership with the goal of enacting revenge on Susan Lee and Francis Tower, he didn't really have a clear idea in his mind about how they should go about it.

However, it appeared from the start that McPhee had been stewing about the incident between he and Tower from the get go and he had a plan, several to choose from actually, of how to get back at the recluse. It took very little tweaking in order to make Susan a co-recipient of his vengeful intentions.

Those intentions had now become Ron's intentions as well, but his participation in the plan to send a message to the people living at 517 Sycamore consisted mostly of acting as a laborer and a driver, an Igor to McPhee's Doctor Frankenstein, a

Renfield to McPhee's Count Dracula.

As of fifteen minutes ago when Ron went for the beer that was now warming in his hand, McPhee was snoring up a storm on the fold-out sofa-bed in the living room of Ron's single-story house. It was the house that Ron grew up in and was full of fucked up memories. When McPhee pressured him into letting him stay there Ron snorted. *Why not, what was one more fucked up memory?*

As bad as his childhood and teen years were, this house was the one constant in Ron's life. His father had bought it on a G. I. loan after serving as an infantryman for two tours in the Vietnam War, or police action, or conflict or, as his father called it, "The Great Gook Hunt." That was his father, a man of expression. He always came up with the jazziest things to say, or to call people. While all of Ron's friends' mothers were being labeled with run of the mill monikers like "Nagging Bitch" and "Ball and Chain," Ron's mother had the pleasure of hearing expressions like "Flapping Jabberwocky" and "Walking Jizz Bank" coming her way. While his friends' fathers were yelling "Little Shit" and "Punk Ass" at their sons, he was answering to "Afterbirth Junior" and "Yapping Cum Stain." Yes, his father had a way with words. Except for the day he cut out on them.

He had very little to say on that day. Just "Get the fuck out of my way you Babylonian Meat-choker," accented with a brutal slap to his mother's face, of course. His witty pearls of verbal expression were always accompanied by sharp kicks, open-handed smacks, gnarly backhands, or jabbing punches to serve as punctuation. They were how he got his point across. Just in case you didn't hear it, he wanted to make sure you felt it and he "accentuated" the hell out of his son and his cowering mother the entire time he was around.

At least dear old Dad had been nice enough to sign over the house to Mother before he retreated from his domestic station. As his mother later found out, his father had taken his name off the deed weeks before he left them. The abandonment was carefully planned and executed, like the assaults on the nameless hills that make up the dense jungles of Vietnam in the stories his father told to nobody in particular while hitting the sauce.

The day his father left was one of the happiest of Ron's life, he smiled and quietly hummed the entire time as he prepared an ice pack to ease the pain and swelling in his mother's jaw from dear old Dad's parting shot. In Ron's thirteen-year-old mind his father leaving for good would mean a fresh start for him and his mother. No more screaming and yelling, hitting and kicking, no more abuse whatsoever at the hands of the paternal tyrant.

Unfortunately, that wasn't the way his mother saw things. Like many women of her generation she chose to feel guilty for the failure of her marriage. If only she had tried harder, maybe Ron's father wouldn't have been so mean to them; if she had been a better cook, if she had made herself more attractive in his eyes, if she had kept a cleaner house, if she had said things more pleasing to her man's ears, if she had pleased him more in the bedroom. These failings made the abuse and final abandonment her fault and because of her failure to make her husband happy she and her son were now sentenced to live on their own. She felt she didn't deserve to be happy and, in fact, she deserved to be punished. But with her husband now gone, there was no one there to mete out her just deserts. So she took it upon herself to punish herself.

From the day Ron's father left to the day she died, the ex-Missus Rhodes endeavored to punish herself with excessive amounts of alcohol and meaningless sexual encounters. With no breadwinner to bring home the bacon, Ron and his mother relied upon the social welfare system, but very few of the food stamps provided by the state went towards food. His mother sold the food stamps, sometimes for as little as twenty-five cents on the dollar, to support her non-stop intake of gin, vodka, and boxes of wine. If not for school lunches Ron would probably have died from malnutrition.

The electric and gas bills were paid by the men who took turns visiting Missus Rhodes's bedroom. After all, a few bucks a month wasn't much of a sacrifice in exchange for an unlimited source of drunken rutting with a halfway attractive divorcee. Missus Rhodes became so infamous around town that men would actually pass each other in the hall leading to the broken woman's bedroom.

The men would often stop and exchange a few words with the teenage boy sitting in the living room in front of the TV watching reruns of *Dragnet* or *Get Smart*. At the end of these short exchanges they would give Ron a couple of bucks to go towards the household. Over evolutions of this routine Ron had become his own mother's pimp of sorts. On occasion one of the men would pick up the staggering Missus Rhodes for a night on the town and a horizontal romp back at his place, as a change of scenery, and it was on one of these nights when his mother's body finally gave out on her.

The autopsy concluded that it was acute accumulated alcohol poisoning and the coroner was amazed that she had lasted as long as she did considering the advanced diseased state of her liver and kidneys. At the time of her death the autopsy revealed Missus Rhodes also exhibited the first stage symptoms of ovarian cancer, four venereal diseases, and a bladder infection.

With the demise of Mother, Ron became a sixteen-year-old high school dropout living on his own. But at least he had the house. The connections he made through his mother's promiscuity had set him up with the connections to make a decent living by selling and dealing drugs; mostly lightweight stuff like reefer, hash, and various prescription medications. He also charged drug users rent to allow them to store their stashes at his place away from the prying eyes of family members and co-workers, though he rarely allowed them to use their drugs of choice in the house. He was strictly take-out.

Ron wasn't selling and storing drugs because he liked it. He knew the dangers involved and his observances of drug use, along with the aftereffects, made him anti-drug as far as his own behavior was concerned. Once he was old enough to get a legitimate job he severed all of ties with dealers and suppliers and ceased acting as a stash house. While he never succumbed to the temptations of drug use, his mother's behavior left a deep impression on his mind. In his opinion all women were whores under the right circumstances, weak and subject to the whims of the masculine gender. That is what fueled his desire to get revenge on Susan. That is why he had that crazy, filthy, dog-killing derelict sleeping on his sofa bed. But what McPhee had in mind was atrocious, even to a macho man like Ron.

He had liked Susan, liked her a lot, to be honest. If it hadn't been for having a kid he might have made the necessary moves to make the relationship permanent. He wasn't sure that it had been a good idea to bring McPhee in on this after he'd seen what the man was capable of. The man was just fucking nuts. It was bad enough to poison the dog like he did, but what he did to the dog once they returned with it to Ron's garage; the results now residing in plastic bags in Ron's freezer.

What the bum had in mind was not only criminal, but it was horribly beyond the bounds of sane, civilized reason. McPhee was going for shock value. Ron was no longer sure that he wanted to subject Susan to what McPhee had in mind, in fact, he was thinking of warning her. It was too late to call it off altogether; McPhee would just add Ron to his list of people to get even with and Ron didn't want that hanging over him, but it might be possible to leave Susan out of it. Francis Tower, the nut on the fifth floor, was the only one McPhee cared about; he didn't give a rat's ass about Susan or Ron's humiliation in front of the nigger mailman.

Yes, he could warn her away. He couldn't tell her that anything was about to go down, but he could try to steer her away from being at 517 Sycamore on Saturday, tomorrow. He'd have to see her tonight; now, while McPhee was snoring away on the sofa bed. And he knew exactly where to find her.

Susan had a bone to pick with Francis. All of those morning

cigarettes she was bumming off of him were changing from a calming, morning ritual in his kitchen into a full-blown, tobacco-craving habit... again! She had quit smoking while married to Harry and had gone years without the sweet nicotine-packed temptress tobacco, not that she hadn't thought about the wonderfully unhealthy habit from time to time.

Once an addict always an addict, she sighed as she stepped through the back door of the Paramount Hotel laundry and into the stairwell that led up to the ground floor service lot behind the building, lighting up the Marlboro she had coaxed from her pack on the walk to the door. Only after the door closed behind her and the flame from the cigarette lighter died did she realize that the stairwell was in full darkness. She'd have to remember to tell maintenance about it so they could change the bulb. Until then she'd just have to smoke at the top of the stairs where there was plenty of light coming from the parking lot lights. The Paramount Hotel was in a decent neighborhood, but whackjobs knew no boundaries and a petite, attractive women hunkered in the dark was more of a temptation than your average rapist/murderer/weirdo could resist.

She spotted Ron's black Mustang convertible only a two-second-long sprint away as soon as she reached the top of the stairs. She did a quick, half-panicked scan of the lot imagining him pouncing upon her from any one of the shadows or from behind the garbage dumpsters, but there was no sudden stalker charge from any direction. On her second less-panicked scan of the lot she spotted the silhouette of Ron's head in his car. As if he knew that she had finally gotten her wits under control the driver's side window of the Mustang rolled down with an electric hum.

"Susan! Hi!" Ron called from the car.

"Hello, Ron. What are you doing here?" She backed one step down the stairs.

"Hold on, Susan, please. I'm not here to give you any trouble."

"Oh, yeah? Like you weren't trying to cause trouble at my

place the other day?"

"Hey, okay, you're right, I have that coming. I acted like a real ass. I'm man enough to admit that. I was just really pissed off, you know? I'm over it now... really."

"Well, okay, but what are you doing here?"

"I just thought—"

"Don't say you thought we might be able to fix things. We're over, Ron. I'm sorry, but that's the way it has to be. You know full well there is no way we can be together again; if we were ever together to begin with!"

Ron took a long, silent look at Susan and when he spoke again his tone had changed to counter her determination. "That's NOT what I was going to say, Susan. I was just going to... you know what, fuck it!"

"Don't get mad, Ron. I'm sorry. I should have let you finish what you were saying. I can give you a few minutes."

"Let me? Give me?" Ron's casual tone was quickly spiraling back into angry mode.

"I just mean I have to get back inside for work, that's all. I just came out for a quick smoke break."

"Smoke break? Since when do you smoke?"

"I've been bumming smokes off of Francis. Francis Tower, the man in my building. I—"

"Yeah, I know who Tower is; the new man. Let's you smoke, huh? Well, isn't that just dandy?" Ron had an unsettling way of making goofy old words like dandy drip with venom.

Susan felt this encounter quickly turning into a rerun of the day in the lobby, except this time there was no Marshall the Mailman to come to her rescue. "It's not like that, Ron, I told you that the other day. I really need to get back in now." She let her voice drop sedately, hoping it would rub off on her steaming ex. But the man behind the wheel was already eerily calm.

"Right, Susan. You go on back to folding the laundry. Forget that I even came by." The electric hum of the window started up again and right before the window was all the way up he muttered, "That's what I get for trying to warn you, you whore." The Mustang's engine roared to life and Ron pealed out of the parking space with squalling tires.

Susan quickly glanced at the black marks left by the Mustang before looking up to follow the car's taillights out of the parking lot and out onto the street. The window of the Mustang obstructed Ron's voice enough that she wasn't quite sure she clearly heard his parting shot. She heard "whore" clearly enough, but did he say something about a warning? She was already late getting back in from her smoke break, but Susan's hands unthinkingly went for the pack of cigarettes and lighter in the pocket of her uniform. Her hands were shaking slightly as she lit the butt, but the shaking subsided with the first glorious drag.

XIX

"For the last time, it's none of your goddamned business. I don't have to explain myself to you... you moochy scumbag."

"I beg to differ, pretty boy. I wake up in the middle of the night and your car's gone. Until we're done with what we have to do, we stick together like Chang and Eng, you got that?"

"John and who?"

"Chang, dipshit. Chang and Eng, the Siamese twins? Never mind, brainiac. Just say, 'Yes, McPhee. I understand, McPhee.'"

"Fine, McPhee. I got ya'. I'm going to go get a little sleep now."

"Before you do, you need take the mutt out of the freezer. We wanna' make sure he's good and thawed out before we head over tomorrow."

"Cripes. Fine, but I still don't think it's a good idea to do this in the middle of the fuckin' day, man."

"How many times do I have to explain it to you, Rhodes?"

"I don't need it explained, *McPhee. I just think it would be better to do it in the middle of the night when there is less of a chance of getting caught. You might like the idea of a nice warm jail cell and regular meals, but that isn't my idea of a summer vacation."*

"Right, yeah, a couple of guys lugging buckets around in the middle of the night isn't going to draw any attention. Listen fucknuts, we've been over this already, but I'll say it again for the retards. Your ex will be sleeping after her shift, right?"

"Right, once she finishes up doing her morning work for Tower. Then Tower and the Lee brat will be busy for hours with the dude's animals. I got all that, but what about everyone else in the building? And the mailman?"

"You can set your watch by that mailman; he's in an out before 8:30 every morning. As for the other residents in the building, the fourth floor is vacant, as is the other unit on the first floor. That leaves the second and third floor units. Three of those four units have old fogies living in them. You could have a shootout in the lobby and those shut-ins wouldn't even take their eyes off their TVs. The last of those four units is occupied by a young couple and their baby. Daddy works Saturdays, out by eight in the morning. The mom's got her hands full with the rugrat. I've never seen her out of the apartment before one in the afternoon at the earliest."

"Okay, but Tower sends Chava on errands, too, right? What if the kid catches us?"

"Listen, I've been watching the place for weeks. The kid ALWAYS does the errands in the morning; out and back before noon, she doesn't come out again until late afternoon with the garbage."

"Yeah, but—"

"Knock it off for fuck's sake. You go on like a whiney little bitch. I said I've been watching the place for weeks. I've seen everyone in the building, I've watched them, studied them, and they've all seen me on numerous occasions, except Tower of course. That stupid Asian kid has even said 'hi' and given me change a few times. Even if they do see me outside the place they'll think nothing of it. As far as they know I'm just the local bum rambling through as usual; rummaging through the garbage or some shit like that. We go in at twelve-fifteen and we do our thing, we are out by twelve-thirty, nobody the wiser."

"And you're sure the basement access door will be unlocked? How can you be sure?"

"'Cause the lock is busted, courtesy of your tire iron. I made sure of that. I broke it yesterday when I was over watching the place. They don't have a full-time maintenance guy, so they won't notice it's broken until after we're long gone. We come up behind the building from Briar Street, through the alley. We go into the basement through the access door and then up into the lobby. Nobody will even see us go in the building. The place behind 517 Sycamore is an accounting firm, nobody there on Saturdays. I have it all thought out, Rhodes."

"I know. I know—"

"I know you know! So what's the fuckin' problem? You wouldn't be having second thoughts, would you? Surely you wouldn't be so moronic as to think you could back out on me now, would you?"

"No, man... it's just—"

"Just nothing, you little shit. It's too late to change your mind now. You back out now and you're gonna see my bad side. You don't want that, Rhodes."

"Don't threaten me, you fucker. I'm not backin' out on anything. It's just so goddamned sick."

"It's meant to be sick, that's the whole fuckin' point. We're showin' 'em we mean business. Now go take the mutt out of the freezer."

Francis sat at his kitchen table puffing away at his tenth or eleventh cigarette of the morning. It was only six o'clock, but he had already gone through half a pack of cigarettes and nearly a whole pot of coffee.

On the tabletop in front of him lay an edge-worn 8 x 10 photograph of himself with Mindy and Melissa, most likely taken by Terry, but he wasn't sure. It was their last picture together and the photo was taken only a couple of weeks before their deaths. It was the only representation of their long-lost faces that he kept in the apartment. Like Lorraine and Terry, he visited them on their birthdays and on the anniversary of the day they died. Unlike his brother and sister-in-law, however, he did his visiting via the courtesy of Kodak. He kept the picture hidden away down low in his stack of *National Geographic* magazines.

There were times that he came across the picture by chance while searching for old articles on sea otters or Mount Fuji, which led to hours of sitting in his easy chair smoking and staring at their faces. These unscheduled visits with the 8 x 10 didn't do him much good, but he couldn't help get drawn into studying their smiling faces, as well as his own. He looked like a different guy in the photo, which he certainly had been.

He had hundreds of other photographs of his wife and daughter, but they were all in storage in the fourth floor apartment units right below him, along with everything else he had owned before being institutionalized at the Harper Institute. It wasn't even the best picture he had of them; it was slightly out of focus, his own eyes were partially closed and it was taken in a nondescript wooded setting, maybe during a walk at the park near the home they shared or maybe even in the backyard of that home with its tall shade trees.

After all of the hours he had spent staring at the photo Francis had never been able to pinpoint the exact location of where it was taken or verify who the person had been manning the camera. The reason he cherished this photo over the others was simply because it was the last one taken of them all together. It was the closest he could get to them, the closest representation of them from a time when they lived and breathed and laughed and spoke; mere weeks before he would betray and deliver them over to specter death.

Staring at the photo, Francis allowed himself a rare moment of remembrance on how he and Mindy had done everything right. Of how they met and dated for over a year, falling in love in the process. They were both students at the time, he a business major preparing for his long-planned entry into the family commercial property business and she was an education major with plans to teach elementary school.

He proposed to her one moonlit night, on one knee with ring in hand. They agreed to marry after they had both graduated, to settle down in the vicinity of Tower Properties' home office and to wait until they were comfortable with domestic life, emotionally and financially, before they would have a child. Once they had their professional lives under control they abandoned all forms of birth control and it wasn't long before Melissa came along. The pregnancy was normal and Melissa arrived on time with all ten fingers and ten toes, healthy and plump. What every new parent hopes for.

For the next seven years they lived happily in their family home with the shade trees out back, a comfortable nuclear unit. Francis and Mindy were both content with their chosen careers and Melissa was growing to be a wonderfully bright freckle-faced kid. They had Terry, Lorraine and their kids only fifteen minutes away by car and the two families spent a lot of time together. They couldn't ask for anything more.

Unfortunately, careful planning doesn't allow for the random happenstances of the world. And it was one of these random happenstances, when everyone's guard was down, sedated by the happiness and the blindness to horror provided by living well, that it all came crashing down on their heads.

All he had left was their photo and the tons of baggage heaped upon the survivor of life's horrors. So, he was up early, drinking coffee and chain smoking in preparation for the moment when he was to come face-to-face with the seven-year-old results of random happenstance.

Will their graves be under a shade tree? Will the grass be green and freshly mown? What color would the stones be? Will there be flowers? Am I going to collapse into a jangled raw ball of dead nerve endings? He didn't think so. He was going to simply visit the graves of his wife and child, with flowers for each, like everyone else in the world that had lost someone they loved. Someone they betrayed. Someone they had lost to random happenstance.

He wasn't alone on his visit to the graves, and not because Terry and the others would be there. He was going to be only one of the countless living making the slow amble to a plot of grass-covered dirt that day. He wasn't alone in his suffering, but still his suffering was his own. That was the selfishness of it all. It was the selfishness of the suffering that drove him to attempt suicide so many times, the desire to disseminate the feeling, to wipe it away. With death he would be in the same boat as Mindy and Melissa.

That was wrong though. He knew that now. It was weak. Killing himself would have been even more selfish than mourning those he had lost. His fault or not, his job now was to live the best that he could. Keep going for Mindy and Melissa. Live and try to be happy in place of those who could no longer do so. They wouldn't want him dead, and he should abide by their wishes. That's the least he could do.

Francis got up from the kitchen table, emptied the used grounds out of the coffee maker, and put on a fresh pot. While it was brewing he took the picture of him with his family, the picture taken in an unknown location by an unknown person, over to the stack of *National Geographic* magazines. He lifted more than half of the magazines up, gave the faces another long look and then placed the photo on top of the cover of an issue sporting a fresco depicting Alexander the Great.

See you next time. He gently replaced the rest of the stack on top of them.

Francis couldn't remember the last time he had cut a work day short by choice. For the past four years every one of his days were completely consumed by the tasks involved in taking care of the gliders, the birds, Luis, Merlin, Constance, Felicia, and all of the other creatures who depended upon him as their one and only lifeline. For the three years before that while he was in the Harper Institute his only thoughts were concerned with the misery of his existence and the means of bringing that misery to an end, which wasn't exactly work but the thoughts took up all of his time nonetheless.

He felt weirdly off from the moment Susan arrived to make him breakfast. He rushed through it; forgoing their now habitual coffee, cigarette, and bull session after he had finished eating. The only reason that he could even recall having pancakes that morning was because the taste of maple syrup still lingered on his tongue, which goes to show that he didn't take his usual amount of time to brush his teeth either.

Chava showed up half an hour earlier than usual and, with the enlisted help of the animal-care novice Susan, the three of them rushed through making sure that all of the animals had food and water. Constance was good for another few days but Luis, a few of the reptiles, and the scorpions required their allotment of pinkies. Susan didn't hesitate at giving Francis a hand with offering up the blind morsels, which greatly surprised Francis and gave him reason to respect her more than he already did. Thus he came to the conclusion that Chava's squeamishness concerning this chore was passed onto the girl genetically through the dearly departed Harry; if such a thing could be passed on, that is.

Susan in turn was surprised to see how nimbly Francis was now getting around. She suspected that he no longer really needed the cane, but still carried it around with him as sort of a precautionary safety blanket.

Or maybe he was trying to justify still having us around? She was unexpectedly moved by her thought.

While helping Francis and Chava with their chores she couldn't help but also notice the changes that had taken place in her daughter over the past month plus change. She and Francis worked together like a well-oiled machine; moving from cage to cage and tank to tank, and though Chava was small for her age, she seemed to have matured quite a bit and this made her seem larger in her eyes somehow.

Susan found it amusing how Chava was showing off for her, bantering back and forth with Francis about animal-related information only the two of them knew and physically handling creatures that would have previously made her shriek in terror and disgust; showing her mother how important she was to the operation. Susan couldn't help but beam.

By 9:30 that morning all of the animals, including Francis and the Lees, were fed and watered. At ten minutes to ten the three descended the five flights of stairs with Francis in the lead; ready to meet Terry and his family out in front of 517 Sycamore at ten sharp for the picnic and the visit to Mindy and Melissa's graves. After seeing Susan to the door of 101 and wishing her a good sleep, the man and the girl went outside and sat on the stoop with a few minutes to spare before Terry's scheduled arrival.

Francis sat swiveling his head repeatedly to the right and left like it was the first time he had ever seen the street. "I can't remember the last time I did this."

"Did what?" Chava was looking around and trying to get a bead on what was drawing Francis' attention.

"Just sat and looked around. That must sound odd, huh?"

"Yeah, a little bit. But you've been busy."

"Hah, busy. I guess you could say that. Busy as a bee inside my head, pretty much dead and buried on the outside."

"You're not going to get all creepy today are you? 'Cause if you are, maybe I shouldn't go with you guys."

"No, Chava. Don't worry. In fact, I think I'm going to be just the opposite. For the first time in a really long time I feel like I'm one of the living again."

"That's good then. To feel alive, I mean." Chava nodded.

"It is. And I have you and your mom to thank for that. Actually, when you get down to the bare bones of it all, I mostly have Lawrence McPhee to thank for it. As screwed up as that may be."

"McPhee? You've got to be kidding? The crazy jerk that tried to kill you! That McPhee? I wouldn't think you'd have anything nice to say about that guy. I sure wouldn't."

"That's the one. I can't say that he's one of my favorite people, but if he hadn't done what he did I'd still be roaming around on the fifth floor waiting."

"Waiting for what?"

"To up and die, Chava. I've spent the last seven years of my life waiting to die. For the first three of those seven I was trying to move it along on my own, as you well know."

"Yeah, I know. But you're not going to do that again, are you Francis? Even without the animals you wouldn't do that again, right?"

"I wish I could say for sure. Without the animals, I can't say. But, I can say this; I want more than just the animals now. I want to stay friends with you and your mom. Maybe even make some new friends too. I want to be a good brother to Terry and Lorraine, a good uncle to Terry, Jr. and Amy. That's a lot. It's been so long since I wanted anything besides just wanting to die and then just wanting to NOT die. Death; that's all I've thought about since Mindy and Melissa were taken from me."

"Is this going to be hard for you? Seeing their graves for the first time?"

"Yes, I think so. But that's okay. It is supposed to be hard I think. I think that will help make me more normal. I've been hiding from the hard stuff that life throws at people. Normal people do things that are hard, but then continue on with their lives. That's what people do. And I think I'm going to do that today. Strange as it may sound, I'm looking forward to feeling the pain of seeing their graves."

"Looking forward to pain? Not me. I'd like to stay away from it altogether if I had the choice!" Chava frowned up at him.

"You'd think so, but think about it. What better evidence is there of being alive; of being a real person, than feeling pain? Emotionally or physically? As long as it's spaced out over our years, then I think that maybe pain has its rightful place in the human experience. Like with the Daoist Yin-Yang; good cannot exist without bad, and vice versa. The balance of the universe; two sides of the same coin."

"You keep trying to be deep like that and you're going to forget which way is up and finally pop up out of a gopher hole in China! But I'll try my best to enjoy the pain the next time I'm at the dentist."

Francis turned and looked at the grinning Chava. "Well said. You get your sarcasm from your mother," he smiled, "Hey! That looks like Terry coming now. You ready to go?"

"I'm ready if you are."

XX

"Thanks for letting me come with you guys today. I just wish my mom could have come, too. She could use a day out in the air and sunshine. She spends six nights a week down in the basement of that hotel. She hardly ever gets to go outside in the daytime because that's when she sleeps."

"It's no problem, Chava. It's really nice to meet you and we wish your mom could have come, too. Our dad talks about you a lot. He says you've been a big help to Uncle Francis. Your mom, too."

"Uncle Francis? Ha! It's funny to hear him called that, but I bet he's a great uncle."

"Yeah, he used to be before... before Aunt Mindy and Melissa died. We were pretty little at the time, but I remember he was the best. So much fun; always laughing, and making everybody else laugh."

"I wish I could have known him then."

"What's he like now? Isn't it weird spending all day with him? I just can't imagine—"

"It's not weird; not a bad weird, I mean. He didn't talk to me very much at first, but now we talk all the time. He is definitely strange, but not creepy strange. He just looks at things really different; probably 'cause he's spent so much time alone."

"But what's he like? Besides strange?"

"Well, he's... he's Francis. He is very focused on his animal friends. And he doesn't just talk to hear himself speak, you know? He asks me things; my opinions on things. It really took some getting used to. My mom doesn't really do that."

"Our parents don't either. They think they do, but they stop listening after the first sentence or so. They don't really want to know

everything."

"Francis does. He'll keep on asking questions until you're tired of them. In fact, some days I kinda' miss how he was when I first met him; just real quiet. "

"But doesn't it get boring being with just him all day? That seems like it would get old pretty fast."

"It's not just him. There is Mavis and Felicia and Constance and Luis and Oliver and —"

"Huh? Who are they?"

"The animals, of course. Francis has taught me a lot about them. And they have taught me a lot of stuff, too."

"What? What could those pets teach you? They just eat and sleep and poop."

"No, no, Amy! That's like what you said about your parents not listening to you, that's just the surface. They do eat and sleep and poop A LOT, but if you really watch them, they have a lot to teach really. Mavis, the raven, is very independent. She CHOOSES you to be her friend. Felicia, she's a ferret, is all about being fun and crazy. Oliver, he's a sugar glider, is a great leader; very kind, but strict when he has to be. Constance, the boa constrictor; she's a picture of patience. They're all great teachers. I couldn't ask for a better summer school. You ought to ask Francis about coming up to see them. I bet you'd love it there!"

"Maybe I will. What do you think, Terry?"

"I wouldn't mind seeing that snake. We could ask Dad to ask Uncle Francis for us. Or, maybe Chava could ask for us."

"Me? Why me?"

"Come on, you don't know? You're like his best friend or something. I heard my mom and dad talking; they think you remind Uncle Francis of Melissa."

"Huh? "

"Yeah, they think that's one of the reasons Uncle Francis is more, uh... normal now or something."

"Oh—"

"Don't be embarrassed! It's a good thing, we think. If it makes Uncle Francis more like his old self and doesn't make any trouble for *you or your mom; it's not a bad thing, is it?"*

"I guess not. I just didn't think about that, that's all. Hey, uh, could I ask you a question?"

"Sure."

"Um... what happened to your Aunt Mindy and Melissa? How did they die? And why does Francis act like it was his fault?"

"'Cause it kinda' was, but it was an accident. They—"

"Terry! You know we're not supposed to say anything about that. That's Uncle Francis' job to tell people about that! Dad told us not to go blabbing about it. You know they haven't even told US everything, so be quiet."

"Okay. Sorry, Amy."

"No, I'm sorry, Amy. I shouldn't have asked—"

"It's okay, Chava. Only, it should be Uncle Francis who tells you about it if he wants you to know, that's all."

"Hey, look! We're almost there."

Five Towers and a Lee stood silently in front of two matching white, stone markers planted firmly in the grass of the Lush Haven Cemetery. Terrance, his family, and Chava stood in a straight line facing the markers in order of height and evenly spaced; as if they had rehearsed their positions and taken their marks.

This formation put Terrance at one end of the line and the diminutive Chava at the other, with Lorraine, Amy, and Terry, Jr. sandwiched between them. Their military-grade observance of organization was due to the fact that they were, indeed, on an unspoken high alert. Defcon Francis. None of them had a clue as to how Francis was going to react after they reached the graves. Thus far their fears had been unfounded.

When Terrance and his family had arrived at 517 Sycamore to retrieve Francis and Chava, the younger Tower and his family found Francis in good spirits, smiling and talkative. Francis hugged Lorraine and Amy, and then shook hands with Terrance and Terry, Jr. He expressed how nice it was to see them all again before introducing his sister-in-law, niece, and nephew to Chava, who he referred to as his trusted heavy; this earned a smile from Chava at the inside joke.

During the ride over in Terrance's SUV; the adults and the kids broke off into two distinct groups, as adults and kids tend to do. Francis insisted Lorraine take the front seat beside her husband and he rode sitting directly behind her. The SUV had third row seating, so the kids occupied that territory. The adult conversation during the ride was light, very light, for Francis knew nothing about current events. He mostly answered Lorraine's questions concerning the healing of his leg and ribs.

The conversation coming from the third row as the kids got acquainted was steadier, but they spoke mostly in conspiratorial whispers. There were no crossovers in the two conversations going on except for an occasional, "are we almost there?" from Terry Jr.

The walk from the SUV to Mindy and Melissa's plots was done in complete silence. That is when the high alert kicked in and everyone was focused on Francis. Everyone took heartening note that Francis was standing straight, head up, actually carrying his cane rather than leaning on it, and he had a slight smile on his face; as if he was gathering strength from the inside out. They started the walk in a cluster, but as they neared their destination the uniform line they stood in now was formed.

As mourner-in-chief; Francis stood a good eight to ten feet in front of the Towers and the Lee, his eyes looking over the stones marked *Beloved Wife* and *Cherished Daughter*, moving from one to the other precisely in time to his beating heart.

Blood in, Beloved Wife.
Blood out, Cherished Daughter.

It was an exercise in grieving yoga. As the blood moved in and out of his heart the memories and never-to-be memories of his wife and daughter came flooding over him in heavy waves of emotions: happiness, denial, contentment, horror, grief, loneliness, regret, and hope; all taking their turns riding the cyclic tide through the muscle that kept him a participant in this life, whether he wanted it to or not.

The emotions received equal time, a single heartbeat, until their turn came around again. And as these emotions raced through his veins his heart picked up speed; the emotions changed more quickly, his eyes darted frantically from *Beloved Wife* to *Cherished Daughter*. The emotions were switching from one to the other so lightning-fast that they threatened to become one single feeling, one that encompassed all emotions and had no name. At the same moment this nameless emotion carried him to the very limit of coping; Francis' desire to remain upright fled. He fell to his knees, the joints cushioned by the well-tended greens of Lush Haven, his hands grasping his cane to hold up the rest of his body. As a throat-tearing sob began to gather strength deep inside his body Francis heard a flapping come from a tree growing about a dozen feet behind and to the right of *Cherished Daughter*. He looked up and saw a black body with bright, concerned eyes and the miserable sob was halted.

"*Croak!*"

Mavis had come to mourn with her friend.

As Francis smiled up at Mavis cocking her head at him from amongst the leaves Terrance spoke, startling him.

"How did she get here?"

"She flew."

"You know what I mean."

Francis looked up at his younger brother. "She probably saw us get in your SUV and just followed us over. That's my best guess."

Terry stared at the raven. "But how did she get out?"

"She comes and goes as she pleases," came Chava's voice from Francis' other side.

Francis' head swiveled around. "You're like a ninja."

"Ninja are Japanese. I'm Korean."

"Okay. You're like a Korean ninja. Better?"

"You alright, big brother? You need some help getting up?"

"No. I mean, yes, I'm okay. I don't need any help, though. My legs just got real tired all of a sudden, but I'm fine."

"You want us to give you a minute? We can go unload the food at the gazebo; you can see it from here," Terry pointed to the structure only a brief walk away. "Just come on over when you're ready."

"Yes, that'll be fine. I'm going to rest here for a second and I'll be along in a little bit."

"Okay, Francis." Terry turned to his family, "Lorraine, kids, let's go get the food ready while your Uncle Francis visits for a minute. Chava? You coming?"

"Well. Um—" the girl was having trouble finding words and looked to Francis for assistance, rocking back and forth on the heels of her feet.

"She can stay if she wants, Terry."

"Okay. See you two in a little while. Take your time, Francis."

"I will."

Francis remained in the grass on his knees, leaning on his cane as he and Chava watched Terry and his family walk back to the SUV. The Tower family had nearly reached the vehicle before either of them spoke again.

"You sure you're okay?"

"Sure. Sure, I wasn't lying. My legs just got tired. You ever get emotional and all the strength goes out of your body?"

"Yeah, when my dad died. I felt that a little. I know Mom did, too. She fell down at the funeral parlor. Right in front of everybody. It was scary."

"Ah. Yeah, well, it's like that. The brain can't take what it's feeling, so the body gets all confused too, I guess."

As he finished his sentence they heard Mavis croak before hopping from the tree to the ground. She did her bird strut the dozen feet over to where they were positioned in front of the markers. The three of them then trained their eyes on Mindy and Melissa's stones.

"Well; Mavis, Chava, this is Mindy and Melissa. My wife and my daughter. Mindy, Melissa; this is Mavis and Chava, they are good friends of mine."

"Nice to meet you, Missus Tower. Nice to meet you, Melissa." Chava offered small half bow.

"Croak!"

"That was a little weird, but very sweet. Thanks, you two. What's with the bow?"

"Oh. Ha-ha, my family has been here three generations, but we still do some of the Korean stuff."

"It's good. I like it. Maybe I'll start bowing to the jabberjaws cashier when I go to the Pet Emporium. That might shut her up." They both laughed at that, knowing nothing would ever shut jabberjaws up.

After the sounds of their laughter drifted away on the breeze Chava spoke in a serious, very adult, tone, "How did they die, Francis?"

"I killed them, Chava."

"You've said that before. But what are you talking about? If you killed them you'd... You'd be in jail, wouldn't you? So if you killed them, like you say, then it was an accident or something. Am I right?" The girl was getting aggravated at Francis' lack of clarity.

"Why is it so important for you to hear the details? You're being childish."

"It's not childish. I'm only thirteen, so what? Thirteen-year-olds aren't allowed to know things; not allowed to care about what is hurting their friends? You're my friend, Francis, and I want to know. I won't tell anyone if you tell me, not even my mom. But, fine; if you want to keep it to yourself, then just keep it to yourself."

Francis was visibly impressed by Chava's caring, yet curt, words, "That was a very adult thing to say, Chava. Maybe I haven't given you enough credit."

"Nobody gives goofy looking midgets credit."

"Knock it off. Don't get your prepubescent panties in a bunch."

"I'm not! I—"

"I killed them in a car crash."

"Oh."

"I was driving too fast. It was night. I was aggravated about something, I don't even remember what. I don't remember where we were coming home from. Mindy was talking about something for the house; new drapes or a dining room set, I don't remember. Melissa was singing one of her silly songs in the back seat. I was aggravated and I had a headache so I was driving too fast, way over the speed limit. I just wanted to get home to some peace and quiet; get that day over with. We were only a few miles from the house. I took a curve too fast and we left the road—" Francis' eyes lost focus on anything in particular as he retreated into the most horrible moment of his life.

"Francis?" She and Mavis were studying the man's face in an attempt to see where he was heading.

"There was smoke in the car and my face was wet and sticky; blood, but not my blood. It was Mindy's, or Melissa's, or both. Their blood was on my face and on my clothes and the dash and the windshield. It was outside. It didn't belong outside. Because I was impatient and driving too fast, their blood was on the outside. It was my fault, but my blood was still inside where it is supposed to be. I didn't have a scratch on me. I said their names, but they didn't answer. I yelled their names, they didn't answer. I tried to get out of the car but the door was stuck; bent, warped. I couldn't get them to answer me and I was covered in their blood. I had a headache and I wanted quiet and I killed them."

"It was an accident, Francis." Chava's voice cracked through her tears.

"It was my fault." The response was matter-of-fact; his eyes as dry as the Mojave as he spoke.

Mavis croaked sympathetically.

"Yeah, it was your fault, but it was still an accident."

"Thank you, Chava. Thank you for telling me the truth; for seeing it was my fault."

"It's okay."

Francis stopped talking and just looked at *Beloved Wife* and *Cherished Daughter*. Someone finally agreed with him that it was his fault, with minimal argument. He needed to own up to the fault; take responsibility for it, learn to live with it. He didn't need to deny it. To deny the truth. Terry and Lorraine never would let him own up to it. Even Doctor Singh tried to make him deny responsibility. It felt good to have an ally.

Francis let out a wistful sigh. "You know what I miss most, Chava?"

A number of things ran through her head. *His daughter's laughter or smile. His wife holding hands with him as they walked down the street. Evening meals where they talked about their days.* That's what she missed most when she thought about her father. "No, what?"

"I miss looking forward to things. Me and Mindy growing old together. Melissa's graduation from high school, then college. Watching her start out her adult life. I miss looking forward to walking my daughter down the aisle; of having grandchildren. I miss being called sweetheart and I miss being called Dad."

"I think I know how you feel."

"Yeah, I guess you do."

"Francis?"

"Yeah?"

"You can walk me down the aisle if you want. Well, in fifteen or twenty years anyway."

"I'd be honored to do that, Chava," he smiled up at her and extended a hand. "Now help me up. I think my feet went to sleep."

Mavis let out a shrill, relieved croak and took to the air, wheeled around, and made for the gazebo.

XXI

"See what I told you, dipshit? I told you it would be a piece of cake to get in here without anyone seeing us. Abracadabra!"

"Yeah, fine. Let's just get in, do what we're gonna do and get the fuck out. And watch out you don't drip any of that shit on my shoes."

"Prissy fucking bitch. This way, the stairs to the lobby are over here. Now, listen. When we get up there, we have to work fast. Everyone in the building is accounted for but we don't want anyone coming along and ruining our little prank. There'd be no fun in that."

"I'm not so sure this is any kind of fun, you crazy bastard."

"Whatever. Okay, you get to work with the buckets and I'll start spreading the pieces around. Make it as aesthetically pleasing as possible."

"Aesthe-what? Never mind, but let's keep it in the lobby. I don't wanna' chance running into anyone up on the other floors."

"Chickenshit. But, yeah, we'll keep it here in the lobby. NOT because of your pansy-ass reasons, either. Old Doggy boy wasn't very big; don't want to spread him out too thin; don't want to lose the dramatic effect, the shock value. You know?"

"God! McPhee, you're one sick fuck."

"Takes one to know one. Hey, Ron! You wanna' give the door there a knock to see if you're little slant-eyed piece of ass is home. We could make a day of it. From what you've told me about her I wouldn't mind taking a poke at her myself. Whaddya' say? You can even go first, I don't mind sloppy seconds one tiny bit."

"I'll call the cops myself before I'd let that happen."

"Yeah, right. A pretty boy like you in the lock up? They'd love your ass. "

"Whatever. Shit, let's just drop it and stick to the plan."

"Yeah, yeah, yeah. I'm out of dog. You done?"

"I have a little left in this bucket —"

"Hey! Wait a second. Give it to me. I just had an inspiration."

By the time Francis and Chava reached the gazebo, Terrance and Lorraine had unloaded the coolers, spread a white and red-checked tablecloth over the picnic table, and arranged the food on the table buffet style.

As the couple prepared the food, Amy and Terry, Jr. warily studied Mavis who was perched in the rafters of the gazebo eyeing the activities. Terrance didn't mind the big bird, but had tried to shoo her away at Lorraine's request. Mavis merely croaked at him menacingly and flapped her wings whenever he attempted to get near her. She wasn't one to be bullied, especially when a meal was a distinct possibility. He finally gave up after Mavis had fanned him half a dozen times and told Lorraine that if the bird bothered her so much, she could go ahead and try to make it leave. Mavis wasn't causing any trouble and he didn't see the point in acting out an Alfred Hitchcock scene over nothing. The bird would relocate soon enough. Once Francis arrived Mavis would surely want to be near him.

Speak of the devil. Terrance looked up from the condiments to spy Francis and Chava approaching the gazebo. Sure enough, at the appearance of Francis Mavis left the rafters, glided over to the man, and gently perched on his shoulder.

"I was just getting ready to send Terry down to get you. Soup's on, almost. I forgot the baby sweet pickles I picked up for you in the car."

"Excellent! Sweet pickles; love 'em!" Francis wondered how long had it been since he'd had a sweet pickle. He'd have to remember to ask Susan to put them on the grocery list.

Terry jogged over to the SUV to retrieve the pickles. He jogged back to the picnic table with the jar held in the air like a runner in the final leg of a relay race, holding the baton high triumphantly while crossing the finishing line. Everyone took this pickled exuberance as the signal to sit down at the table for lunch. Terry and Lorraine took one of the bench seats with Terry, Jr. sitting between them, while Francis, Chava, and Amy sat across from them. Lorraine dealt out the paper plates Vegas style and everyone got to work with their plastic utensils.

Nobody talked at first. It was one of those situations in which a group witnesses something they are not comfortable talking about and then telepathically agree to a period of silence until someone comes up with something more pleasant, or at least something neutral, to get the conversation going. The short exchange between Terrance and Francis concerning baby sweet pickles was a valiant attempt at normalcy, but the subject couldn't be stretched too awful far. The Tower children kept their focus on the meal relinquishing the responsibility of starting up a conversation after having seen their uncle go to his knees. Chava, as the only non-Tower at the table, sided with the Amy and Terry, Jr.; let the adults lead the way.

"*Croak!*" Mavis became impatient with the silence and started things off.

Francis took the cue from the raven. "Amy? Terry? How are you guys enjoying your summer vacation?"

"It's been pretty good," Amy answered. "I've mostly been hanging out with my friends or at home. We've been riding our bikes a lot."

"Yeah," Terry, Jr. added, "Dad said he'd take us over to the state park. They have a bike trail there that used to be a railway. But they took out the rails and made it a bike trail. Right, Dad?"

"That's right. I figured we'd leave early in the morning and spend the whole day. See how far we can go."

"That actually sounds pretty fun," Chava chimed in.

Amy piped up excitedly, "Hey! Maybe your mom would let you come with us! Or she could come, too!"

Francis took Amy's invitation to go riding with them to Chava as a good sign that the kids liked her and viewed her as a friend. If that is the case, the day was working out like he'd hoped.

"Maybe, she works nights and neither of us have a bike, but I bet we could work something out. I'll talk to her about it after we get home!" Chava looked pleased with the idea.

"I think Francis and I could front you and your mom some bikes," said Terry, "Call it a bonus for the big help you two have been this summer."

"Uncle Francis, you could come too if your ribs don't hurt anymore," Terry, Jr. sounded excited. "What do you think?"

"Uh. Yeah, I could probably do that, Terry. I'd have to work out some stuff, but I think it would be a good time."

"Oh, yeah, Chava? Will Uncle Francis give you time off from working in his man cave to come bicycling with us," joked Amy. Everyone at the table found that funny, even Francis, but he wasn't sure why.

"My man cave? What does that mean?"

"Man and cave," Lorraine explained.

"Right, man and cave, but what's a man cave?" Francis really had no idea what they were talking about.

Terrance joined in to clear things up. "Oh, that's a term nowadays people use to describe a guy's personal space. You know what I mean; a room with sports memorabilia and a pool table; someplace to hang with male friends. You can even buy signs to hang on the door like *Francis' Man Cave: No Women Allowed*, they even have man cave door mats. I have one friend who converted his two-car garage into a man cave. His wife was pretty P. O.'d about it, too. Doesn't like parking on the street. He has a full-service bar and a jukebox in there. I'd do the same, but Lorraine would have my hide."

"You got that right!" Lorraine confirmed.

"Hm...," Francis grinned. "That's not exactly fair, is it?"

"What do you mean?" Lorraine asked.

"Well, come on. The ladies get sewing rooms, quilting circles, and breakfast nooks and... and... doily crannies—"

"Doily cranny?" Terrance queried.

"Yeah, I made that last one up just now. But you see what I mean; nice little parts of the house that conjure pretty, comfortable images when you think about them. Why do we get a cave? It makes it sound like guys are sitting on dirt floors around little campfires. Maybe drawing stick animals on the walls with charred chunks of wood or gnawing on leg bones from their last hunt. I'd rather have a doily cranny."

"Ha ha ha! Yeah, Dad, and I want a gaming nook," added Terry, Jr.

"I don't think it's that bad," Terrance said in defense. "It's just the new expression for a man's den."

"Den isn't so hot either when you think about it. Lions and bears live in dens," Francis countered.

"Come on, why—"

"Terrance?"

"What?"

"You remembered I like sweet pickles, but you forgot I like to kid around?"

Terrance looked at his brother from across the table and realized for the first time in over seven years he was actually seeing his old big brother. His brother as he was before he was torn apart by tragedy one dark night, before his descent into self-loathing and self-destruction. It had been so long since Francis had tried to be funny that Terrance couldn't see that the lame anti-man cave rant was a joke. But, at that moment, it was the funniest damned thing he had ever heard.

"You're right, Francis. I want a doily cranny, too."

Francis smiled at Terrance and then fed Mavis a piece of his sweet pickle.

Susan Lee awoke from her post-shift slumber at 3 p.m. on the button. Her first thought, before she even opened her eyes, was of Chava and how the day with Francis, Terry, and Terry's family was going. Chava rarely went anywhere without her.

Gary R. Gowers

Harry's family was mostly back in South Korea, except for a couple of cousins living on the west coast. Her own parents had passed away and she had no siblings. Any family she had left was also back on the Pacific Rim and she hadn't heard from them in years. Chava wasn't close enough to any of her friends at school to get involved in sleepovers or other social activities. When she stopped and thought about it, she and her daughter lived very lonely lives. They had only each other. But now they had Francis, in a matter of speaking.

Susan threw her feet over the side of the bed and walked to the bathroom she shared with her daughter. She had to admit, Chava was a really good kid. No dirty clothes in the bathroom floor, her towel hung up to dry, no toothpaste residue in the sink, and her bedroom was every bit as neat and clean as the other parts of the apartment where Chava frequented. Susan's own bedroom, however, usually had an ever-growing pile of laundry in a corner and two or three coffee cups or water glasses on the nightstand. These were untidy transgressions her daughter would never allow to happen in her own room.

After relieving her bladder, washing her hands and face, brushing her teeth, and putting on some comfortable sweat pants; Susan went into the kitchen and loaded the toaster with a couple of pieces of wheat bread. She'd have a light snack to hold her over before Chava returned from the picnic and then see if her daughter was hungry enough for some dinner.

Something easy, maybe pizza. They hadn't ordered out for a while and it would make a nice change of pace. Maybe she'd even invite Francis to join them; perhaps the rest of the Tower family, as well. Make an evening of it. She didn't have to work at the laundry tonight, so why not?

While her bread toasted, she liked it almost burnt, she headed for the front door by way of the living room and Harry's memorial portrait. Hopefully one of the elderly people in the building hadn't stolen her Sunday paper for a change. She had a sneaking suspicion they were playing upon their age when they confessed to taking her paper because they got confused. She was pretty sure she was the only one in the building who even bothered to invest in a subscription.

Oh, well. They were always so nice to me and Chava when they ran into each other in the lobby or out in front of 517 Sycamore, so if having my paper stolen on Sundays was the one drawback to her neighbors, so be it, I'll consider myself lucky. There were other people in the city dealing with neighbors far worse than hers. At least she didn't have a meth lab next door or a bunch of tweakers cutting each other up in the halls.

Susan opened her door expecting to NOT see her paper on the floor in front of her door. The paper wasn't there, of course, but what she did see made her scream until the eighty-nine-year-old woman one floor up in 2B felt it was her duty as a concerned citizen to call the police. Well, after she finished reading the comics from the pretty Oriental lady's Sunday paper.

The almost burnt toast went cold in the toaster.

XXII

"Missus Lee, I'm Detective Putnam. Could you please repeat to me what you told Officer Chavez after he responded to your call?"

"Yes. Uh, I don't know very much; just what I found. "

"That would be fine. Anything you tell me could be helpful."

"Okay. I woke up at 3 p.m. I sleep the first part of the day because I work nights—"

"At the Paramount Hotel on Fitzgerald, correct? In the laundry?"

"Yes, detective, I've worked there for the last three years. "

"And would you say you get along with everyone at your workplace? Your co-workers, the managers?"

"I would say so. I mean, I'm not really friends outside of work with anyone, but we are friendly enough on the job."

"And do you have any enemies outside of work? Ex-husbands? Jealous boyfriends? A parent from your daughter's school? Anyone at all?"

"I've only been married once, and he passed away—"

"I'm sorry for your loss."

"Thank you. I don't really know any of the other parents from the school. I have one ex-boyfriend, Ron Rhodes, he also used to work at the Paramount as a shuttle bus driver. We broke it off some weeks ago."

"Did you part as friends?"

"Well, no. He was pretty upset, but I really don't think—"

"Detective Putnam?"

"Mister...?"

"That's Francis Tower, detective. He's the reason I took the call. The assault victim; was pushed into the street and hit by a taxi."

"*Thank you, Chavez. Yes, Mister Tower?*"

"*Detective, I don't think this has anything to do with Susan at all. She just happens to live on the first floor and was the one who found the... vandalism. I have a pretty good idea who did this. And so does Officer Chavez.*"

"*And who would that be, Mister Tower?*"

"*McPhee. The homeless man that pushed me in front of the taxi.*"

"*That's Lawrence McPhee, detective. He has a sheet. A very unstable man. I checked him out after the incident involving Mister Tower.*"

"*I'd like to see your file on this McPhee, Chavez. And why do you believe it was McPhee, Mister Tower?*"

"*The head mounted on the bannister, I recognize that dog. It was McPhee's dog. And the graffiti written in the dog's blood...*"

THANKS FOR THE BURGER

Francis said goodbye to Susan at her door. He didn't disturb Chava, who upon seeing the gory display in the lobby burst into frantic tears and could not be coaxed from her room once she had disappeared inside the Lee's apartment at a full run, slamming her door behind her. That was the best place for her now anyway, a place where she felt sheltered from the horrific craziness just outside her apartment.

If she didn't show up the next day to help with the animals, if she needed some time to herself, he would understand. Susan was calm now but when he, Chava, and Terry had entered the building they found her standing in her doorway shivering from head to toe moving her eyes over the lobby as if she was trying to get a handle on what she was seeing. She had screamed all of the breath out of her body by the time they found her and could only manage a whimper until after they had led her inside and given her a drink of water.

She was finished with being shocked over the mess in the

lobby and, after downing the water, she was able to calmly relate to them how she had gone to the door to retrieve her paper and found instead what looked like a set from a horror movie. Luckily, they had dropped Lorraine and the kids off at home before coming to 517 Sycamore. One traumatized child was enough.

If not for their concern for Chava and Susan, Francis and Terrance may not have handled the lobby very well, either. But their primal manliness lent them the fortitude to see to the welfare of the ladies before they took the time to melt down. The first thing they noticed when they swung open the door of the lobby was the smell. It wasn't the smell of rot. The poor dog hadn't been dead for very long, or it had been frozen or preserved somehow before being used as morbid decor. Instead, the smell was perceived as the taste of pennies on the tongue, with an underlying odor of feces to give it an extra kick.

Pieces of the dog, the legs and the tail, and at least three sections of the body were distributed around the lobby, in corners and spaced evenly across the room. The only piece of the canine not on the floor was the head. It was sitting on the bannister of the first floor staircase with its eyes open towards the entrance and its tongue hanging out, as if begging for a treat it could never hope to chew.

In addition to the body parts, blood had been splashed across the walls like Jackson Pollack had returned from the grave and had traded in paints for bodily fluids. Perhaps the most disturbing detail of the spectacle was that someone had taken the time to write on the white tile above the bank of mailboxes in the dog's blood in all capital letters:

THANKS FOR THE BURGER

Before he even processed the fact that he recognized the head on the bannister as the dog belonging to Lawrence McPhee, the bloody words told him exactly who had been responsible. He had given the dog a cheeseburger and had only trash-talked

McPhee. Francis had no doubt McPhee was responsible for this.

Francis gave Detective Putnam and Officer Chavez the account of what had transpired between he and McPhee. Well, it was mostly for Putnam. Chavez seemed to be a very sharp young man and was able to recall details about the incident that Francis had already forgotten. Other than suggesting strongly that McPhee was the vandal, he had said very little to the police. Terrance, however, walked the police out to their cars after they finished with their questions. He had told Francis he wanted to speak with Chavez after Putnam had left. About what he hadn't said, but Francis was sure his brother would fill him in on it in time.

Francis was on the flight leading to the third floor, so he started digging around in his pockets for the keys to his place. His place. McPhee had found out somehow where he lived. How much hatred did the man carry? How thirsty was he for revenge, to take the trouble to find out where Francis lived? Yes, Francis had insulted McPhee, first by giving the dog food and ignoring McPhee's hunger and then by cutting him down with snide comments. Francis was not proud of the things he had said, but surely causing him to get hit by a taxi and sent to the ER via ambulance was enough to even things up. Apparently not. This was a level of hate Francis knew existed in the world, but he had never found himself on the receiving end.

By the time Francis had returned from the ER with his taped up ribs and leaning on a cane, he had already begun the process of forgetting about what had happened between McPhee and himself. He had recognized the dog, despite the condition the pathetic thing was in, but he doubted if he would know McPhee by sight. What did that say about Francis? No wonder McPhee hated him. McPhee lived on the streets begging for coins to feed himself, as well as to keep himself drunk as often as possible. The man had nothing going on in his life. Before encountering Francis the only power the man probably had was power over how much or how little he made that dog suffer.

When the dog attacked McPhee in Francis' defense, even

that pitiful amount of control was lost to McPhee. The man lived a small life, a small existence. Something like this would represent something huge to him. It would elevate Francis from just an asshole who snubbed him in passing to being as close to an arch-nemesis that McPhee could imagine. It would make Francis a focal point for everything that had gone wrong in McPhee's life. Francis sure had opened up a can of worms that day. *Worms? Hell, a can of cobras.*

McPhee didn't really worry him much, though. The police knew who they were looking for and McPhee would be easy enough to spot and pick up for questioning. It shouldn't take them long to have the man in custody. Francis actually hoped that being arrested for what he'd done could somehow help the man. Some time in jail might dry him out; maybe give him a new perspective. One could hope.

Francis finally reached his door, with very little help from his cane he was happy to notice. As he pushed the key into the lock he wondered if Terry had yet arranged for the cleaning crew to come clear up McPhee's macabre exhibit. Whatever those folks made an hour, he hoped Terry would tip them well. In fact, he'd make a point of recommending it after Terry was finished talking to Chavez.

"*Croak!*"

"Felicia! Get away from there!" Every now and then Felicia took an interest in the shiny silver latch used to hold the top of Constance the boa's tank in place. The little troublemaker just could not ignore shiny objects. Of all the shiny objects on the fifth floor, the latch on the snake's cage is the last one the ferret should be fiddling with. If Felicia managed to get the latch open and Constance got out, well, the ferret could very well end up a boa turd. Francis didn't sit around babysitting Felicia, so more often than not it was Mavis who alerted him to the ferret's death defying activities. Whether she was concerned for the goofy little albino or she just liked to snitch on her, he wasn't sure.

It had been a week since McPhee's act of bloody vandalism took place in the lobby of the building and things had settled back to normal for the most part. On the day it happened he had left Chava alone to process the incident however she saw fit, fully expecting not to see her the next day. The girl's physical size might be small, but her determination and resilience were bigger and stronger than Francis gave her credit for. She was on time the next morning and they talked very little about what had transpired. Instead, the girl chose to focus on what a good time she had on the picnic with Francis, Terry, and Terry's family.

She and Amy had hit it off well despite the two years difference in their ages. Chava looked up to her like a big sister and Amy probably looked at her as the little sister she didn't have, most likely wishing the Korean girl could replace her younger brother; the Prince of Flatulence. Susan had told him Chava and Amy had been talking on the phone pretty much every night, usually for a couple of hours at a time. What is more, two nights ago Amy had invited Chava for a sleepover and Terry had to deliver Chava to her job the next morning. The adults were unanimous in considering this new friendship between the two girls as a wonderful thing and something to be supported and encouraged.

Chava also did not bring up Francis' mini-breakdown at Mindy and Melissa's graves, nor his collapse and his confession in regards to how they died. Francis appreciated this greatly. He was not embarrassed about his show of emotion at the cemetery, but he'd rather not talk about it anymore than they already had. How Chava handled the emotional demonstration at the cemetery and the mess in the building's lobby greatly reinforced his opinions of the girl. She was someone he could count on, someone he could trust; she understood him and did not stress their friendship with the tiresome rehashing of painful incidents.

He was sure they would talk about these things again, in time, but they would let the subjects come up on their own and not force the envelope. These subjects would simply become part of their history together, to be discussed rationally and with understanding of where the other stood in regards to that history. This was a mark of true friendship, and it wasn't lost on him.

Francis was sprinkling food over the pool occupied by the pig nosed turtles when he heard the door to his living quarters open and close. She arrived about an hour later this morning because Susan had wanted to take her daughter grocery shopping before Chava reported for duty and Susan took to her bed for her day's sleep. Francis had already started the day's work, though, and it was going to be a light day. None of the water in the pools needed changing, so it was merely a matter of feeding, watering, and cleaning up of poop. Maybe today would be a good day to check the inventory of various foods, vitamin supplements, pinkies, and miscellaneous supplies. If the stock was severely lacking in some category he'd send Chava to the Pet Emporium, otherwise, he'd let it wait until tomorrow.

"*Croak!*"

"Felicia!"

"What's all the yelling?" asked Chava as she entered the menagerie.

"Oh, it's Felicia. She's messing around with the latch on Constance's tank again."

"Oh, boy. If it wasn't for Mavis that little goofball would have been a snake turd already.".

"I was thinking the same thing. If I could just get it through her pointy little head, but there is no use in...," he stopped mid-sentence and stood staring at Chava.

"What?" The girl looked down at herself then back up at him.

"I don't know. Something is different."

"I don't know what you're talking about. Where are you with the feeding? Did you do the—"

"Are you wearing makeup?"

"No."

"Yes, you are. You're wearing makeup."

"No, I'm not! Yes, a little, so what?" Her voice rose a bit and her cheeks darkened.

"So nothing. Just an observation."

"Okay, then. What do you want me to do? Have you fed the rabbits?"

"Why are you wearing makeup?"

"Why not? I'm thirteen. I can wear makeup if I want to. My mom said it's okay."

"Yeah, okay. But why now all of a sudden?"

"It's not all of a sudden. I've worn makeup before."

"No, you haven't. Not up here at least."

"Okay, I haven't! Up here or anywhere. Amy gave it to me, so I'm trying to learn how to put it on. Okay? It's no big deal so let's just do the work."

"Sure, sure; don't have to get mad. I was just asking."

"What are you smiling at? You've never seen a girl wear makeup before?"

"Of course, I have. Just not you. It looks good, really. I wasn't trying to embarrass you or get you riled up. You can get started on the rabbits if you'd like, I'll finish up with the turtles. After that I want to do an inventory, see if we're running low on anything." He had decided not to press the issue of the makeup. The girl was clearly uncomfortable talking about this sudden development in her appearance.

"Okay."

Francis checked to make sure he hadn't overfed the pig nosed turtles during the exchange with Chava before moving on to Bullet and the other sliders. Chava walked down the aisle between the pools and the cages in the direction of the rabbits. She removed the empty food trays from the cages and set them next to the plastic container and started measuring out scoops of pellets.

"School is starting back up soon," her back was facing Francis. "In a few weeks."

"Yeah, where did the time go, huh?"

"I want to look like a girl at school this year."

His curiosity in regards to the makeup must have struck a nerve. Or, more likely, she had worn the makeup with the express purpose of him noticing it. It seemed to him now that she wanted to talk about it, but had been unsure of how to broach it, thus the defensiveness when he did, in fact, notice she was wearing the makeup. Girls were tough to read and he had never had a chance to go through the trials and tribulations of puberty and burgeoning womanhood with Melissa. The early end to his fatherhood paired with his reclusive lifestyle over the past seven years left him remarkably unschooled in how to deal with this, but he would do the best he could.

"You do look like a girl, Chava."

"You know what I mean. I want to look like a girl, not a kid. Amy says the makeup will make me look more grown up."

"Okay. That might be true, but why would you want to look more grown up? Grown-ups have wrinkles and weird spots and growths on their skin and gray hair. You'll have all that in time, why rush it? What's the hurry?"

"The boys all treat me like a little kid. The girls, too. But it bothers me a lot when the boys do it."

Boys. This is way out of my league! He definitely wasn't prepared for this talk. And wasn't this her mother's department? He couldn't just blow it off, though. The girl wanted to talk about it, so he'd talk about it. He'd just have to proceed with baby steps and attempt not to be too blunt and overly honest as he normally would when asked his opinion. This was brain surgery, not a loose tooth or road rash from falling off a bicycle.

"How is it you want the boys to treat you?"

"I don't know; just not like a bratty little kid. I want them to notice me like they notice the other girls. Think I'm pretty, you know," Chava could barely get the words out because embarrassment was choking the words out of her.

"Ah. I see. You think the boys don't think you are pretty."

"Well, yeah. Last year the kids were always talking about who liked who; this girl is so pretty, that girl is so pretty, none of the boys ever told anybody I was pretty. The most I got was how

I could run fast and I always got perfect scores on the math quizzes."

"Well, let me ask you this. Who is the prettiest girl in your school?"

"That's Tatiana. She's adopted from Russia, I think. She's tall and blond... and... and curvy. The boys can't stop looking at her!"

"Okay, do they ever talk about how fast she can run or how she does on her school work?"

"Never! Because she's so beautiful!"

"And you think the boys noticing her looks is better than the boys noticing your skills?"

"Well, yeah."

"Is this Tatiana stupid?"

"No, not at all. She speaks two languages! She is good at math, too."

"Can she run?"

"Of course. Not as fast as me, but almost. She has really long legs." Chava's face fell into a frown.

"You should consider yourself lucky, then."

"What? How is that lucky?"

"Sunsets are pretty. Art, a lot of it, is pretty. A flower is pretty. They are objects, things. The boys view poor Tatiana as a thing, that's how. You want people to look at you like you're a thing?"

"Well, no, I guess not, but—"

"The boys see you are a fast runner and see you are smart. They see you as a PERSON with skills. They don't see you as an object. This is a good thing, Chava, because later, after you have become more... more... um... well, physically developed... you'll have beauty on top of skills and brains!" As he spoke he became animated, swinging his arms around and talking with his hands. This seemed to help drive the point home and Chava could not stop herself from smiling.

"You really think so? You think I'll be pretty?"

"You're already pretty. I already told you that, but soon,

kid, you're gonna be a knock out. I wouldn't worry about it. Your mom is going to go crazy trying to keep the boys from the door."

"Poor Tatiana."

"Yeah, poor Tatiana."

"*Croak!*"

"Felicia!" they yelled in unison.

McPhee was keeping to the alleys during the day and only chanced the main streets to hit strangers up for spare change and dollar bills after dark had fallen. *A guy still has to drink after all.*

Yes, he was being sought by the police, but he still had to make a living. His eyes were constantly scanning the traffic on the streets for police vehicles and the pedestrians on the sidewalks for officers in their tidy blue uniforms. His being guilty had made everyone else a suspect.

He knew before carrying out his bloody escapade with Ron Rhodes that the cops would be searching for him soon afterwards. Using the same dog and leaving the burger message was stupid, from a criminal's perspective. McPhee's purpose, however, was not to carry out a petty act of anonymous vandalism. He wanted Francis Tower to know it had been he who had left the message in the lobby, that McPhee knew where he lived, and that he was more than capable of going the distance in search of retribution. He was not one-hundred percent certain Tower would recognize the dog, especially as blood-soaked as the animal was, so his sudden inspiration to leave the message on the wall over the mailboxes in the dog's blood would insure Tower knew who was responsible.

He was sure the police had put two and two together before the mess had even been cleaned up, which means they were looking for him. *Or were they?* McPhee doubted they were trying very hard to find him. Not because they didn't want to apprehend him and punish him, but because they figured he would lay low as he made his way out of the city and away from the crime scene and the punishment that was sure to follow. If that is the case, the police could not be more wrong. McPhee had no intentions of leaving the city. In fact, he was going to go back to the apartment building on 517 Sycamore to carry out the second part of his plan.

Throwing a scare into Tower was not enough. That did not equal the humiliation dealt McPhee on the street by the recluse all those weeks ago. The freak needed to be punished further, needed to experience the full force of McPhee's revenge. And that is why he was sticking to the alleys and laying low. They thought he was on the run and this would lull Tower, and the cops, into a false sense of security. That would make his next visit all the sweeter. The unexpected surprise; he couldn't wait to see the look on Tower's face.

Soon he would be giving Rhodes a visit. McPhee doubted very much that he and Rhodes could be linked together. The only ones who had seen them associate were Sid and the waitresses down at *Stew's*, and that was only once. The police would not know to ask questions at the bar. Why would they? He had thought at first to try to implicate Rhodes in the dog prank, but why should that dipshit get any glory? Besides, with Rhodes not being involved, as far as the police knew, McPhee had a safe place to sleep during the day if he needed one and an accomplice in the second visit to the apartment building.

He'd figure out what to do about Rhodes after finishing things with Tower. Rhodes could not be trusted, that much was clear to him. The pretty boy didn't show much fortitude while dealing with the dog, nearly tossed his cookies putting the mutt on display, and his refusal to fuck with the ex-girlfriend when they had a golden opportunity to do so demonstrated he wasn't man enough to go all the way. Yeah, Rhodes would have to go. And maybe after Rhodes was dealt with McPhee could just load the man's pretty car up with whatever valuables he could find in the dick's house and drive on out of the city as pretty as you please.

Just a little longer, Tower. Get nice and comfortable up there on your fifth floor. Feed your pets, enjoy your time with the gooks. Fool yourself into thinking it is all over and you've seen the last of me. Get all healed up, if you're not already. I'm coming for you, you son of a bitch, and I'm going to make that bump from the taxi seem like a smooch on the forehead from your momma. I'll be writing messages in your blood next time.

It was going to be beautiful.

XXIII

"Would someone like to explain to me what this is all about?"

"What's with the raised hackles? The derisive hisses and nips? The glares?"

"You can't be serious?"

"Neglecting you? Now, you guys know better than that. Yes, since the taxi put me partially out of commission there have been some other faces around here. Don't act like you don't like the girl. And the mother has done nothing but ooh *and* aah *all over you. You should all be ashamed of yourselves!"*

"CROAK!"

"Thank you, Mavis! The voice of reason, as usual. You're all just a little jealous, I get that. For so long I've only had eyes and mind for you, but that hasn't changed. My mind has been on some other things as of late, but you still need me and I still need you. No, that hasn't changed between us. Not at all."

"I know, I know. There have been changes for sure, but they have been good changes."

"I'll tell you right now getting banged up was no picnic, but it brought Susan and Chava into our lives. What's more, my brother is more than just my caretaker again. He was taking care of me while I was taking care of you. The difference is, I CHOSE to take you in and care for you. Terry never chose to do the things he has done for me. Without him I'd still be locked up in a white-walled institution or dead in the ground and you would all be scattered around in other homes and probably not cared for quite so well."

"You are coming off a bit ungrateful."

"Luis, you'd probably be living in some high school science lab

being mishandled by teenagers; never knowing when one of them was going to flip shit and squash you. You have to admit, you've had it very easy here with me and that won't change."

"But I've got news for you, and all of you need to hear this and hear it good, there are going to be some other new faces around here and you're just going to have to learn to adjust to that; be a little more flexible and understanding about what I need. It's not only about what you need. My niece and nephew, Terry's kids, they want to see you. They want to get to know you. And I've told them they could."

"Calm down! You're carrying on and you don't even know why! Just childish pouting, that's what it is! And it isn't going to fly!"

"CROAK!"

"Hear that? Mavis is fine with it! Trust her if you don't believe me. If you'd just show a little faith; I've been good to you, Chava has been good to you. Amy and Terry, Jr. will be good to you, too. Won't it be nice to have some fresh blood around here? Bullet! Wipe that smirk off your pointy little face! You know what I mean! I see you nipping at those kids and you'll find yourself in a five-gallon tank all by yourself! Don't make me put you in time out!"

"Alright, then, that's more like it! I knew you were better than that; all of you. Just be patient and give them a chance. I really need this. I'm doing better, getting better, and I need my family back; my human family!"

"So I'm asking, for all I've done for you, let me out."

"I'm ready to leave the cage."

"Another pancake?"

"No thanks. I'm stuffed."

Francis and Susan were eating breakfast in Francis' kitchen. The morning repast had settled into a comfortable routine for the two neighbors. They were usually a little groggy at the start of the meal; Francis because he hadn't finished his first cup of coffee yet and Susan because she was coming off her night shift at the laundry. By the time they were half-way through whatever the woman cooked for them the caffeine had kicked in, bringing Francis to life, and Susan perked up as she caught her second wind. By that time the two were chatting about anything and everything under the sun. There had even been a few instances in which Francis actually assisted with the preparation of breakfast, though Susan limited him to cracking eggs, or stirring batter, or pouring out coffee and juice. Francis imagined this is how meals went down in their apartment, Susan in the lead with Chava as the assistant. Poor Chava, always the assistant. *That's basically what kids are, apprentices to life,* he mused.

"Susan."

"Francis?"

"Great pancakes."

"Thank you, Francis. You did seem to enjoy them."

"My wife used to make them with bananas cut up in them. Banana pancakes."

"Oh! Would you like me to make you some banana pancakes next time? I never thought about it because Chava doesn't like them."

"No, that's okay. Yours are fine just the way they are. I don't even remember if I really liked the banana pancakes. Melissa liked them, that's why Mindy made them that way."

The two sat looking at their coffee cups in silence. The subject of Mindy and Melissa rarely came up, and when it did it always made them a little uncomfortable; Francis because he wasn't used to talking about them and Susan because she didn't want to push Francis into talking about them. They let the names of his departed family drift on into the ether.

"The day the police interviewed us in your apartment..."

"Yeah."

"I noticed there was a black ribbon arranged on Harry's portrait, the one hanging in the living room. Is that a Korean thing because he passed away?"

"Yes, that's it exactly. But I think other cultures do it to. I'm not sure. Why?"

"I was just wondering."

"Francis?"

"Susan?"

"If you don't mind me asking, why don't you have pictures of Melissa or Mindy; or one of the three of you?"

"I have one of us. It's in my stack of *National Geographic* over by my chair and I have a lot of photos in the storage down on the fourth floor."

"But why don't you have any hanging in here?"

Francis' eyebrows knotted up and he stared at his coffee cup like he was trying to refill it through the power of thought.

"I'm sorry, Francis. You don't have to answer that."

"No, no, it's okay. I'm just not sure. I don't like to look at them I guess. Not all the time."

"I know exactly how you feel. It took some weeks before I was able to hang the portrait of Harry. And I used to look at it every time I walked through the room. Now, now it's more like he's there when I want to look. It gets easier. And it's nice being able to turn my head and see him there if I want to."

"You think I should hang a picture of them?"

"Only if you want to."

"I'll think about it."

And he would think about it. He was sure Susan could help him find a nice spot to hang it. Somewhere he could see them when he wanted to, but not be confronted with them every time he entered the room. Since his visit to their graves maybe he could look at them a little easier; with less guilt maybe. Without feeling like they were judging him in some way. Maybe instead of feeling like hell for his role in wiping their smiles from the face of the earth, he could merely appreciate the beauty in their faces. Yes. He would definitely give it some thought.

"On the topic of spouses…"

"Yes?"

"What's your maiden name?"

"Lee."

"Did you change it back after Harry died?"

"No. His family name was Lee also."

"Were you cousins or something?" Francis chuckled at his own joke.

"Nope," she gave him a playful scowl, "we were both just Lees. Over in Korea, Lee is like Jones or Smith here. More Chins than a Chinese phonebook, so to speak." They both smiled at that. "Besides, even if I'd been a Cho or a Kim, I probably wouldn't have changed my name. That's a Korean custom; maybe the Chinese do it, too. A wife doesn't take the husband's name after marriage."

"No kidding? What about kids? If you had been a Cho, would it be Chava Cho or Chava Lee?"

"She'd still be a Lee. The kid is always given the father's family name. In East Asia, it's all about continuing the man's bloodline."

"No different here."

"I guess not, now that I think about it. It may be even more about the man here; even the wife changes her name. That's slowly changing though, I think. I work with a woman; her name is Janet Pulaski-Menard. Pulaski is her maiden name."

"In the battle for gender equality, I suppose the hyphen is a way of meeting halfway; lets the woman keep her identity and gives the man the illusion of partial ownership." Francis shrugged.

"I've heard there are some men who have taken their wife's name, changed theirs instead. I don't know any men who have done that though, or would even have been willing to do that."

"I'd do it. What's in a name?"

"Yeah, if you ever get married again maybe you'll be Francis Washington...or Francis Suzuki, Francis Pulaski."

"If I become a polygamist I can be Francis Washington-Suzuki-Pulaski."

"Oh, God. Can you imagine? Three wives?"

"No way I could eat three breakfasts."

"I don't know; the way you scarf down pancakes you might be able to handle it. But keep it simple, just you and one woman is enough."

"Yeah. Simple is best. Just call me Francis L—"

Before Francis could embarrass himself by finishing that ill-conceived sentence Chava announced her arrival with the sound of the key sliding home in the lock.

"Croak!!"

Mavis' voluminous announcement that Felicia was, once again, playing around with the silver latch on Constance's tank startled both Francis and Chava. Their heads snapped up and around in the general direction of where the boa's tank was arranged along the wall.

"Felicia!" they yelled in unison.

They couldn't see whether or not the ferret had responded to their dual-toned accusatory hullabaloo, but they heard the *click click clickety click* of her toenails as she scurried along the floor, obviously as startled by their yells as the two humans had been by the raven's croak. Hearing the sound of Felicia's retreat, the two went back to what they were doing.

Francis was examining Jethro the toad's habitat, considering whether or not it was time to move the bulbous amphibian to a new tank, and Chava was standing in the sugar glider enclosure letting the small marsupials use her for a tree. Oliver was sitting atop her head overseeing the festivities. Even the stand-offish Martin was participating, running up and down Chava's legs, occasionally leaping from the left leg to the right and back again.

The animals were very active that morning. Not only were the sugar gliders in a happily agitated state, but the parakeets, cockatiels, and finches were singing in a chorus; nearly in tune for a change. Every wheel in every cage and tank was spinning frantically under rodent power. The turtles, both sliders and pig noses were swimming laps in their pools fast enough to make small slapping noises as water gently lapped up against the sides of their pools. Sunlight was streaming in through the glass in the ceiling and windows. The entire population of the fifth floor was in fine spirits. To top it off, which gladdened Chava greatly, no pinkies or other rodents of any size were scheduled for demise today. Nobody had to meet their end on this fine, sunny day.

The upbeat mood of the animals was contagious. Chava was giggling like the young girl she happened to be as the sugar gliders had their fun. She tweeted and squeaked back at the birds, causing them to sing even louder. Francis went about his work with a bounce in his step, the strings of Stravinsky playing softly on the stereo. For the first time since his incident with the taxi he had left his cane back in his living quarters. It was left hooked on the side of the kitchen table, abandoned like a bad memory best forgotten.

"*Croak*!!"

"Felicia!!"

"Chava! Can you come over here for a second?"

"Coming!" The girl took several moments to gently dislodge the multiple grips the mini-horde of sugar gliders had on her. She saved Oliver for last, pulling the small creature out of her hair, his toenails running through the coal black strands like the teeth of a comb. She held Oliver up to her face in both hands, kissed him on the nose and gently deposited him on the branch of a non-human tree. She made sure to carefully fasten both locks on the enclosure door after stepping out. Sugar gliders had escaped before and it was not easy to corral them once they had the entire room to duck and weave out of the way of their pursuers. Once the door was secure she walked over to where Francis was staring at Jethro the toad.

"What's up?"

"Well, I'm trying to decide whether or not to move Jethro's chubby butt to a larger tank. What do you think?"

Chava was always amused at the way Francis put so much thought and consideration into each decision he made in relation to his animals. He once spent nearly three hours weighing the pros and cons of different heat rocks. The longer oval rocks allowed his reptiles to place more of their body on the rock, while the shorter thicker rocks put out more heat. He eventually decided on the longer rocks seeing as he never let the room get below a balmy 80 degrees anyway. Chava had picked up something of Francis' methodology concerning the care of the animals, so she stood there staring intently down at the toad. Jethro stared back at them, moving his eyes from one human face to the other. The look on his face, not afraid, was just not sure why he was the center of so much attention.

"Hmm. You know he really doesn't do much; a hop or two to eat a pinkie. He barely moves when he poops, just enough so he's not sitting in it."

"Yeah."

"Are they that lazy outside? I mean, in the wild? How in the heck do they not just get eaten?"

Jethro seemed slightly offended at Chava's remarks concerning his lack of vitality and did a little side hop just to show he could do it whenever he wanted to, and for no reason at all. The hop seemed to sap his strength, though, and so he just went back to staring back at them.

"Oh, they get eaten. But, no; they are more active in the wild. Outside captivity he'd have to hunt down his food, search for a mate, and escape predators."

"That's what he needs."

"What does he need?"

"A girlfriend!" Chava smiled. This seemed to get Jethro's full attention and the toad locked eyes solidly with Chava as if willing her to continue with that line of thought.

"*Croak!!*"

"Felicia!!" they yelled in unison again.

"You know, you might have something there. I've never had a breeding pair of toads—"

"*Croak!!*"

"Felicia!!"

"...the Pet Emporium should have some information on it.

When you go there tomorrow ask them…"

"*Croak!!*"

"Felicia!!"

"*Cro—*"

A frantic flapping of wings and the sounds of a struggle came from the far wall in the direction of Constance's tank. Francis and Chava whipped their heads around to see Felicia come running full speed in their direction, her toenails making the *click click clickety click* sound as she bounded down the aisle.

Francis started to move towards the sound of the commotion. He hurried towards the boa's tank, all signs of his tender ribs and stiff leg obliterated. "Lock Felicia up, Chava!"

Chava scooped Felicia up in one hand and noticed the albino was shivering from the tip of her pointy nose to the end of her fluffy tail. She jogged the ten or twelve steps to the ferret's wire cage, just above the rabbits, and plopped her down inside and fastened it shut. She moved to join Francis, but she wasn't even half way to him before he raised his hand to halt her advance, and then he spoke, his voice low, serious and cracking. She had never heard him speak in this tone before and she knew in an instant that something very terrible had happened.

"Chava. Please. Go home."

Francis leaned over and gently picked up the large snake and placed her back in her tank. He took a moment, looking up at the sun shining through the glass panes. *Such a beautiful day.* His eyes found the open window Mavis used to enter and exit the fifth floor. And then he started to cry.

Tears were flowing freely as he turned and looked at his friend laying on the floor. The crying turned to a light sobbing as he picked up the black, broken body of the wonderful creature who had been his best friend for so long. He cradled Mavis in the crook of his arm and found the nearest stool. As he sat he hugged her lightly against his chest and buried his face in her downy breast and let the soft feathers soak up his tears.

Francis, Chava, and Susan sat on the bench facing the small animal cemetery on the roof of the fifth floor. Long before Susan had arrived for breakfast that morning, even before the sun had peaked up over the buildings to the east, Francis had been on the roof digging with a trowel. The grave he had dug for Mavis was near the front of the cemetery, closest to the bench. He knew this was a feeble attempt to hold onto his friend as he was digging; keeping her as close as possible, but letting go had never been his strong suit.

Once the grave was finished he carried Mavis up the spiral staircase and laid her next to the grave so she could rest and be warmed in the morning sun. He chose not to encase her in a box or container of any sort. Mavis was never a pet, never really domesticated. She came and went as she pleased; putting her in a box would feel like he was containing her somehow, though she would never take to the skies again. So aside from folding her wings to her sides and smoothing down her feathers, his friend would be buried as is.

"I'm so sorry, Francis," comforted Susan.

"Thanks, Susan." He was fully aware the woman was putting off sleep after a long night in the laundry and he appreciated this act of friendship. "She was very special. I'm glad you came." Chava just gazed at the still body of Mavis and said nothing.

"You know, Chava. After Mavis started coming around I did a little research on ravens. The raven is featured prominently in Native American lore and mythology. They represent something to nearly every tribe in North America. What they symbolize varies from tribe to tribe, but the raven is always in their stories somewhere. I still have the books if you'd like to take a look."

His attempt at getting Chava to talk failed completely. Not

even a nod, yea or nay, to acknowledge she had heard his words. The girl was obviously saddened by what happened to Mavis, maybe even a little in shock. Francis shuddered to think what her reaction would have been like if she had seen what he had seen on the floor next to Constance's tank.

Apparently, Felicia had finally managed to fully unlatch the top of the tank and Constance had escaped. Constrictors, ferrets, and dead ravens don't speak English, so he would never fully understand what had happened. The best he could guess was the snake escaped and targeted Felicia as just the right size for a meal. From all the flapping and croaking they had heard, Mavis had most likely intervened on behalf of the ferret to draw the snake's attention. When he found the results of this confrontation the raven was no longer in the snake's deadly embrace. Constance had released Mavis and was crawling away from the crushed body of the bird, showing no interest in making a meal of her. The bird had obviously startled Constance. Mavis had done too good of a job pulling Felicia from the jaws of death, literally. None of this could ever be confirmed, of course, but that did not change the results. Constance was back in her tank, Felicia was still alive, and Mavis was dead. That was the reality of the situation and there was nothing to do but accept things as they were.

In the spirit of acceptance and moving on, Francis continued, "In some tribes the raven is a trickster because it has the power to change forms, so it can take a human form and cause all kinds of trouble. For others, a raven carries magic and messages from the heavens to the people it feels deserve the knowledge. Still, for other tribes, the raven is called on to assist in healing rituals; such as when a member of the tribe is wounded on a hunt. The one I like the most, what I saw in Mavis when I think about it, ravens are the keepers of secrets. They help people figure out answers to our most inner thoughts. Thoughts we aren't willing to face or harmful things we keep secret. I used to tell Mavis everything. In her way, she probably knew more about me than anybody; more than Terry, more than

Doctor Singh—"

"I hate her!"

Susan was the first to address the girl, "Hate who, sweetheart?"

"Constance."

"That's natural, Chava—"

"Yeah, it's natural, Chava. When I first saw what had happened, I won't lie to you, I wanted to hurt, even kill Constance. But that's not right."

"It is right. She deserves to be punished! Look at Mavis!"

"That's grief for a friend. That doesn't make it right. Listen, you still have trouble with feeding pinkies to Luis and the others, right?"

"Yeah—"

"Well, what I think happened is Constance got out, tried to eat Felicia, and Mavis stopped it. You can't hate Constance for wanting to eat Felicia, that's just nature. And you can't hate Constance for defending herself against Mavis. Knowing Mavis, I'm sure she went pretty hard at Constance with her claws and beating with her wings. It probably scared the crap out of Constance."

"I guess, but—"

"You can't hate creatures for doing what comes naturally to them. We don't have to like it. I wish it hadn't happened, but it wasn't Constance's fault really. We could fault Felicia's curiosity; she's the one who unlatched the lid to the tank, right? It could be my fault. I knew Felicia couldn't resist the shiny latch, but I never got around to painting it black or something. We both knew Felicia couldn't resist it. We both yelled at her on a daily basis. Is it your fault, too? No, Chava, sometimes things happen, and yes, there is fault, but it is shared. That's the way things are. I'll understand if you don't want anything to do with Constance anymore, but she has never shown you any type of aggression and she wouldn't understand, or even care, if you stopped showing an interest. She's not going to feel guilt over something that came naturally to her. So how can she be punished?"

"I guess she can't. I just feel so sorry for Mavis."

"Me, too. Just because I don't blame Constance for anything; it doesn't mean I don't feel awful about losing Mavis. She was my friend. And Mavis did understand friendship; if she didn't, she would be alive now. She died helping a friend, you know. And can you think of a better reason to die than helping a friend?"

Francis stood and walked over to Mavis, lifted her, and gently placed her in the grave. Felicia had arrived at some point during the vigil and was now standing at the edge of the small cemetery on the roof, a piece of unchewed licorice at her feet.

XIV

"Good afternoon, old friend."

"The last few days have been rough, what with coming to terms with losing you. That's going to sting for a good long while; right on the heels of what happened in the lobby and the search for McPhee, crazy bastard. Chava seems to be coming around. She flat out refused to feed Constance today though and I can't say as I really blame her. She's just a kid, after all. Constance killed you, pretty simple in her mind, but things are never that simple. At least she'll look at Constance and she hasn't brought up punishment since your funeral. She'll understand better as the grief fades. For her sake I hope it fades sooner rather than later."

"Susan was great at your funeral; very supportive, very understanding. She even held my hand for a minute. Just the comfort of a person who cares about the fact that you're going through something, that's all it really was. "

"But could it be more? Not the handholding, that was something she'd probably do for any friend, but could it become something more if I wanted it to? If we wanted it to? Our conversations at breakfast have become very friendly and natural; comfortable even. I'd lie if I said I didn't look forward to her coming upstairs each morning. I know I'll miss it after school starts. I actually don't need her help anymore. Why haven't either of us mentioned this? She must know I'm getting around just fine now. Chava has been coming with me to the Pet Emporium rather than going there by herself for me. Does Susan enjoy the breakfasts as much as I do? Is that possible?"

"I haven't had to think about this kind of thing since before Mindy and I got married. I think Mindy would like her; that's

something, too. Should I ask her about it tomorrow at breakfast? Or is that too aggressive? What if she doesn't feel that way at all? It would probably freak her out; just months ago I was the crazy recluse who lived on the fifth floor. How would she react if I asked her on a date? Is that even the right terminology anymore? I don't freaking know."

"I'll ask Terry. That's what I'll do. A third party opinion. That's probably the best way to go. He'll tell me if I'm being delusional. I think. Won't he?"

"I need a cigarette."

"How is Francis doing?"

"Fine, Mom."

"Is he really doing fine? He's not acting like before?"

"No, Mom. He's acting fine. We did the work as usual; he talked about The Three Stooges *and* Abbott and Costello, *whoever they are, and his roommate from college; a guy named Liam had a boxer named Canyon; caught his own bed on fire once."*

"What? A boxer caught his bed on fire?"

"No, his dog was a boxer; Liam caught his own bed on fire. You're not really listening are you?"

"I'm listening. I was just wondering something."

"Wondering what?"

"Just something about Francis."

"What about him?"

"Nothing, sweetie. Really."

"Moooooom, do you like *Francis?*

"Stop it."

"Mom and Francis sitting in a tree—"

"Chava!"

"Then why're you smiling like that and blushing! K-I-S-S-I-N-G!!"

"You're such a brat."

"Are you going to ask Francis out?"

"Ask Francis, what?"

"*Seriously, you should.*"

"*Chava! I don't... how can... where would we even go on a date? The man hasn't gone anywhere except the Pet Emporium, hospitals, and a cemetery in the last seven years. What does he like to do?*

"*So, you ARE thinking about asking him out.*"

"*I didn't say... stop putting words in my mouth!*"

"*You want me to find out for you? I can ask him if he wants to go on a date with you.*"

"*PLEASE! I'm not going to have you asking him things like that! Besides... I never said — *"

"*Wow. Take it easy, Mom. I was just playing with you.*"

"*Sorry, sorry... I just — *"

"*Love sure makes people crazy!*"

"*Chava!!*"

Officer Chavez had to pee. He'd had to pee for the last forty-five minutes or so. He put off driving down to the convenience store to use the restroom because there was something off about 517 Sycamore.

On the day Chavez and Detective Putnam responded to the vandalism call at the address Terrance Tower had taken him aside to ask a personal favor. Tower was concerned about his brother and the Lee family. While it was fairly obvious Lawrence McPhee was responsible for what took place in the lobby of the building, Tower was realistic in being concerned about how long it would take for the police to take the homeless man into custody. He had asked Chavez to moonlight, as often as his time allowed, by keeping an eye on the building, especially as far as who entered and departed the premises. And for the last several weeks Chavez had been doing just that.

During his off hours, every other day or so, he would sit in his personal vehicle outside the five story building and watch. Tower trusted him to report an accurate account of the hours he spent doing this in return for the sum agreed upon by the two men.

Thus far, the time Chavez spent watching the building had been uneventful. He saw Francis Tower and the Lees on several occasions, as well as the other confirmed, mostly elderly, residents. Only once did he leave his car; and that was to investigate a man lingering at the side of the building near the garbage dumpster. It had been a homeless man, but it hadn't been McPhee. Chavez, as well as the others involved in the case, were fairly certain McPhee had fled the city. That is typically how his surveillance of the building had gone; he'd watch for a few uneventful hours and then be on his way once hunger or the urge to relieve himself came upon him.

But now something was off. It was the delivery man. Francis Tower often had groceries delivered, and it wasn't unusual for different delivery people to make the five story walk up to the man's apartment. This time, however, the delivery man had been inside for too long. It was normally a ten or fifteen minute stop for them, tops. This time was different. The man went in the front door just over half an hour ago. *Why was he taking so long?*

Chavez could not think of an acceptable reason and strongly felt the urge to go up and check, but Tower had asked him to try not to let his brother know the building was being watched. He had tried to reach Terrance Tower on his cellphone at least half a dozen times but it went straight to voicemail. This put Chavez in a pickle. Break the established protocol and make himself known to Francis Tower or follow his gut.

Chavez reached across the passenger seat, opened his glove box, and removed his off duty piece. He held the .40 Glock loosely in his right hand for a few moments as he studied the windows on the fifth floor.

Always follow your gut. He swung the door of his car open.

Francis and Susan sat at the kitchen table having coffee; the breakfast dishes washed and drying on the rack. Francis thoughtfully rolled an unlit cigarette between his fingertips, his lighter poised in his other hand, but also unlit. He seemed troubled.

"How're you doing, Francis?" He had been his usual self that morning, but there seemed to be an underlying sadness that he was trying to mask from her.

"Fine, Susan. Just fine. I miss Mavis though, you know."

"Yeah, so does Chava. She was talking about her again this morning, about how funny she looked pecking at the dog treats you guys fed her."

"Yeah, she really liked the liver flavored treats the best, go figure," he chuckled, thinking back.

"Hey, Francis?"

"Yeah?"

"Do you like movies?"

"Sure, haven't seen any recent ones. Hell, I haven't seen anything new in years, but, yeah, I like movies."

"You want to go see one with me?"

"At a theater?"

Before Susan could reply to his obvious bid to stall for time there was a knock at the door. It was right around the time for Chava to show up for her day's work and Susan had wanted to ask Francis to the movies before the girl arrived. She didn't want her daughter poking fun at her while she asked him out on a date and, at the same time, she didn't want to make Francis uncomfortable with whichever answer, be it yes or no, he was prepared to give.

"There's Chava." Francis turned quickly toward the door.

"Yes, I suppose it is." Based on his obvious relief at the arrival of her daughter, she couldn't help thinking he had been going to answer her invitation with a big, fat no. "I'll get it."

"She lose her key or something?"

"Dunno." Susan crossed the room to the door and turned the knob.

A split-second following the *clack* signaling the door was

unlocked it burst open. Susan was spun around towards the interior of the apartment facing Francis with an arm firmly wrapped around her neck. An arm she recognized. She didn't ponder the arm for long though. She could see to her right that entering immediately after the arm that grabbed her was Lawrence McPhee in all his stenchful glory. He was grinning through his scummy teeth, eyes wide with excitement. To her horror she also saw her daughter; McPhee's left arm draped casually over Chava's left shoulder, his right hand holding an ice pick scant inches from her tender, exposed throat. McPhee kicked the door closed with the heel of his foot and looked directly at Francis.

"Well now, isn't this cozy." The filthy man chuckled.

Francis was on his feet standing next to the kitchen by this time. He was visibly shaken by the intrusion of the insane man. "McPhee. What do you think you're doing?"

"Oh, that's a good question, Francis Tower. But let me answer with a few questions of my own. You in the mood to die today, you fucking faggot? And which one of these fine ladies would you like to see bleed before it's your turn? The gook bitch, or the gook pup? Doesn't make no difference to me!" McPhee hissed as his hand moved the tip of the ice pick slightly closer to Chava's throat.

"Hey McPhee, you didn't say anything about hurting Susan or the kid." Ron Rhodes answered before Francis could speak.

"Rhodes? Did anybody pull your fucking string?"

"You didn't say ANYTHING about hurting Susan or the kid!" Ron's eyes darted between his ex and her daughter. "I didn't sign up for no goddamned triple homicide."

"Keep it up, Rhodes. I'll make it a quadruple! Catch my drift, dipshit? So, what? You think I'm going to do Tower here and then just let the two bitches walk? Walk straight to a phone and call the cops? Are you really that fucking stupid? Nah, Rhodes, you know they gotta' die, too."

Ron Rhodes saw where this was going and he was trying to figure out a way for everyone, including Tower to get out of this alive. He had agreed to come along on this second visit to 517 Sycamore because McPhee claimed to have evidence linking Ron to the vandalism in the lobby, evidence that would clear McPhee and lay all the blame at Ron's feet. Ron had no idea what evidence could accomplish this exactly, but McPhee had proven to be far more intelligent and resourceful than his appearance suggested. If he had known that this was what McPhee had in mind, he would have just called the bluff. Now he found himself involved in something he had no idea how to deal with. *How do you defuse a crazy man like McPhee?* Ron could only think of one way.

"No, they don't! Nobody has to die." Ron released Susan, pushing her back towards Francis. He reached into the grocery delivery jacket he'd stolen and withdrew a collapsible baton, the spring steel variety muggers liked to use. He gave a quick snap of his wrist extending the baton to full length and turned to face McPhee.

Then there was another knock at the door that made everyone, even McPhee, jump and they all froze in place. McPhee made a show of moving the point of the ice pick even closer to Chava's throat, letting everyone know what would happen if they called out to whoever was knocking on the door.

He jerked his head at Ron, silently instructing him to position himself to the side of the door. He nodded at Francis. Francis shook his head from side to side. McPhee nodded again, punctuating his order by placing the point of the ice pick actually against the skin of Chava's throat.

"Who is it?" Francis called, his eyes burning with anger.

"Mister Tower?"

"Yes, this is Francis Tower."

"Mister Tower, this is Officer Chavez. Could you let me in, please?"

"I'm a little busy right now, officer."

"Mister Tower, please open the door or I'll be coming in by force if need be."

Francis looked at McPhee. The dirty man just smirked,

shrugged his shoulders and glanced down at the top of Chava's head.

"It's open, officer."

The door opened and Chavez entered, his Glock in his right hand and pointed at the floor. Before he had a chance to survey the room Ron's baton whizzed through the air and caught him on the back of his head, knocking him to the floor, the pistol flying free from his hand.

"Well, I'll be," giggled McPhee, "it's the wetback cop from before. Now this IS turning out to be a good day."

The giggle didn't linger in McPhee's throat when everyone in the room, besides the stunned Officer Chavez, noticed the Glock had slid across the floor after having left the policeman's grip and came to rest at Francis' feet. Francis bent down, his eyes still moving from McPhee to Ron Rhodes and back again, and picked up the weapon and extended it before him at arm's length.

"Shit." Ron's eyes widened at the lack of expression on the armed man's face.

Ears and eyes and tongues turned towards the door. Tongues flicked and noses twitched, trying to catch a scent of what was transpiring beyond their vision. The animals; rodents and reptiles, avians and arachnids, amphibians and marsupials - stood, sat, lay and perched in motionless agitation. Warmth, grooming, food, and water were forgotten as they focused their full attention on the voices and noises coming from behind the door. Some things are bigger than immediate needs, some things are more important than momentary gratification. Something was happening beyond the door, something beyond their sight and smell, and this made them afraid. There is nothing more terrifying than the unknown.

XXV

It was only a matter of time. This was no surprise. The inevitable drop of the other shoe. Only the form the drop was taking held surprise for him, but not the drop itself.

He knew it was coming.

There was always a price to pay for happiness; just as misery was rewarded in time. That's the way the world worked; a balance that every person had to learn to accept.

He had had everything he needed and took it for granted and lost it the night Mindy and Melissa died. He paid for the blissful years with his family with the erosion of his sanity and his will to live. He paid for that happiness with years in the Harper Institute. A false existence, a medically enforced existence perpetrated by Doctor Singh and permitted by Terrance. It kept him biologically alive until a new upswing.

Little Demon entered his life and he was saved, momentarily. The animals became his life. Constance, Luis, Bullet, Oliver, Felicia, Jethro, Mavis, all of them. They became his purpose, if not true happiness. They had made him involved enough to continue on with life, such as it were.

He paid for this contentment with his first encounter with Lawrence McPhee and the taxi cab.

This physical pain heralded the entrance of Susan and Chava Lee into his life. Resistant at first, but over time he had begun to feel... feel... FEEL. He had felt again.

This newfound reason to go on, to continue the process of existence, these feelings; the world had to take Mavis from him in trade. The bigger the happiness, the bigger the sacrifice to balance things out in the cosmos. Obviously, however, the cosmos was not satisfied with the taking of Mavis and wanted more. But how much more?

That is what Francis was about to find out.

His hope was it wasn't the time for Susan, Chava, or Officer Chavez to experience a fatal downswing in their own existences; that it wasn't time for the other shoe to drop for them.

"Francis, don't..." The sight of McPhee holding an ice pick to her daughter's throat and Francis pointing the Glock in the girl's general direction had her on the edge of losing her breakfast, passing out, and going nuts all at once.

"It's okay, Susan. I won't let anything happen to her." He was deathly afraid when he had first picked the weapon up off the floor, but the weight of the pistol in his hand and the instant effect it had on the expressions worn on the faces of McPhee and Ron Rhodes gave him the feeling that the tide had turned and the ball was now in his court.

"You won't, huh? You really think I give a fuck if you shoot me? You really think I won't stick this in your little friend here? Scramble her brains a little, just because you might shoot me? You think you're the only crazy fuck in this room, cocksucker?"

"No, I think you're the only crazy f... person in this room. And I know for a fact that you're not going to hurt her, or Susan, or the officer."

"Is that so? That's a fact is it?"

"It is. Because if you hurt her I'm going to put a bullet in your head and you'll never have the chance to kill me; that's what you really want, McPhee. Killing my friends won't be enough for you. If you know anything about me; if you know why I live up here, and I'm sure you do. You're not stupid. I know you did your research, which means you know I've been through pain before. Some heavy, heavy pain. Giving me more pain isn't going to satisfy your sick desires, asshole, but killing me might. Killing me for treating a skinny, old mutt better than I treated you. For treating you like you were nothing, for showing people what a worthless piece of shit you are. A filthy, powerless, impotent bitch."

Ron Rhodes saw the blood rising in McPhee's face. "Yeah, McPhee, the freak is right. Let's let the girls go. I'll take them downstairs and make sure they don't make any calls. You can stay up here and deal with Tower. Take your time with him, get your jollies. The fucker totally disrespected you, man."

Tower was not totally surprised to find Ron working with him on this. He was a jilted, angry ex, not a murderous lunatic. Ron didn't want Susan, Chava, or Chavez, and probably not even Francis himself, killed. What's more, he didn't want the ire of the police coming down on him for his role as an accomplice if McPhee's intentions were realized. The police took the death of a fellow officer particularly personal. Francis was certain Rhodes had been involved in enough nefarious goings-ons to know this.

"Listen to your friend there. It's me you are after. Even if you manage to kill the girls and this police officer," Francis motioned towards Chavez on the floor, "witnesses or not, the cops are going to know it was you. They'll figure out quick enough you haven't left town and came back here."

McPhee continued to glare at Francis with his rheumy, piggy eyes. The man was carefully processing what Francis and Ron Rhodes had said, and he believed the words to be true. He was here for Tower. He didn't give a rat's ass about the woman, or her brat, or even the cop.

Though it sure would be fun to ventilate a cop. McPhee glanced at the spic do-gooder; he was starting to stir and moan a little. *That big fucker sure could take a hit. A smack on the head like the one Rhodes delivered would have knocked most guys out for hours, if not killed them outright.* If he was going to make his move it was going to have to be soon.

"Okay, Tower. How about this. The bitches can go, wait, not yet," Susan had already taken half a step towards McPhee to retrieve Chava. "They can go, and Rhodes, you will go with them. Don't give me any of that 'I'll keep them from calling the cops bullshit'. We both know you're a chicken shit and don't have the balls to go through with jack. I'm just tired of looking at your fucking face."

"What about Officer Chavez?" Francis stared calmly at the bum.

"If you wanna' see these ladies walk out of here that's where you're going to have to do a little... compromising."

"How so?"

"The cop stays right where he is, spread out like a nice big wetback rug. These three leave," he motioned vaguely in the direction of the door. "And then you put down the gun and I put down my little pig sticker here."

"And then?"

"Well, then we have it out. One crazy fuck to another. Settle things without any distractions. Whaddya say?" McPhee smiled broad and wide, like a shark about to have his first meal in weeks.

"And Officer Chavez?"

"What good is a contest without a prize, huh? You take me out, the cop walks out with you. I take you out, then; well, I don't call it a pig sticker for nothing."

Francis surveyed the faces in the room. Ron's eyes were wide and telling him this was the best deal they were going to get. Susan's eyes were brimming with tears, she didn't see any other way out for her daughter. Chava's face was a pure mask of fear. Francis looked down at Chavez and, surprisingly, the police officer's eyes were partially open. The big cop gave Francis a barely perceptible nod of the head. The nod told him to take the deal. Francis supposed Chavez operated under the widely held belief police officers had that they signed up for such shit as this and it was their job to get innocents out of the way. What a way to make a living. Francis turned back to McPhee.

"Fine. Deal."

"Alrighty then. Rhodes, open the door and you and these two ladies," he shoved Chava towards Susan, "can get the fuck out. And close the door behind you."

Chava finally spoke, "Francis?"

"It's okay, Chava. You go with your mom."

"Francis, no! He's going to kill you—" the girl uttered in a very mature whisper.

"Remember the farmer, Chava? Nobody can tell. Go on now." Francis smiled at her. And not a forced smile of false reassurance, but a genuine smile that told her everything was going to be just fine.

Just before reaching the lobby Susan Lee stopped in her tracks, turned around on the steps, and punched Ron Rhodes in the testicles. Ron doubled over without making a sound and rolled head-first down the six remaining steps and came to rest on the lobby floor. Susan and Chava reached the ground floor, and Susan reached her leg back preparing to launch Ron's head for a field goal.

"Mom!" Chava grabbed Susan's arm.

Susan looked at her daughter. Both of them had tears flowing freely down their faces.

"The phone Mom! Don't waste time on this... this... DICK!"

"Yuh...yuh...," Ron grunted up from the floor in agreement.

"Fine. I'll grab my cell! You go out to the street, Chava. We'll call from there! You're going to jail, motherfucker," she added for Ron's benefit. Susan reasoned calling from the street was the way to go. If McPhee killed Francis and the police took their time getting there, she didn't want to be cornered in the apartment with a blood-crazed McPhee at the door. He'd have the police officer's gun in addition to his pig sticker.

Susan was through her front door in a flash, snatched her cellphone from the kitchen table and sprinted back towards the lobby and the front door of 517 Sycamore. Before she moved through the door she stopped, looked back towards the steps for the briefest of moments and muttered a prayer for Francis.

Francis on the fifth floor.

CLACK!

The sound the door made as McPhee locked it echoed in Francis' ears. McPhee paused, took a deep breath, and turned around to face Francis, the smile gone from his face. All that remained was malice and the promise of cruel intent.

"Tell me, McPhee. Is this all really about a dog and a cheeseburger?" Francis was now holding the Glock pointed directly at the man.

"I'll be honest with you, Tower. It's probably not."

"Then why? Why me?"

"You were there."

"Where?"

"At my breaking point. You think you're the only one who has suffered? I've suffered for years; been on the streets for years; watched people pretend not to see me for years; and then you chose that mangy animal over me. A fellow human being! Those years piled up on me, Tower. You broke the camel's back, so to speak."

"So it could have been anyone, that's what you're saying."

"Yeah, I guess I am."

Francis took a quick moment to reflect on the point McPhee had just made. It could have been anyone; Susan walking home from the laundry; the blabbermouth at the Pet Emporium heading to work; one of the old folks living at 517 Sycamore; Chava out for a walk. But it had been him.

It had been Fate stirring the contents of life's pot. Fate had chosen him, a man who had been searching for death for years, and death had come in this form; the form of another man fed up with his own existence. Fate had taken his family away from him all those years before and Fate had brought him the friendship of the Lees. Personal experience had taught Francis not to fight Fate. And he wasn't about to start now. Susan and

Chava were out of harm's way. Rhodes was a scumbag, but he helped get the women out of the room. Chavez was coming around; making a few noises and moving a bit. Francis was sure he could keep McPhee busy long enough for the Lees to put some distance between themselves and the 5th floor and, who knows, maybe the big cop would find his feet soon. There was also the off-chance that McPhee would go through with the deal to lay down arms. In any case, Fate had brought him and McPhee to this point. He was going to go through with the deal he had made, whether McPhee chose to or not. So much had happened beyond his control and he was going to make his own choice this time. This is what Fate had brought to the table and he was choosing to follow Fate's lead. Let the chips fall where they may.

The men stood and studied each other silently for a moment longer. There was the briefest flicker of recognition between the two, the discovery of something in common, but neither could put their finger on it. Perhaps it was nothing more than the fact that they were two broken men; one on the mend and one beyond fixing.

"Okay, Tower. A deal is a deal. Slide the gun over there; away from the cop, if you don't mind."

"And you'll do the same with the pick?"

"Yeah, a deal is a deal, like I said. But you first. Hot lead trumps pointy kitchen utensil."

"Right."

Francis knelt down and placed the Glock on the floor in front of him. With his right foot he kicked the weapon to his left knowing as he did it that McPhee was not going to follow suit with the ice pick, but he no longer cared. This was going to end one way or another. And Francis was right. McPhee watched the Glock slide across the floor and then broke into another ghastly smile and directed the sneer at Francis, as he did the ice pick was held up at chest level in front of him.

Chavez let out a desperate moan as if in the hopes that his incomprehensible plea would somehow halt this madness or at least stall it long enough for him to come to Francis' aid. Neither Francis nor McPhee took notice of the police officer's entreaty or struggles to rise.

"I know exactly what I'm going to write on the wall in your blood, Tower." McPhee's voice was strangely even and inhuman in tone. All sanity had left the man and had been replaced by the primal urge to kill. Not for survival, but for the sheer thrill, an urge Francis' friends on the other side of the door would never have understood in a million years. This was an urge owned in whole by humanity, practiced by humanity, and coveted by humanity.

"Come on then. I've been waiting for you long enough," Francis calmly replied, arms slightly lifted from his sides, palms turned upward and feet spaced apart, ready to receive the attack.

McPhee advanced at a slow even pace across the room in Francis' direction, but his smile left him. Francis was smiling right back at him. There was no look of terror, pleading puppy dog eyes, or a mouth wide open to beg for mercy; none of the responses he expected, none of the responses a sane person would display. Instead, his face sported a genuinely peaceful smile. A smile of acceptance.

XXVI

"I wasn't conscious throughout the entire incident, sir."

"Well, tell us what you do remember, Officer Chavez. What you included in your written report."

"Yes, sir. Well, I remember something being off about the delivery man from the grocery store. He was taking too long to deliver to the fifth floor, so I decided to check it out."

"Okay, one moment. To clarify, you were off duty and doing surveillance for Mister... Mister Terrance Tower. Correct?"

"Yes, sir. My captain was aware of my activities and supported it seeing as it was directly connected to the manhunt for Lawrence McPhee."

"Fine. Continue."

"I went into 517 Sycamore to check out the delivery man, who, as it turns out, was Ron Rhodes wearing a uniform jacket he stole from the grocery locker room. I went to the fifth floor and knocked on the door. Francis Tower answered from the other side. He told me the door was open and I went in. I'm assuming McPhee and Rhodes were in charge of the situation at that point and used the safety of the Lees as leverage to force Mister Tower to lead me into an ambush. As I entered the apartment I was struck from behind, on the back of the head. The assailant, Ron Rhodes, used a collapsible baton."

"And you're expected to make a full recovery?"

"Yes, sir. He rung my bell pretty good, but I'll be at one-hundred percent once the headache goes away."

"Good to hear. Continue."

"Then it was nothing but mumbles and blurs for a time. The next thing I remember clearly was Francis Tower agreeing to give up my off

duty piece, a .40 Glock, in exchange for McPhee allowing the Lees to leave the apartment. Ron Rhodes went with them. Before he actually agreed to the deal I motioned, nodded rather, to Mister Tower to encourage him to agree to the deal. I felt it was best to get the Lees out of the apartment in any way possible, even at the expense of Mister Tower's life and my own. I don't know, however, whether my nod was recognized as a signal by Mister Tower or had any bearing on his decision."

"So, Mister Tower handed the Glock over to McPhee after the Lees and Rhodes left the apartment?"

"No, sir."

"No?"

"No. McPhee wanted some sort of hand-to-hand showdown He wasn't interested in the Glock, but he didn't hold up his end. Mister Tower gave up the Glock, but McPhee, that piece of shit —"

"Officer Chavez."

"Apologies. McPhee did NOT set aside the ice pick as per the arrangement. The two men exchanged words for a few moments. I couldn't make them out very well. I did make out McPhee claiming Mister Tower had broken the camel's back. I'm not sure what that meant."

"And after they finished conversing?"

"Well, that's when McPhee went for Mister Tower with the ice pick."

"Mister Tower made no attempt to ward off Mister McPhee's attack?"

"Not that I could see, sir. He just smiled."

"Smiled?"

"Yes, sir. He smiled like... like it was okay. I don't know if that makes any sense. When McPhee reached him and stabbed him with the pick the first time Mister Tower grabbed onto McPhee's coat and just held him. McPhee stabbed Mister Tower with the ice pick several times. I can't say how many times exactly; at least half a dozen, maybe more."

"It was a total of eight times, officer. I'm assuming it was at this time that you were able to go to Mister Tower's assistance?"

"Yes, sir. When I saw Mister Tower not doing anything and the

259

ice pick, um... enter his body; it must have been adrenaline or something, I don't know. I was able to half crawl and half lunge myself in their direction. I got my hands around McPhee and brought him to the floor."

"You were not stabbed or injured in the take down, though?"

"No, sir."

"Can you explain the trauma done to Mister McPhee's face?"

"That occurred as I was subduing him, sir. He resisted arrest and I used the appropriate amount of necessary force *I felt the situation called for."*

"I see. And where was Mister Tower at this time?"

"As I bea... subdued McPhee, Mister Tower slumped to the floor. He was losing a great amount of blood."

"And did he say anything to you? Any last words before he expired?"

"Yes, sir. They are included in the written report, but if you don't mind I'd rather not repeat them now. The words were meant for those special to him.

Officer Chavez parked his squad car directly in front of the steps at 517 Sycamore. He stepped out of the car and looked up at the fifth floor windows of the building and noted stained glass at the top of the panels. Blue stained glass. He wondered to himself how he had never noticed the blue glass before. Chavez realized his concentration on the blue glass was just a way to put off completing his errand.

Terrance Tower and the Lees had agreed to meet with him this afternoon at the Lees' apartment. He had a kind face and a soft speaking voice and had always been skilled at delivering unwholesome news to the loved ones of victims; it was part of the job, but he always dreaded it. Most of his fellow officers felt the same way. At least he wasn't delivering news that Francis Tower had died, those inside 517 Sycamore were already well aware of that. He was there to deliver Tower's last words, which felt like an even greater responsibility. He wanted to do it right. He was prepared for their responses, whatever emotions might rear their heads. He just hoped he could keep his own emotions in check. Francis Tower had been harmless; a troubled man to be sure, but a good man by all accounts. It hurt Chavez as a person, to his core, to see another good man die the way he did, so brutally and without mercy.

Terrance Tower and Susan Lee had been anxiously waiting for him it seemed. Susan Lee opened the door to the apartment before the echo of his knock had even completely dissipated from the lobby. The woman smiled and stepped aside so the large police officer could enter.

"You wanted to see us, Officer Chavez?"

"Yes. Would you mind if I had a seat?"

"Oh, of course. I'm sorry, please, take that chair. Would you like some coffee? Terry and I are having some, it's no trouble."

"No, thank you, Missus Lee."

"Officer Chavez." Terrence extended his hand.

The officer clasped the offered hand. "Mister Tower. I'm very sorry for the loss of your brother, sir. I wish I could have done more."

"Officer, don't apologize. You did what you could. And if it wasn't for you, McPhee could still be out there on the streets, a danger to others, instead of locked up in the maximum security wing of the Harper Institute. You did everything in your power."

"Thank you, Mister Tower, still—"

"But you said on the phone you had something to tell us." Terry really felt no blame for Francis' death belonged on Chavez' shoulders; it was all McPhee.

"Yes, sir. Is your daughter here, Missus Lee? She needs to hear this, as well."

"Oh, yes, she's here. One sec." Susan went down the hall and returned after only moments with Chava in tow.

"Hi, Chava," smiled Chavez.

Chava smiled back. It was a tired smile, but a smile

nonetheless, "Hi, Officer Chavez."

"Okay, well, I didn't have a chance to tell you this before because I was having my head checked out from where Rhodes hit me; then the paperwork, the debriefing... anyway. Um... Mister Tower, Francis, asked me to pass on some messages. As you are aware, he didn't pass right away, and he talked a little. I made most of it out."

"Oh." Terry sighed.

"Yes, um... Mister Tower, I was to tell you; you are doing a great job with your kids, Amy and Terry, Jr. Francis loved them and your wife, Lorraine, very much and he wished he hadn't wasted those years away from them. Also, he wanted to thank you for looking out for him, that he knows he had been a pain in... well... a pain in the ass much of the time. You didn't have to do what you did for him and he knew that, and he loved you for it. You were the best little brother any guy could ask for." Chavez paused signifying the end of the message.

"Thank you, Officer Chavez," Terry's eyes were filled with tears. "Thank you very much."

"Yes, sir."

Chavez cleared his throat before he continued, "Missus Lee."

"Yes?"

"Francis wanted me to tell you thank you for taking care of him and he's sorry he made you turn, um... orange? Turn orange on a regular basis? I'm not sure if I heard that last part right; he was smiling when he said it though, so, I—"

Susan smiled. "It's okay, officer. You heard right. He was such a weirdo."

"He also said he's sorry he won't get to go to the movies with you."

"Oh... wow... he was going to say yes, Chava." Her daughter smiled at that.

"Go to the movies? Since when?" Terry's face was scrunched up in confusion.

"I'll tell you later." Susan was beaming.

Chavez then turned to Chava, who was still standing in the hall where it met the living room.

"Chava, he told me to tell you... to... um... to not be too sad if you can help it and that he was your Mavis. Again, I have no idea what that might mean. Does it mean anything to you?"

Chava's face took on a new vitality and the sadness in her eyes melted away.

"Yes, it does. It means I was his friend."

Terrance Tower stood in front of *Beloved Wife*, *Cherished Daughter* and *Loving Husband* at Lush Haven Cemetery. He hadn't been to Francis' grave since the day he was buried nearly three weeks ago. Somehow he felt Francis would be just as annoyed by frequent visits in death as he was when he was alive. An absurd thought, but old habits die hard.

"Mindy, Melissa. Hi, Francis I thought I'd come by and give you an update on things; things I know you'd care about. Um... Lorraine and the kids are doing fine. They miss you. Sometimes I think it might have been better if you hadn't reconnected with them, you know? They were really looking forward to spending time with you, the kids in particular. But, of course, there was no way to know things were going to turn out the way they did, huh? But.. .uh... at least Amy and Chava are still friends, they yak on the phone for hours; the usual teenage girl stuff. I won't bore you with it. "

Terry looked up at the sky and cleared his throat. "Speaking of Chava and Susan... the Lees, I mean. They moved out of 517 Sycamore. They didn't want to stay in the building after all the bad crap that went down there. I can't say as I blame them. I helped them find a new place over on West Columbia; a little house, not an apartment. I'm not sure if you remember the place, it's right down the street from Dad's first real estate office. I also offered Susan a job at our company. I know you'd approve. She's working the phones right now, but I think she's taking an interest in possibly becoming one of our agents. I think she'd be great at it. She and Lorraine have become pretty close."

The surviving Tower looked back down at his brother's grave. "Lawrence McPhee; he's in the Harper Institute. Doctor Singh told me he spends most of his time locked in the solitary section of the maximum security wing. It seems you made some good friends there, whether you were aware of it or not. Another patient by the name of Martin beat McPhee senseless with a chair after he found out what he did to you; put him in the infirmary for three days. After that Doctor Singh decided to keep him separate from the other patients. He told me McPhee will most likely never know the feeling of free air ever again. The man is just too far gone; I don't have to tell you that."

Birds chirping in the branches of the surrounding trees brought a sad smile to his face. "The other one, Ron Rhodes, Susan's ex. He's going to do some time, but how much time is the question. For starters, Rhodes has confessed to helping McPhee butcher the dog and vandalize 517 Sycamore. He also admitted to letting McPhee in through the service entrance door when he went in disguised as the delivery guy. According to Chavez they are not sure what to do with him. He assaulted Chavez, that's pretty serious, but he did help get Susan and Chava away from McPhee and is being as upfront and cooperative as possible, most likely trying to save his own skin somehow, but Chavez is willing to try to help get him a lighter sentence. I don't know if that's the right thing to do or not, but that's Chavez' call, I guess. Hell of a nice guy, that one."

Terry let out a deep sigh. The next topic was something he knew his brother would be very concerned about. "As for your animals; Chava asked if she could have the ferret, the albino. I told her yes, of course. Most of the others have been adopted out already. To good homes, I assure you. Believe it or not, that big hairy spider got adopted out fast. I thought I was going to end up with him myself! Thank goodness that wasn't the case. I don't think I could have slept with him in the house. Your, uh... colony of sugar gliders; they actually found a place in the zoo, and they named the enclosure after you. I thought that was pretty cool. The big snake, too. The zoo accepted her as a mate for a male they have. Looks like love is in the air."

"Nobody is living in your apartment. I don't know if I'm going to rent it out or not. I'm not even sure what I'd do with the pet cemetery on the roof; don't really want to disturb your friends, but that's okay... I'll figure out something to do with it."

A sudden flapping in the tree behind and to the right of *Cherished Daughter* caused Terrance to look up with a start. He half-expected to see a big black raven sitting in the branches waiting for a picnic lunch, but it was only a blue jay.

"I miss you, big brother."

He turned and walked back to his SUV, hands in his pockets.

EPILOGUE

Chava sat on the park bench, her attention divided between watching the storm brewing to the west and the playground equipment directly in front of her. The storm had been gathering since before arriving at the park. First some dark clouds moving into a huddle, like black sheep circling the wagons to ward off marauding wolves. Now, however, the banks of clouds were starting to light up periodically as lightning flashed from the center of the storm.

The woman had decided it best to head home before the storm got any closer when she heard a flapping and a croak come from the nearest tree. Her gaze fell on a large raven with twinkling eyes. The big bird had its head cocked her way, studying her like it knew her face but couldn't quite place it.

"You remind me of someone I used to know. A good friend."

"*Croak!*"

"You be careful out here. There's a storm coming."

She stood up, raised her arms over her head and gave her back a good stretch before calling out in the direction of the big yellow slide on the playground, "Francis! Come on, honey! It's time to go home!"

"Okay, Mom!" A little boy came running, a broad grin splayed across his face. He was a little small for his age, but he'd grow up just fine.

Life went on.

"A Weave for Depression"

When Gary requested I read his first novel *5th Floor Francis*, I was intrigued by his title and his black raven totem sitting enigmatically on its cover. My being a lover of literature and a poet added to Gary's seduction and my inability to refuse his call. His knowing that I have been a practicing psychiatrist for over forty (40) years, treating adults, adolescents, and children for all forms of psychiatric disorders, Gary appealed to my well experienced psychiatric mind to read this with my discerning eye and my full blown sleuthing curiosity. I readily consented.

Gary wanted me to verify and to corroborate the description of depression in *5th Floor Francis*. Was it clinically accurate, true to form to my own real experiences with my patients? Did he describe the true agonies and deep emotional sufferings of human depression? Did *5th Floor Francis* realistically depict the terrible ravages of this serious mental disorder? Did he depict the deeply insidious "cognitive/feeling" condition suffered by millions and millions of people? One that has dogged our human species for many thousands of years, sapping their will to hope, to strive, to desire, to live life fully for their future when there is no future, nothing but blackness.

Sometimes unfortunately, even in the face of all heroic efforts, depression brings a tragic and a terrifying self-inflicted death to the depressed person, defeating families and professionals alike; leaving all in mutual helplessness and sorrow, that lives on forever in all those left behind. Words can never express the defeat that depression reaps: the killer that kills both the deceased and the living left in its wake.

And so, page-by-page, of *5th Floor Francis* I joined in the battle with Francis; struggled with him, cheered him on, hoped with him, and even prayed for him. I had empathy, compassion, and understanding for him as a reader and simultaneously as a psychiatric-physician objectively following my patient (a participant-observer if you will) strategizing for his most optimal psychiatric treatment. And all along intellectually knowing the complexity of depression: that the "brain/mind" is one organic entity composed of 100 billion neurons, trillions of neuronal synapses and neurotransmitters that orchestrate the "brain/mind "to sing and to give shape, form, and function to his present tortured self.

And simultaneously in the very same moment Francis' "brain/mind" gives him his sense of a conscious Self, his unique psychological character and personality which originate his thoughts, his ideas, and his dreams. Taken together, these two facets of his "brain/mind" generate Frances' agonizing depressive, suicidal feelings/affects/emotions. Residing therein is Frances' essence of this total humanity.

So I lived along with Francis from the hospital to his 5th floor apartment, the psychiatrist-physician-me experiencing the severity of his debilitating depression, one that had brought him to death's door by a massive imbalance of his neurotransmitters precipitated by a horrendous external tragic trauma. The adage "what happens on the outside also happens on the inside and vice versa" applies to what happened to Francis three years before I met him. This was the self-punitive depressive whirlwind; the precipitating etiology which triggered his multiple near death attempts the psychiatric hospital was attempting to stem when I made his acquaintance through Gary. Francis was the classic chronic depressive suicidal semi-psychotic patient drowning in his self-loathing and unrelenting, unforgiving guilt.

Psychiatric hospital treatment, 24 hour self-protection, multiple anti-depressant medications, talking psychotherapy (the only "scalpel" psychiatrists have), and a combination of adjunctive therapies including pet therapy were employed over three long years. Kudos to Dr. Singh, Francis' exemplary psychiatrist, who tirelessly persevered in holding the torch of hope and life with unwavering dedication and commitment. (I honor Dr. Singh and thank Gary for portraying our psychiatric profession in the highest humanistic light possible!) Dr. Singh never gave up! No physician can. He fought for his patient even as Francis had given up. And finally, creatively, Dr. Singh blew into Francis an inspiration that struck a resurrecting cord somewhere deep in Francis activating a lifesaving challenge; an ember that turned back the shadow of his depression and gave Francis the will to live for another, rather than for himself.

And so Francis begins his life once again safely outside of the hospital with his sole purpose larger than his own: giving of himself to others. Gary guides us through the ensuing vicissitudes as Francis begins to live onward in his 5th floor home. Slowly, as Francis ventures out of his depressive solitary shell, we begin to live along day by day in his expanding world of companions, of alter egos, relatives, and the forging of his new living bonds. And always, his ever present black raven silently watches over him.

Gary skillfully captured me and led me inexorably to a pivotal emotional moment halfway through the book: the first climax when Francis reveals the horrific guilt ridden trauma that threw his "brain/mind", his total essence, into a major psychotic depression. Francis' emotional disclosure personally caught me completely by surprise. Its weight crushed me! My humanity, not my psychiatry, burst forth into a torrent of tears. Sobbing, I felt deeply in my heart the trauma, the pain, the agony, and the unremitting terror when Francis articulated the gravity of his action. Even as I write about it now, I tear up and feel it again and again. This is the greatest compliment to Gary's writing. As he said to me: "I made a psychiatrist cry!"

This is what depression does even to the most dispassionate and "distant" psychiatrist. Gary managed superbly and sometimes painfully slow to bring me into the throes and the maelstrom of Francis' life: his life before; his life in the psychiatric hospital, and his life in his 5th floor residence. He then proceeds to describe the opening and healing experiences Francis subsequently had. Hope against hope, I relished and celebrated the positive future Gary was intimating for Francis.

And yet these forebodings, these fears, and these worries hung in between the empty spaces of this novel. They lingered and floated and new foreshadowing heightened my worries, nagged at me, and kept upsetting me. Little by little Gary led us down the only path of resolution Francis' depression could take.

Francis' unresolved mental ambivalence continued to be very deep and pervasive: driven by the neuroscience of his dysfunctional brain and by the psychology of his inner punitive Self which generated his terminal destructiveness, his unforgiving ideas, thoughts and his feelings.

In the end Francis felt that a certain "cosmic" order had to be fulfilled. A certain re-balancing, a righting of the scale, if you will, had to occur for Francis to feel that his soul's yin and yang could find the eternal peace he needed to surrender into the eternal unconsciousness. Did Francis finally feel he had to assuage his guilt by sacrificing himself into his final smile?

Gary ends *5th Floor Francis* on this note of mystery and awe.

Paul J. Kachoris, M.D. is a triple board certified child, adolescent, and adult psychiatrist in the "original" practice of psychiatry; treating the whole patient with both psychotherapy for the psyche/mind and with psychotropic medications for the brain as needed. Dr. Kachoris has been in continuous clinical psychiatric practice for more than forty years. During his professional career, he has held multiple clinical and administrative positions in both inpatient and outpatient psychiatric settings. Presently he is devoting himself to his outpatient practice and pursuing his many interests in poetry, the humanities, neuroscience, men's studies, and leading men's weekend retreats.

Depression Awareness

Depression has a direct impact on the daily life of more than 18 million Americans and an estimated 350 million people worldwide. The disease causes pain not only on the one afflicted, but also on those who care about them. Medical professionals have termed the condition "depressive disorder," or "clinical depression." This is a real illness and is in no way a sign of weakness. Most people who experience depression need treatment to get better.

Depression can strike at any age, but most often begins in the teens or early 20s or 30s. A lot of factors can play a role in depression, including genetics, brain biology and chemistry, and life events such as trauma, loss of a loved one, a difficult relationship, an early childhood experience, or any stressful situation. Depression has been known to pop up with other illnesses. Sometimes medications taken to treat other conditions may cause side effects that contribute to depression.

Sadness is only a small part of the disease. Some people with depression may not even feel sadness at all. Depression has many other symptoms, including physical ones. Symptoms of depression may include:

- Appetite and/or weight changes
- Decreased energy, fatigue, being "slowed down"
- Difficulty concentrating, remembering, making decisions
- Difficulty sleeping, early-morning awakening, or oversleeping
- Feelings of guilt, worthlessness, helplessness
- Feelings of hopelessness, pessimism
- Loss of interest or pleasure in hobbies and activities
- Persistent physical symptoms
- Persistent sad, anxious, or "empty" mood
- Restlessness, irritability
- Thoughts of death or suicide, suicide attempts

Certain medications, and some medical conditions, such as viruses or a thyroid disorder, can cause the same symptoms as depression. A doctor can rule out these possibilities by doing a physical exam, interview, and lab tests. If the doctor can find no medical condition that may be causing the depression, the next step is a psychological evaluation.

Major depressive disorder is one of the most common mental disorders in the United States. Living with depression can seem overwhelming at times, so a solid support system can be instrumental. In addition to treatment, joining a support group can be very helpful. These are not psychotherapy groups, but some may find the added support helpful. At the meetings, people share experiences, feelings, information, and coping strategies for living with depression. *Always check with a doctor before taking any medical advice that is heard in a group setting. Joining a support group does not replace medical advice or treatment prescribed by a doctor!*

Caring for someone with depression is not easy. Some of those suffering from depression may need constant support for a long period of time. The most important thing is to make sure friends or relatives get diagnosed and a treatment in place.

Things to do to help friends and family suffering from depression:

- Never dismiss feelings, but point out realities and offer hope
- Never ignore comments about suicide and report them to their therapist or doctor
- Offer emotional support, understanding, patience, and encouragement
- Provide assistance in getting to doctors' appointments
- Remind them that with time and treatment, the depression will lift
- Talk to them, and listen carefully
- Invite them to outings, and other activities

National Suicide Prevention Lifeline
1-800-273-TALK (8255)

If you feel you are in a crisis, whether or not you are thinking about killing yourself, please call the Lifeline. People have called for help with substance abuse, economic worries, relationship and family problems, sexual orientation, illness, getting over abuse, depression, mental and physical illness, and even loneliness.

When you dial, you are calling the crisis center in the Lifeline network closest to your location. After you call, you will hear a message saying you have reached the National Suicide Prevention Lifeline. You will hear hold music while your call is being routed. You will be helped by a skilled, trained crisis worker who will listen to your problems and will tell you about mental health services in your area. Your call is confidential and free.

Veterans Crisis Line
1-800-273-8255

The Veterans Crisis Line connects Veterans in crisis and their families and friends with qualified, caring Department of Veterans Affairs responders through a confidential toll-free hotline.

Veterans and their loved ones can call 1-800-273-8255 and *Press 1* or send a text message to 838255 to receive confidential support.

Online support for veterans and their families can be found by visiting www.veteranscrisisline.net.

Veterans Crisis Line
1-800-273-8255

Gary R. Gowers was born on Grand Avenue in St. Louis, MO in 1970. He attended Cleveland Jr Naval ROTC High School for two years, where he learned he never wanted to join the military. He spent another two years at Owensville High School, where he learned it was easy to complete homework on a rural school bus route.

He started college at Southwest Missouri State University in Springfield, MO on a whim; where he learned college is no fun unless your parents pay for it. He did graduate with a BA in History and this led him to leave for South Korea in 1997 for a one-year ESL teaching contract. One year turned into more than 15 years, during which time he taught ESL to thousands of students, wrote 18 textbooks, appeared on several South Korean television programs, and offered up his baritone vocals doing voice-over work.

During this time he also traveled around the world seeing the sights and meeting interesting people in Europe, Asia, North America, and Oceania. Most importantly, he met and married the love of his life, Cho Kyung-sook.

5th Floor Francis is Gary's first published work of fiction and draws heavily from his own personal battles with loss, loneliness, and depression. To read *5th Floor Francis* is to see into the heart and mind of a self-proclaimed lovable loser who just happened to get lucky a few times.